And when he saw her, Tony grinned, as if it were all a big joke. "Kelly, I was just telling them all how I *accidently* fell in the goldfish pond. Diane here has just offered to take me home for some dry clothes."

"That's all right," Kelly said, quickly taking him by the arm and propelling him out of the apartment. "I'll do it."

Once the door was closed behind them, Tony grinned even more broadly. "Had to come back, didn't you? Afraid you'd drowned me, I'll bet."

"Drowned? That pool was only a foot deep. When I decide to drown you, Mr. Campbell, I will push you into the deepest pool in the known world."

"Saints preserve us," Tony cried in mock horror as he pulled her close. "Will the woman never shut up?" Then he put his lips to hers, and Kelly knew she was where she'd wanted to be all night—in his arms.

ABOUT THE AUTHOR

"Well, we just took the sexiest man we could imagine, paired him with the pluckiest heroine we could dream up and squared them off against each other in New York, the world's most glamorous and romantic city. And after that, *Between Two Moons* just wrote itself," says Joyce Gleit, who—with Herma Werner— forms the writing team known as Eve Gladstone. Both Joyce and Herma are married and worked in the fashion industry before becoming romance writers.

Books by Eve Gladstone

HARLEQUIN SUPERROMANCE
297–ALL'S FAIR
324–ONE HOT SUMMER
349–AFTER ALL THESE YEARS
380–WOULDN'T IT BE LOVELY

HARLEQUIN INTRIGUE
23–A TASTE OF DECEPTION
49–CHECKPOINT
75–OPERATION S.N.A.R.E.
111–ENIGMA

Don't miss any of our special offers. Write to us at the following address for information on our newest releases.

Harlequin Reader Service
901 Fuhrmann Blvd., P.O. Box 1397, Buffalo, NY 14240
Canadian address: P.O. Box 603,
Fort Erie, Ont. L2A 5X3

Between Two Moons

EVE GLADSTONE

Harlequin Books

TORONTO • NEW YORK • LONDON
AMSTERDAM • PARIS • SYDNEY • HAMBURG
STOCKHOLM • ATHENS • TOKYO • MILAN

Published August 1990

ISBN 0-373-70414-3

Copyright © 1990 by Joyce Gleit and Herma Werner. All rights reserved.
Except for use in any review, the reproduction or utilization
of this work in whole or in part in any form by any electronic,
mechanical or other means, now known or hereafter invented,
including xerography, photocopying and recording,
or in any information storage or retrieval system, is forbidden without
the permission of the publisher, Harlequin Enterprises Limited,
225 Duncan Mill Road, Don Mills, Ontario, Canada M3B 3K9.

All the characters in this book have no existence outside the
imagination of the author and have no relation whatsoever to
anyone bearing the same name or names. They are not even
distantly inspired by any individual known or unknown to the
author, and all incidents are pure invention.

® are Trademarks registered in the United States Patent and
Trademark Office and in other countries.

Printed in U.S.A.

For Stefanie.
Friday's child, loving and giving,
may the gods shine on you.

CHAPTER ONE

"SPLENDID SIGHT, the Temple of Dendur in the moonlight. And it's a blue moon at that."

At the stranger's words, Kelly Aldrich gazed across the reflecting pool. She'd been too busy seeing to the table arrangements to think of the temple as anything but a stage set.

"Yes, of course it is," she said, not hiding the sudden awe in her voice. "How perfectly beautiful, and how wrong we are to surround it by all this—this *nonsense*," she added, gesturing to the party tables groaning under the weight of huge vases of flowers and elegant place settings. Across the pool, standing in silent majesty beneath the night sky, was a small, ancient Egyptian temple. A gift to the people of New York from the Egyptian government, it had been removed stone by stone and reconstructed in a glass-roofed atrium of the Metropolitan Museum of Art.

The north side of this atrium had been transformed with masses of palm fronds into a dreamy evocation of ancient Egypt—all part of the elaborate floral decorations for this evening's party. As atmospheric as the temporary additions were, a faint shiver crawled along Kelly's arms. The quiet, mysterious setting had been violated somehow. Oh, well, she decided, all in the name of charity, and a good one at that. The party would be over soon enough, the tables and flowers and palm fronds carried away, and the temple would be returned to its solitary splendor under the light cast by the moon.

"I suppose it is a bit of a folly," the stranger went on. "An ancient pile of stone used as a prop for a charity affair." He spoke with a British accent, his voice a warm baritone. Kelly turned to him, wondering just who he was and how he had materialized in the quiet court of Dendur. She was struck at once by a certain animal energy that radiated from the man standing next to her, a restlessness that spoke of adventure. The tuxedo he wore was impeccably tailored. He was tall, light-haired and handsome with glittering eyes that might have been gray or hazel and that scrutinized her with a directness she found overwhelming. Whether he caught her surprise or not, he continued talking without missing a beat. "And it's all surrounded by the gray towers of the city. If you listen closely, you can hear the sounds of airplanes overhead and fire engines in the distance—to say nothing of the music of police sirens. It takes a leap of the imagination to see the Temple of Dendur as anything but the relic it is."

"I wonder if they had parties way back in the Second Dynasty, complete with silver service and crystal," she mused. "You wouldn't be here about the flowers, would you?" She knew the question was foolish, but she *had* been waiting for someone from Manhattan Florists.

The stranger went over to a table and broke off an orchid from one of the elaborate arrangements. Then he presented it to Kelly with a bow. "Am I here about the flowers? All things are possible under a blue moon."

"You can't be from the florists. You've just committed the gravest sin this side of...of the moon. See? You've made everything lopsided...and orchids at umpteen dollars apiece! Not to mention that Mrs. Laurence is sitting at this table." Kelly contemplated the richly concocted centerpieces of sultry orchids, lemongrass, forced goldenrod and Queen Anne's lace.

"I'm not quite certain I agree with you," he said, "as to the arrangement being lopsided. I'd say it's a bit of an improvement. I'm speaking as an authority, you understand. The lotus was the sacred flower of the ancient Egyptians, I believe, not orchids."

"You're no authority." She put the orchid down, lifted the bouquet and its wide-lipped vase and marched over to a table in the far corner, one with a distant view of the temple that would surely be cut off by dozens of distinguished heads. She made the exchange adroitly, uttering a little apology to the guests who would sit at the table, and brought back an especially florid centerpiece. Mrs. Laurence chaired the Job-Up committee and would be the most distinguished head visible that night.

"There. No one will ever know the difference," she said. The dropped orchid still lay abandoned on the table.

"Especially Mrs. Laurence, who possesses a fine greenhouse in Westport," the stranger said.

"You know her, then?" Kelly examined him curiously, wondering how many more surprises he had in store for her. "Mrs. Laurence."

"And her greenhouse," he agreed, and took the hand she offered in a firm, dry clasp.

"I'm Kelly Aldrich."

"And I'm Anthony Campbell. Pleased to meet you."

They stood for a moment, smiling at each other. Then, giving in to an uncanny feeling that he knew her or knew something about her, and feeling faintly embarrassed, Kelly drew her eyes away. That was when she remembered the orchid. She frowned, and for a moment the incongruity of the evening, of the gloss and terrible expense for a charity dinner even if it was for Job-Up, passed over her as though the soft lights in the atrium were flickering out one by one.

"Something wrong?" Tony asked the question quietly, his hand still holding hers.

"You're not with Manhattan Florists."

"I'm beginning to wish I were." He released her hand and picked up the orchid, a small delicate flower with brown tiger spots on beige-and-pink petals. He reached over, draped her long brown hair behind her ear and tucked the flower in. "There. That's what florists should be doing instead of stuffing all this excess into vases."

"Excess?" Kelly used the word more sharply than she'd intended because in a single word he'd expressed what she knew to be the truth. "When you're asking people to reach into their pockets for money, you have to go to some lengths to amuse, entertain and charm them." It was an old argument, but a perfectly serviceable one, even with all the holes that she knew could be shot through it. "Holding a fashion show and a charity dinner at the Metropolitan Museum of

Art is . . . is . . . de rigueur. Oh," she groaned, "I can't believe I just said that."

He smiled indulgently. "You did and succeeded very well at your appointed task, especially in the area of amusing, entertaining and definitely charming me."

Her hand fluttered briefly to the orchid. She wished that the entire structure in which they stood would tumble down and end the curious dreamlike state she was in. But when she spoke, Kelly's voice had its usual practical edge. "You realize, of course, that I'm not above begging for a check."

"For Job-Up, correct? I believe that's the charity at the tail end of all this."

"Exactly, like leg up. Formed to keep artistically talented high school kids in school where they belong. Can I count on you?"

"Oh, absolutely. I'm all for keeping kids out of trouble and in school. What I'll need is the pertinent information, such as your address and telephone number."

"You might want to pass the check along to Mrs. Laurence," Kelly said. "Just make out something with four or five very large figures to Job-Up."

"Provided it's not going to be used for flowers or other vegetation, certainly. What do you expect from Manhattan Florists that hasn't already been accomplished?"

"Oh, that." Kelly laughed. The idea was suddenly almost too foolish to discuss, but she plowed bravely on. "We'd also contracted for separate little stalks of freesia to be placed alongside each napkin. For fragrance. They weren't delivered. But," she added, "I suppose you'd call it overkill. After all, there's all that scent of lamb cooking as you come down the galleries. The freesia might just confuse your taste buds."

"The scent of lamb, of course," he said. "I was wondering at the sudden bout of nostalgia I've been feeling for home and hearth. It's the smell of cooking lamb—the last thing I'd expect in a museum devoted to the world's great art."

Kelly laughed. "I'm happy to say it's not part of an exhibit. Our caterer has set up shop, and I suppose he's busy roasting the main course."

"Just when does dinner begin?"

"Actually, I'm afraid not for another hour. First there's the fashion show in the Medieval Court." Kelly stopped and looked curiously at him. "Are you attending the dinner?"

"Yes, as a matter of fact, I am."

"And the fashion show?"

"That, too."

Something was a little off kilter, she thought. Was he a reporter? Had she been saying too much? No, of course she hadn't, but sometimes it was tiresome, this odd feeling of always being on her guard, of always holding herself in readiness for some unspecified disaster. Her responsibilities weighed too heavily upon her. She'd lost her youth and her freedom and had grown old at thirty-one. She turned and stared once more at the pool. If only she could tear off her clothes and dive into the black water. Maybe if she swam to the other side, she'd emerge as an Egyptian princess in some strange, wonderful place and time.

But all she did was turn back to the handsome stranger standing there smiling at her, as though he alone were responsible for her mood—a mood she couldn't afford when she had so much at stake. She was flustered by his friendly scrutiny and had to stop herself from explaining why she was there. She had rushed back from the Medieval Court where the fashion show was to be held, merely to check the table seating.

"Let's see," she said, "the place cards, if you'll excuse me. My schedule is really running tight."

"Please, don't let me interfere."

Kelly picked up her clipboard and began to inspect the place cards. Her assistant had seen to the complete seating plan, but Kelly wanted to make certain that the central tables were given to the most generous donors to Job-Up.

Everything was to her satisfaction, but still something bothered her. For the first time she was thinking of the incongruity of holding a charity event in the Met, of holding an event to benefit New York's underclass in one of the cathedrals of the city's upper class.

"Orchids and golden rod—hothouse flowers and common weeds. These bouquets express the theme of the evening rather well, don't they?" Tony Campbell commented, as though reading her mind.

"Yes," she said, looking at him in surprise. "But how beautifully the exotic and the commonplace meld together. You do agree, don't you?"

She thought his eyes, whose color still eluded her, were shining with an intensity that had nothing to do with their conversation. He didn't answer her, and to break the momentary spell, she dusted her hands. "I'm about done here," she told him. "If you'll excuse me, I must get back to work. There are dozens of things . . ." She let the sentence dangle.

"I'll come along."

"How'd you get in here, anyway? This is off-limits," she asked him over her shoulder as she hurried out of the temple court and into the darkened galleries beyond. Kelly was aware of her heels clicking along the marble floor. She was equally aware of the tall man beside her and his quiet, easy gait.

"One only has to assume an air of unmistakable authority," he said. "No one—not the museum guards certainly—will question a tuxedo and a faint air of intense concentration. It's all quite simple, actually."

The music of a violin and harp playing something appropriately ancient could be heard as they approached the Medieval Court. "Are you a gate-crasher then?" she asked, turning briefly and studying him.

He shook his head.

"Reporter?"

"No, again. I came on behalf of Gregory Solow."

"Oh, don't tell me," she groaned. "He missed his flight." Gregory was due in from England and had promised to return in time to host the event.

"Business," Tony said, shrugging helplessly.

"Damn, what in the world does he think this is? Oh, I'm sorry," she said. "It's none of your affair, is it?"

"I'm taking his place—" he began, but Kelly glanced at her watch and saw she was running late.

"Fine," she said. "We're at table three. Mrs. Laurence's table, as a matter of fact. Just give her a killing smile. I'll see you later."

She went at a near run toward the Medieval Court, certain he hadn't moved an inch and, in fact, was watching her closely.

Once in the court, she was waylaid by Gail Ester-brook, her assistant, and dragged quickly back to the makeshift dressing room. There Kelly spent the next fifteen minutes checking over the models and their clothes. She had dallied back at the temple, knowing how tight her schedule was, and even now, still couldn't quite shake the curious magic that had come over her. Her staff, luckily, had been a lot busier.

Except, of course, for Isabella, who stood in the corner with a faint, grudging expression on her face. Fear, thought Kelly. She doesn't want to be here. She's frightened, afraid of making a mistake, and she doesn't trust a soul, not even me. Kelly went over to the teenager and put an arm around her shoulder. "One dress, Isabella. And to think it's your own design. That's something you can carry around with you for your whole life—a dress shown at the Metropolitan Museum of Art."

"But I hate the dress, Miss Aldrich. It stinks. It doesn't look the way I wanted it to."

"The dress doesn't stink," Kelly said patiently, giving her an extra hug. "And it's being worn by the most glamorous model in New York. Look, I don't have time to talk, but you've trusted me until now, haven't you?" The girl gave her a dubious smile. Kelly laughed. "Okay, why don't you try to help Marie with the accessories?"

Isabella shrugged and made her way across the small dressing room. She'd get underfoot and probably make a mess of things, but Kelly wouldn't give up on her. Isabella was what Job-Up was all about. The youngster was gifted, and Kelly had elected to be her mentor. Isabella was going to finish high school, then was going on to fashion studies. She'd succeed in spite of herself. Discipline, that was all she needed, Kelly told herself, and Kelly possessed discipline enough for two.

Kelly glanced once more at her watch. "Time. Let's get the fashion show on the road."

"Time, everyone," Gail echoed as the activity in the small, crowded room suddenly speeded up and became more purposeful.

Kelly briefly examined herself in the long, standing mirror that had been brought in for the evening. Someone she didn't quite know stared back at her, someone she'd met at a party or who shopped at Lambs, someone with discriminating taste but a slightly goofy expression on her face. And there was an orchid tucked behind the stranger's ear.

But, that was no stranger in the mirror. That was old Kelly Aldrich all right, with the same brown hair and brown eyes. Only she'd been pushed slightly off kilter by a man with a killing smile.

"I was wondering about that orchid," Gail said. "Looks very sexy, Kelly."

"Does it?"

"Yeah. Very humanizing, a flower in the hair."

"Good Lord, have I been inhuman?"

Gail laughed. She was a dark-haired, sturdy individual, impressed by no one and utterly trustworthy. "Not inhuman, Kelly, just too damn perfect."

"Oh—oh, perfect, what a horrible thing to say." Kelly left the orchid in place. She wore tiny pearl earrings, usually hidden by her hair, and a mauve gown with a deep V-neckline. She stuck her tongue out at herself, a gesture to remind herself just who she was, turned and clapped her hands loudly, half hoping the sound might awaken her from her strange mood. "Okay, everybody, let's go. Music ready?"

"Music ready," Gail said.

"Then let's move." Almost automatically Kelly glanced over at Isabella, the one possible glitch in what should be a smooth forty minutes. The teenager was sifting through the jewelry box. For a moment Kelly's heart sank, but then she brightened. No, the operative word was *trust*, and Isabella would turn into a responsible human being if it were the last thing Kelly ever did.

She took a deep breath and stepped through the lacy Spanish gates and onto the runway that ran the length of the court. All three hundred guests, seated in gilt chairs on either side of the runway, applauded enthusiastically. For the past hour they'd been entertained in the museum's Great Hall, where drinks and hors d'oeuvres had been served with a lavish hand.

The scent of expensive perfume mingled with the musty fragrance of a couple dozen candles burning throughout the court. The beatific expressions of the medieval statues lent a softness to the atmosphere, as though the plaster saints were tolerating the lavish event because it was all for a good cause.

Kelly smiled, hoping the goofy expression she'd seen in the mirror earlier had been a mirage and that what the audience saw was the Kelly Aldrich they expected, the person who told them how to wear their hair and what clothes to buy, the president of Lambs, their favorite shopping emporium.

As the applause died, the music, a recorded array of ancient dances, began, and the first model walked out onto the runway. Kelly started her commentary quickly, saving her Job-Up pitch for when Isabella's dress would come on view. Kelly had selected summery linens and cottons, ranging from cool business suits to soft-skirted dresses. As a result, Isabella's dress, coming halfway through the event, was strange and stunning, a little off-key yet perfectly suited to the show. Very short and skintight, the dress was made of gold Lurex with wide, capped sleeves pleated at the shoulders. The model shimmered down the runway. Sexy and youthful, the garment spoke of a young girl's yearning. The applause was gratifying, underscoring Kelly's belief in young designers. Isabella's saucy little dress led perfectly into an impassioned pitch for Job-Up.

The fashion show closed after twenty additional minutes of evening clothes, ending with the traditional white bridal gown.

"Did they get their money's worth?" Kelly asked Gail immediately after in the dressing room where the models changed into their street clothes, and where the dresses and accessories were carefully boxed.

"Isabella's in the ladies' room having hysterics," Gail responded. "Convinced her life is over, for reasons not quite understood."

"Damn. Look, Gail, would you see she gets home in one piece?"

"She's coming home with me, remember?"

Kelly remembered. Isabella lived on Staten Island, and Gail had volunteered to let her stay overnight in her Manhattan apartment so that the girl wouldn't have to make the long trip home late at night.

Gail reached out and touched her arm. "Kelly, it really went off well, and the pitch for Job-Up and Isabella was perfect. The dress freaked the ladies out—not quite in the Lambs style, but maybe they'll ante up more money, anyway."

Kelly leaned over and spontaneously kissed her assistant on the cheek. "See you tomorrow." The orchid tumbled from her hair to the ground. She bent to pick it up. "Worse for the wear," she said, showing it to Gail.

"Just a second." Gail took the flower and placed it at the low-cut V of Kelly's neckline. "There you go, my dear. You have a penchant for being so correct that I sometimes want to scream."

"What's come over you, Gail? That's the second time tonight you've reamed me out for doing my job."

Gail shook her head. "Tired is all. Aren't you?"

"I'd have to stop and think about it and I don't dare."

"Kelly you're going to have to slow down one of these days."

"Slow down? I don't even know the meaning of the words. Something about traffic? Danger ahead?" She stopped, a long, low shiver spreading across her skin. Danger ahead—what an extraordinary idea. "Never mind," she told Gail. "As a matter of fact, I'm planning a week's holidays in Great Britain."

"Miracle of miracles. When?"

"Next month."

"Have a nice trip."

They parted with friendly grins, and Kelly returned to the Medieval Court to discover that the crowd had thinned considerably and was now ambling through the galleries to the Temple of Dendur.

"Nice show, Kelly." Mrs. Laurence, a white-haired elegantly groomed dowager, came up to her, smiling. "Especially Isabella's sexy little number. You could hear the gasps in the audience when the model sauntered out, but I can think of a dozen husbands who'll order it for their mistresses."

"Mrs. Laurence!" Kelly feigned shock at such a notion. Then she remembered Tony Campbell, who would be sitting with her instead of Gregory. "By the way," she said, "Mr. Campbell will be at your table. I believe you know him."

"Tony." The woman's face brightened. "Marvelous."

Well that settled that, Kelly thought. Mr. Campbell—Tony—was all right. Certainly no gate-crasher. But what was Mrs. Laurence saying now?

"I was stunned at the news, of course, Kelly. You and Gregory certainly know how to keep a secret. Well, never mind, that's your business. See you later." Mrs. Laurence hurried away, calling out to her nephew, who was several steps behind her.

Kelly gazed curiously after the woman. *Stunned at the news?* She had no idea what Mrs. Laurence was talking about. She was about to go after her when Anthony Campbell materialized.

"Here you are," he said. "Ready?"

Her heart gave a funny little leap, as though he were solely responsible for the way everyone seemed to be behaving. "Ready? Good heavens, for what?"

"Blue moon," he admonished her. "Does things with the memory. I'm your table partner."

"Right," she said. "I just saw Mrs. Laurence and told her the good news. She said—" Kelly stopped. Just what had Mrs. Laurence said? "Come along, then." She beckoned him to follow her through the long galleries leading to the Great Hall, forcing herself not to linger on the way to examine the Saracen jewelry, icons and gold boxes on exhibit.

She couldn't remember when she'd last had the time to wander aimlessly through the impressive halls of the museum, tasting of its treasures as one would a buffet of gourmet foods.

"Kelly, *fantastico!*" She turned and recognized one of Lambs' best customers, a businesswoman Kelly's age who bought her entire working wardrobe at the store.

"Thanks," Kelly called out gaily, tucking back into her mind the dream of wandering through the museum alone, getting to know it, seeing the Temple of Dendur without tables and party decorations, perhaps even in the moonlight when she might conjure up ancient Egypt and commune with the spirits.

"Let's have lunch soon," her customer said, going quickly past her. "We'll have to talk about what's going to happen now."

"Now?" Kelly threw a glance at Tony, whose expression remained immobile. Her customer was gone before Kelly remembered Mrs. Laurence's curious remark.

She had no time to think as several more guests stopped to compliment her. On the wave of their enthusiasm she managed to win some pledges for Job-Up and promises of volunteer work.

If the museum wasn't quite the appropriate place for a charity event, it was still the most exciting—and her customers clearly thought so, too. "Not bad for an evening's work," she told Tony when they reached the Great Hall. "Enough compliments to live on for a year."

"Compliments and pledges all in the same breath," he said admiringly. "You really know how to work a room, or should I say a gallery?"

"That's what it's all about, knowing how to uncurl a few tight fists. The program makes a great deal of sense because it's one-on-one. Find a kid's talent, go with it, and the kid's whole family benefits, too—"

"Hold it," Tony said, pulling up short. "You've already sold me ten different ways."

She laughed apologetically. "Sorry, I guess I'm a little keyed up. I get that way about this time of night. As a matter of fact, before an event of this size, I really get very little sleep."

"Then what the doctor suggests is a breath of fresh air."

"That's just what I plan on," Kelly told him, "but it'll have to come later, in that little space of time when I hail a cab a couple of hours from now. Let's go, Mr. Campbell, I think dinner is waiting."

"Kelly, I've got a better idea concerning dinner," he said. They were standing in the near-empty Great Hall.

"Oh, don't worry about it," Kelly said. "I never eat at these things."

"Food that bad?"

"That good. I've no appetite." In fact, she hadn't eaten properly in days, only toying with food she ordered into the office and finding it impossible to eat food she raided from her refrigerator at home. "Oh, don't worry," she said. "Tomorrow morning I'll wake up ravenous."

"I'm not thinking about tomorrow morning. I'm thinking about now. I suppose we can expect an hour of boring speeches."

"Some self-congratulation, anyway," she admitted. "We've arranged for the president of Job-Up to handle that, thank goodness. I'm out of it, except for smiling. And afterward there'll be lots of table-hopping, music, ambience so thick and treacly you could cut it with a wooden teaspoon."

"They won't even know you're gone," he said.

"Thank you. There's nothing I like better than knowing I'll never be missed."

"Let's go."

"But—"

"But, nothing. Do you really want to spend the evening smiling, even though you don't feel it?"

"Tell me you're a psychiatrist," she said.

"Is that what you'd like me to be?"

"If I had a choice, a magician."

"What if I told you I'm a salesman and I'm about to convince you to do something reason insists you can't, that is to get the devil out of here?"

Kelly caught sight of Gail moving through the Great Hall with a red-nosed Isabella in tow. "Nobody has ever accused me of not being able to make up my own mind," she said in a thoughtful tone. Then she added, "Well, at least not in a long time."

"Blue moon," he said in a soft, cajoling voice. "Let's go out and count the stars."

"This is New York," Kelly told him. "The one thing you don't see are stars."

He gave her an unexpected look of impatience, and Kelly realized that in another moment he'd disappear like the good leprechaun he was.

"Don't move," she said, and went rapidly over to her assistant. "Gail, everything taken care of? Clothes on their way back to the store?"

"All taken care of. We're going in to dinner now." Kelly had set aside a table for some of her senior staff at the rear of the gallery.

"There are a couple of empty seats at table six, my seat and Mr. Solow's. How about treating yourself and Isabella to a very posh center table at the festivities? Be my substitute, apologize for my absence, tell them a sudden migraine forced me to retreat."

"Be the hostess?" Gail looked at her in horror. "Where's Mr. Gregory, anyway?"

"Still in England, for all I know. You'll have to hold down the fort."

"But—" Gail began.

"But me no buts. This is an emergency. I'll be back a little later."

Unexpectedly the idea seemed to appeal to Gail, who owned a motorcycle and liked to skydive in her spare time. She smoothed her pretty black dress. "Okay, how about it, Isabellita? You game?"

Isabella sniffed, then rubbed her nose. "Look at the way I'm dressed."

"Go ahead," Kelly said, smiling encouragingly at her. "The dress you're wearing is perfect, and you know it. Have a ball. And *don't* worry."

Isabella held back, but Gail took her firmly by the elbow. "This night is going to make history for you, Isabellita."

Kelly waited while her assistant and the teenager made their way through the court in a curiously tentative gait, as though they'd unexpectedly found themselves walking on eggs.

Tony Campbell came over and regarded her with interest. "What was that about?"

"Just gave away a couple of seats at my table, yours included."

"Well, I'm making progress," he said, smiling. He took her arm. "Come on. We're out to have our own little feast. I happen to know a charming, romantic place for two."

Kelly continued to watch the retreating figures. Would Isabella know how to behave herself? Would she know which fork to use or how to reach for a piece of bread and how to butter it? The teenager was wearing a spare little dress that showed off her figure and beautiful legs. Nothing wrong there. And Isabella was ambitious. She was the best of the kids in the Job-Up program, with plenty of talent and an instinct about knowing how to present herself. So far.

When Kelly was growing up, her father had drummed manners and social mores into the Aldrich troop. "You're not going to make fools of yourselves when the time comes," he'd tell them. And when the time came she had been prepared. She didn't have Isabella's creative ability, but she'd been prepared for success.

Suddenly Kelly wondered now if she'd done the right thing in sending Gail and Isabella to sit with Mrs. Laurence. She almost ran after them, but Tony pulled her up short with a question.

"What's the problem? You look as if you've just seen trouble and it's come in wearing horns and carrying a pitchfork."

"I'm hoping we're not wide of the mark, that's all." She shook her head. "No, that's Job-Up's best shot on her way into the most elegant dinner being held in New York." Then she added with a self-deprecating laugh, "This evening, anyway."

"Let's go," he said, "before you change their minds for them." He drew her toward the exit. "Incidentally, I like your flower. I especially like the way you're wearing it."

Grappling with the idea of going off with him just like that, she fingered the orchid, murmuring a little absentmindedly, "This? It's about as wilted as I feel at the moment."

"Come on. Second thoughts are the last things you want to have just now."

He was right, she thought, matching her stride to his, they were. What was that clever little poem her mother had written?

Think.
And think once more.
Then all is lost.
What for?

CHAPTER TWO

THE SKY WAS the off-blue of New York nights, never quite dark because of the haze and the lights shining from its skyscrapers. The stars were pale, but the moon was full—round and bright. Kelly looked around the sea of bodies on the great lawn in Central Park. Candles dotted the night and occasional balloons announced a party here and there. The park was edged with baronial apartment houses on three sides, while the distant north side was hidden by trees. At the southern portion of the field was the makeshift band shell, empty for the moment of musicians. Kelly and Tony had missed the first two works being presented by the New York Philharmonic.

"Romantic place for two?" she asked. "Looks more like two hundred thousand."

"With you around, what makes you think I'd know the difference?"

Kelly groaned. "Ouch. You can sell me the Empire State Building sooner than that line. In fact, where's the bread? You just dished out enough honey for me to slather it on. Where will we sit, anyway?"

He pointed somewhere off to the left. "In that space just abandoned by that couple with the crying baby, and not a minute too soon."

"Was that a crying baby? Thank heavens. I thought it was the music."

"Come on." He took her hand and led her past some bicyclists leaning against their wheels, around an ice cream truck and behind a vendor selling hot dogs.

"Funny, these summer concerts in the park have been going on for years," Kelly said, "and I've never had the time to attend even one. What a perfectly beautiful evening for it, too."

"Ordered up just for you," Tony said. "Hold on tight. It's going to take a lot of fancy maneuvering to get to that spot before someone else does."

"You're sure you know what you're doing?"

"I always know what I'm doing."

"Somehow," she said, releasing his hand and finding it easier to hold on to his jacket, "I think you do."

They picked their way around blankets filled with people finishing up the last of their dinners, landing at last at the postage stamp spot that had just been vacated. As Kelly was about to sit down, Tony said, "Allow me." He whipped off his tuxedo jacket and spread it on the ground. *"Mademoiselle."* He made a deep, elaborate bow.

"Monsieur." Kelly sat down, arranging her long skirt, aware of people watching them quietly. "Pretty picture we make," she declared. "Me in my gown and you in your tux. They must think we're putting on the ritz."

"Just what we're doing," he said, reaching for the bottle of champagne he had cadged from the barman at the Hotel Carlyle where he was staying. "And they don't even know we've turned down a gourmet dinner for three hundred."

"Three hundred *plus* of New York's richest, if not finest."

"And here we are playing hooky." He reached for the shopping bag that held a long French bread and a wedge of Brie, also cadged from the hotel on their way to the park. "It's not the food, Kelly. It's the company." He handed her a wineglass, deftly opened the champagne and offered her some.

"The trouble is that Job-Up is my baby. And to think I walked out on it. I'll never be able to explain myself."

"Pretend you were there if anyone asks. Stare them down and dare them to disagree."

"I'm beginning to understand your modus operandi, Mr. Campbell."

"No," he told her after a slight hesitation, "I'm afraid my modus is a lot more complicated than you think." Then, as though to stop her from questioning him, he raised his glass. "Cheers."

"Cheers. Oh, look, the musicians are coming back on stage."

"Cheers and cheese," Tony said, breaking off a piece of bread for her. "No eating allowed during the singing." He handed her a slice of cheese with some bread and watched with an amused smile as she hungrily wolfed it down.

"No eating *allowed* or no eating *aloud*?" Kelly reached for the program. "What's next? Ah, Tchaikovsky, the *1812 Overture*. Wonderful. It says with fireworks. Fireworks, imagine! I love this evening. Notice how remarkably quiet it is, considering the amount of people?"

"And the unknowing believe New Yorkers are incapable of behaving themselves," Tony said.

"Some can, some can't," Kelly said, "like everywhere else." Far off in the distance a fire engine screamed. High above an airplane made its way east to La Guardia Airport. Lights twinkled in apartment windows. "But," she added, "it is the most exciting city in the world."

"Especially if you're on top of it." His voice had a sudden cool edge to it that surprised her.

"And aren't you on top of it, Mr. Campbell?"

"What do you think?"

She tilted her head and regarded him. "I'll take a ballpark guess. Yes. Do you want to add to my store of knowledge about you, which right now adds up to nothing?"

"I would, but our attention is required," he said, nodding to the podium and the conductor who stood there, a tiny figure under the distant, lighted canopy.

Again Kelly guessed Tony was holding back deliberately. He had been at the Temple of Dendur, not just because of Gregory, but for some other reason. Gazing thoughtfully at him, she asked, "How did this happen? I mean, my sitting here with you and a bottle of champagne and two hundred thousand people. I don't even know who you are. I mean, I've taken it for granted that you are who you said you are and that you know Gregory and that you're standing in for him and, of course, Mrs. Laurence did recognize your name, but—" She stopped. "Oh, dear. I don't think I should be enjoying myself."

He laughed. "You Puritan you."

"But who *are* you?"

He nodded at the stage without answering. The conductor raised his baton. The first note was struck on a sudden movement of brisk spring air that sliced through the park. Kelly shivered and hugged her arms. In another quick movement, as the music flowed out from strategically placed loudspeakers, Tony Campbell had pulled her back against him, sheltering her between his arms.

"But—" she began, and tried halfheartedly to pull away.

He put his finger to her lips. "Shh."

Kelly gave up and leaned limply back into him, as though the day had begun with just this ending in mind. She closed her eyes and let the music engulf her.

SHE WAS ALONE at the far end of the Medieval Court. Beyond the Spanish gates, under a cool beam of light cast by the full moon, music rose from the statues, each playing a musical instrument—an oboe, French horn, flute, violin—in a dialogue that echoed across the huge hall. Kelly was entranced. She felt enveloped in a warm cocoon. She didn't dare move. If she were to make the slightest gesture, the music would stop and it would all disappear. Kelly sighed and let the music soar.

Then all of a sudden there was a great crash of sound. Kelly opened her eyes slowly, uncertain where she was. It took a few seconds to remember she was in Central Park, sheltered in Tony Campbell's arms. She felt his lips against her hair. But a sudden burst of light above caught her unawares.

Fireworks and the crash of cannons almost obliterated the music. The applause and the shouts of ex-

citement faded to background noise. She needn't come
fully awake, not yet. How wonderful to be part of this
huge, anonymous crowd, to be without worry, without the adding machine and computers that seemed to
inhabit her head twenty-four hours a day, to be held
by strong arms, to take in Tony's masculine scent and
to feel his lips against her hair. The music reached a
great crescendo as bursts of light obliterated the sky.

Had she lost all sense? What was she doing here?

"Hey, sleepyhead, the party's over." Tony's voice
was close to her ear. She felt the softness of his breath
and tried to deny the sensation it produced.

Kelly struggled out of his arms and got quickly to
her feet. "Oh, no," she said, faintly embarrassed yet
wondering why she felt so wonderful. "I slept through
it all. But then," she added, stretching luxuriously, "I
didn't really. I mean, the music penetrated my sub-
conscious. It was there all along. I had the most delicious dream."

"I was in your dream, I hope."

"As a matter of fact, you weren't."

"Too bad. I had the distinct impression you were
smiling."

"I'm sure I *was* smiling."

"But not over me. Pity." He took their food bag
and deposited it in a container as they joined the
crowd making its way out of the park.

"I won't even apologize for falling asleep," Kelly
said. "It's been a long day."

"The kind you usually have."

"Right," she agreed. "The kind I usually have and
usually don't fall asleep over. Look," she said, point-

ing to a rise off to the left, "there's the museum. We ought to go back. What time is it?"

He glanced at his watch. "Eleven. Damn."

Kelly found him frowning. "Is anything wrong?"

"No, no," he said hastily but quickened his pace. "I should find a telephone."

"There'll be one on the avenue. Or in the museum." She was aware of an almost imperceptible change in his mood. Because of the crowd edging out of the park, they were obliged to walk single file along the footpath. She moved ahead of him, her mind working furiously. He'd had a date and was now worrying about how to handle her.

Kelly stepped off the path entirely, angling to the left to a rise outside the museum where there were fewer people. She felt Tony at her back and turned to him. "I think I ought to be there to say goodbye to my guests. Gregory would have a fit if he knew what I'd done."

"I wouldn't worry about Gregory."

She stopped short and gazed back at him. "Oh, wouldn't you?" Tony hooked his jacket on one finger over his shoulder. He had removed his tie and his shirt collar was open. A lock of hair had fallen over his forehead. In the soft, night-illuminated light, she thought with a strange little twist of her heart that Tony Campbell was the most sensual, attractive man she had ever met, and in another few minutes the adventure would be over.

"Just let me make my phone call and then we'll talk a little more," he said.

But when they reached Fifth Avenue, Kelly saw the limousines lined up in front of the museum, which meant the Job-Up charity affair was still under way. "Make your phone call," she said. "I'm going back."

He glanced at his watch again, a gesture that struck her as particularly grating because it was one she often made herself. Watch, time, the little hand and the big hand, move on to the next unit, the next category, keep moving folks, Kelly Aldrich coming through.

She began to walk along the avenue toward the museum entrance, feeling the folds of her long skirt swish lightly against her legs. Tony took her bare arm. "Chilly?" he asked.

She shook her head. There were scores of people on the street and on the stairs leading to the front entrance. The fountains on either side played and shivered in the night air. The museum was dramatically lit by spotlights, a huge temple to the god of art, but Kelly found herself reluctant to go back inside.

The door to the Great Hall opened, and Mrs. Laurence stepped out, followed by her nephew. A chauffeur whipped to attention in front of his limousine. Kelly was aware of Tony's hand tightening around her bare arm.

She remembered Mrs. Laurence's cryptic words and experienced a moment of fear. Who was this man, this Anthony Campbell, who hadn't answered her questions? She'd believed every word he'd said about Gregory. She gazed at the front entrance again. Perhaps Gregory Solow would come out after all, wondering where she had gone off to. She was now chilled by the memory of her sending Gail and Isabella back to Gregory's table without checking out Tony's story. What in the world had happened to her this evening?

She glanced involuntarily up at the moon. Moon madness? It couldn't be.

Mrs. Laurence's progress down the stairs made up Kelly's mind for her. She had the feeling she was Cinderella and had stayed too long at the ball. If she wasn't careful, she'd turn into a pumpkin. She was aware of the tightness in her voice when she spoke to Tony. "I'll manage some reasonable excuse tomorrow about why I wasn't there. The truth, for instance, that I was dragged away by a complete stranger to the sound of violins and cannons."

"Couldn't have thought of a better one," he said, releasing his grip on her arm. "They'll never believe the truth, and that's when you can feel very smug."

Kelly saw a cab heading down the avenue. She darted into the street and hailed it. By the time Tony came up to her, she had given her address to the driver and they were pulling away from the curb. She waved through the open window and didn't turn around as the cab sped away. The orchid, she found, had fallen into her lap.

"DARLING, YOU'RE LATE." Diane Bourne offered her cheek for a kiss, held both hands out to Tony Campbell and then drew him into her apartment.

"Sorry." He didn't even try to offer a decent apology, because there was no clever way to explain Kelly Aldrich falling asleep in his arms at a concert for two hundred thousand in Central Park. And he had no explanation for the fact that he hadn't wanted to awaken her, but sat there holding her, feeling her featherweight and her slight, even breathing, smelling the soft, clean scent of her shiny hair.

He'd promised Gregory Solow he'd talk to Kelly before the news broke in the morning edition of the *Wall Street Journal*. And he hadn't. And he couldn't explain to himself why. In fact, there was no way to examine what he *had* done, either. His behavior was aberrant—not his usual style at all.

"Worthwhile, I hope," Diane went on, "your showing up an hour late. Darling," she said, standing back and observing him with a disconcerted look in her eye, "no tie, shirt collar loose, your jacket slung over your shoulder as though you've just trekked the Sahara—what in the world's going on?"

He gave her a sudden crooked grin. "Blue moon," he told her. "You know what a blue moon is."

"An unhappy moon, I suppose." She let go of his hands and led the way into her living room. She was a tall, slender woman in her late-thirties whose long, flowing hair was still the bright red of her youth. She was sophisticated, beautiful and witty, and at the moment Tony wanted to be a thousand miles away from her. He wanted to escape from New York and from his future, too.

Diane Bourne and he had been friends for years, occasionally more than friends. She'd floated through life, he realized, suddenly seeing her in a new way. She was fun and she was predictable and she lacked commitment. Perhaps until that very moment he had found her superficiality the most attractive thing about her.

But then he'd gone to the museum looking for Kelly Aldrich, but what he'd found he hadn't been looking for at all. Gregory Solow had said Kelly was attractive, but then so was Diane. He'd said Kelly was clever and witty, but then so was Diane. But Kelly Aldrich had a certain fragility, which he'd responded to immediately. Now he knew he would have to break off his relationship with Diane. It was that simple. One moment he'd stopped into the court of Dendur, and the next moment he'd felt his life had changed irrevocably.

Too bad that by morning Kelly would be his sworn enemy. But perhaps that, too, was why he found her so appealing.

"A blue moon," he explained, following Diane, "occurs in a month when there are two full moons, one at the beginning, one at the end. Come on." He put his arm loosely around her shoulders and directed her through the living room onto the terrace. "There." He pointed to the sky and the moon that had wheeled lower toward the horizon.

"And it brings madness with it, I suppose."

"No," he told her. "I think it brings something magical, a feeling of life being out of joint—but charmingly so."

"I wonder." Diane regarded him with the same look of bewilderment as before.

"You wonder what?"

"Exactly what happened tonight at that charity dinner?"

"It was very charitable."

She glanced back at the moon again, then walked back into the living room. "Something more happened tonight, didn't it?" Her tone was wistful. "I feel a disclaimer coming on. Rather in the form of, 'We're great friends, but...'" She picked up a decanter of cognac from the cocktail table and poured some into a snifter, which she handed him with a sympathetic smile.

Tony met her eyes for an instant and then looked away. "Diane, I . . ." he hesitated.

She gave a sharp little laugh and didn't let him continue. "I stopped at Lambs today. Funny, often as I've been in the store, I never really looked at it. I mean, looked into every nook and cranny."

Tony rocked the glass slowly in his hand before taking his first sip. "And what opinion did you form?"

"It's very beautiful, all of a piece. Displays are stunning. Whoever's running it has exquisite taste. There was this wonderful silk paisley jacket. Never mind. I've always had the distinct impression one could outfit one's seasonal wardrobe there from head to toe and come out looking incredibly smart. Darling, I know," she added with a little laugh. "It's all Greek to you. Not up your alley. What in hell do you intend to do with the place?"

"The most valuable thing about Lambs is its real estate."

"You know, Tony, you can be a cold, calculating number when you want to."

"Shh. Don't tell anyone."

"Really," she said. "You're a shark, aren't you?"

"No, I just know nothing about fashion, and if there's one thing I've learned, it's not to attempt to operate out of my league."

"You mean you've finally discovered something out of your league?"

Tony smiled. "For a public relations person, you know very little about the way I work or Terro, either."

"On the contrary, I know a hell of a lot about the way you work," she said, lightly kissing his cheek.

He laughed, shaking his head. "I sometimes think you're a little too clever for your own good, Diane."

"You're paying me to learn everything," she said, reminding him that she had been hired to write a vanity book on the company.

"My brother hired you," he said, "not I."

"And you still don't approve of the idea of selling the name of Terro to the American public."

"There's no need to tell the American public we've arrived on its shores."

"Perhaps you're right, but tell that to your brother, not to me."

He could call Kelly on the telephone, ask to see her, tell her before morning broke, help ease the pain if he could. But, no, in the end, she was Gregory's problem, not his. His offering to help out had been spontaneous... and out of line. Kelly Aldrich was simply not his to confront, not quite yet. What else he had to do with her would happen inevitably, and in good time.

"Tony, you're drifting."

Damn, he'd better shake himself out of it.

"You'd better scoot, my boy," she said. The expression on her face let him know that she understood something had happened tonight in which she had no part. "Friends?" she asked. "Friends but no longer lovers?"

"Always friends." He kissed her lightly on the cheek and left. Something had happened, but he'd put no name to it, not yet.

THE APARTMENT HELD four rooms, each of which had a floor-to-ceiling view of the East River with nothing to obstruct it, neither building nor highway. Her view, in fact, was like that of a ship's prow with nothing but the water below.

Upon entering her apartment Kelly did as always: she dropped her bag onto the foyer table and made her way into the darkened living room and over to the window, where she stood for a moment admiring her view. Directly below was the black lane of the river, with the island in the center and the shoreline of Queens just beyond. A skyscraper had recently been built in downtown Queens, disturbing its otherwise flat landscape.

But it wasn't the skyline or even the river she was thinking about; it was Tony Campbell and the way he had persuaded her with a smile to abandon her duty, to walk away from more than three hundred paying guests. What a mess, she thought. Her telephone would ring off the hook in the morning, and even the truth, which Tony agreed was perfectly serviceable, would sound like a blatant lie.

"I left the party with the most extraordinarily handsome man," she said, trying the words out loud. "I'd have abandoned my job, my friends and my reputation for such a man, but he's a chimera. He doesn't exist. And, anyway, at the end of the night I ran away from him because he looked at his watch."

She turned from the river view, then closed her eyes and conjured up Tony Campbell quickly. Light hair, strong chin with a decided cleft, a long indentation in his right cheek that served for a dimple, but she was uncertain of the color of his eyes. Gray or perhaps amber, she decided. And when he'd drawn her back against him, the feel of his arms around her had been so natural, so calming, so coddling, that she had instantly fallen asleep. Fallen asleep.

Kelly went into her bedroom and switched on the bedside lamp. The decor was all white and the curtainless window reflected the room back at her. She could see herself in the black glass, and behind her, the white bed, white walls hung with pale paintings, white carpet. The pristine room didn't even allow for a mussed bed.

She stripped her gown off quickly, letting it lie in a puddle at her feet. Then her bra and panties, which she tossed onto a chair. She hadn't moved but surveyed her trim, lithe figure in the black window glass high above the river where no one could see her. Quiet, lately virginal Kelly Aldrich, successful thirty-one-year-old president of that gem of a store, Lambs, Kelly Aldrich, protégé of Gregory Solow, recent widower and her frequent escort to charity balls, private dinner parties, the opera, the ballet, concerts.

Just who was Anthony Campbell? How did he know Gregory? Why, in fact, had Gregory sent him to the museum as his messenger—a complete stranger? A call to her office would have sufficed.

Was it possible Tony was a gate-crasher, after all? A gigolo? Had he stolen her away from the museum to make love to her, to ensnare her? Single, successful businesswoman in need of a man—was it advertised all over town? The idea made no sense. After all, Gregory, hadn't appeared.

Or had he? Perhaps he'd been at the table waiting for her when Gail and Isabella showed up. If so, it was a nice mess she'd gotten herself into.

She turned from the window, went to the closet and reached for her worn chenille bathrobe, her favorite because it removed all her pretensions. She'd call Gregory's number now, at midnight, and if he was home, apologize.

Gregory's butler answered the telephone on the first ring. "Is Mr. Solow in?" Kelly asked. "This is Kelly Aldrich. I know it's late," she added apologetically. The butler knew her voice, of course, but it was a formal game they played.

"I'm sorry, Ms Aldrich. He hasn't returned yet."

"You mean from England."

"I believe he missed the flight out."

"Did he say when he'd be in?"

"I believe tomorrow."

"Thank you," she said. "Just tell him I called." She hung up, feeling silly for doubting Gregory.

She stood quietly for a long moment and gazed at her reflection in the window. In her chenille bathrobe with the sleeves pushed up, she seemed young and fragile. She touched her cheek; it was unnaturally warm. Was it possible to fall in love under the spell of the moon? How else could she account for her behavior tonight? She turned away.

It seemed to her that she could still feel the warmth of his arms around her, his voice in her ear, the touch of his lips against her hair.

She'd always been cool and controlled, the ramrod kid who was going to move to the top and then think about falling in love. She'd accomplished at thirty-one the very thing her whole life had been in preparation for; falling in love hadn't happened, however. No one had scaled the pinnacle to present himself as an object of desire. But then, falling in love wasn't arranged the same way as a business deal.

She thought of Warren Bedford, whom she dated occasionally. He was out of the country at the moment on business. In a matter of time they'd begin to date more often and after a while he'd propose and she'd have to decide whether she wanted to marry him. They had everything in common, from a love of music to the dream of a house in the country. But having everything in common was obviously not enough.

She hugged her arms, feeling an unexpected sense of longing, feeling a queer, helpless love for a complete stranger, a man she might never see again.

Tony Campbell was staying at the Hotel Carlyle, or said he was. For all she really knew, he could be the maître d'. Who was he, she wondered, and why in the world had she let him take her away from the museum? And why had she run away from him?

Kelly went into her kitchen to brew a soothing cup of green tea and stood staring at it while it steeped, her brow creased in a frown. During the past couple of months Gregory had been increasingly absent from Lambs, leaving its management to Kelly. From the moment she'd received her promotion, he'd told her, "You're the president, my dear. The ball's in your court." He'd repeated the words just before this last trip abroad—a trip he'd already extended beyond his original deadline.

Gregory had always felt that Lambs was the ruby in the crown of Solow Enterprises, and he kept on top of its operations—or he had until his wife, Suzanne, died six months previously. Nothing had been the same since then. Her death hadn't been a shock; she'd been ill from the time when Gregory had hired Kelly straight out of the M.B.A. program at New York University. But even with the years to steel himself against the inevitable, Gregory's grief had been overwhelming.

"The ball's in my court," Kelly told him when he'd been preparing to leave for England—repeating his words. "I don't think I'm ready to run with it alone," she said. "I'm kind of used to popping it off you."

He smiled, although the lines around his eyes told her the smile came hard. "What I saw in you seven years ago when I hired you was determination, intelligence and pluck. They're still the most telling things about you, Kelly. I handed you the title of president because I believe you're right for the job. Trust me the way I trust you. I have to rely on you more than ever."

His heavy-lidded eyes shrewdly took her in. He knows me better than my father ever did, she realized as she allowed a pliant smile to let him know she wouldn't argue further. She studied his melancholy face. He'd lost weight and his silver hair some of its luster. He seemed considerably older than his years. He was tired, worn to the bone, she decided.

He'd been right about giving her complete authority. Lambs hadn't gone under, and after a while Kelly became used to making decisions alone and sticking to them. More and more Lambs came to reflect her image, and profits had increased right along with her sense of power and certitude.

But this night should have been Gregory's as well as hers, and they had both run out on it. The whole evening seemed out of kilter, as if the earth had tilted on its axis and was stubbornly refusing to right itself.

When the tea had the dark, dry taste she liked, she poured herself a cup and grabbed a book and went into her bedroom. She wasn't sleepy but nevertheless climbed into bed, propping herself up.

Not being sleepy had little to do with Gregory or the charity event; it had to do with a man she'd never met before that evening, the man who had kidnapped her, held her in his arms, and then . . . and then . . . *glanced at his watch*, as though it were midnight and he'd turn into a pumpkin. Only it was she, Cinderella, who'd grabbed the coach and escaped home.

CHAPTER THREE

THE SILVERY LIGHT DISAPPEARED. For a long while the world lay dark. Then the slow mounting toward sunrise began. In a dreamless sleep Kelly turned restlessly when the first rays of the sun burst through her window. She awakened quickly, without her usual slow coming back to life of other mornings.

A glance at her clock told her she could stay in bed another hour. But it was a pot of coffee she craved, a full, head-clearing pot. She climbed out of bed and made for the shower. First things first.

"Cold showers, that's what you want. Every morning a cold shower. Gets you awake and ready to cope." That had been her father's morning lecture to the three of them, Kelly, Victor and Jim, siblings in the Aldrich household. And every morning Daniel would see them up and out and on their way to school, bright-eyed—thanks to the cold showers—and ready for success.

Kelly had hated cold showers then, and she hated them now, but all of her father's orders had stuck, at least to some extent, so she compromised with lukewarm showers.

As she stood under the stream of water, she recalled how she'd left Tony Campbell standing in front of the museum while she'd raced for a cab. She hadn't said goodbye, or, thank you, or even, have a nice day. She'd decided he had a date, and that was sufficient reason for her to grab the first coach that had come along. It must have been momentary moon madness. If she'd had her wits about her, she'd have invited him back to her apartment to make the phone call and found out what it was all about.

Not true, of course, was her decision twenty minutes later when she sat in the kitchen with her cup of coffee. She wouldn't have invited him home. She'd have lingered, uncertain, waiting for him to make the first move.

The thump of the morning newspapers being delivered hit the front door. Kelly stepped out into the hallway, collected them and scanned the headlines on her way back to the kitchen. But not eagerly. She didn't expect coverage of her charity event until the next day. She unfolded the *Wall Street Journal* and sat down at her kitchen table with her cup of coffee at her elbow.

The name Solow struck her at once, but she was concentrating on the party and thought the paper had somehow managed an early story on it, after all. But a second glance told her something quite different: Solow Enterprises Sold to Terro Limited.

She flattened the paper on the table and bent over it. Nothing quite registered. It can't be, she told herself. Then she remembered Mrs. Laurence's remark: "Stunned at the news."

And someone else last night had said something about how things were going to be changed. She stared down at the story:

Solow Enterprises, with major holdings in New York real estate, hotels and Lambs, a small, exclusive department store on Manhattan's Fifty-seventh Street, has been acquired by British conglomerate Terro Limited, its chairman, Sebastian Campbell, said today.

Kelly felt beads of sweat form on her forehead. She reached for the *New York Times* and pulled out the business section. The story was inside on page three. Not front-page stuff to anyone but Kelly Aldrich.

"Stunned at the news" was putting it mildly. As Kelly carefully read both stories, a heavy, throbbing pressure in her chest told her she needed to get some answers right away. She glanced at the time and realized she'd be pulling Rudy Marchetta out of bed, but it wouldn't be the first time.

The phone was answered on the first ring. Gregory's lawyer had scarcely time to mutter his name when Kelly said, "How come everybody knows except me?" *Everybody* meaning Mrs. Laurence and the people she had gossiped to the night before.

"Did they call you, too?"

"If you mean Terro, no. I had to read it in the *Wall Street Journal*."

"Six in the morning, Kelly, they woke me with a phone call from London. That's the reason I never became a doctor. I didn't want phone calls at six in the morning."

"You mean Gregory called you."

"Not unless he's had a sex change recently. A very lovely English voice invited me to a meeting at the Pierre at nine this morning, suite 1009. When I began to ask questions, I was told in polite British terms that I'd learn everything at the meeting. Then I read the story, and now I know as much as you do.''

"You mean Gregory never consulted you about selling his business? Last night at the Met Mrs. Laurence was one step ahead of us. She knew and apparently told everybody else.''

"Mrs. Laurence sits on the board of directors of the universe, Kelly. She knows everything.''

And obviously she sits on Terro's board, too, thought Kelly.

"As for Gregory," Rudy went on, "he's the sole owner of Solow Enterprises. If he wants to sell it, he doesn't have to consult me or anyone else. He hasn't any stockholders, no board, no nothing. He can do any damn thing he wants.''

"It's strangely underhanded and not like him,'' Kelly snapped.

"He pays me a salary to do his bidding and you, too. He doesn't owe us any explanations.''

Oh, yes, he does, she thought. *Yes, he does.*

"And, incidentally, I was told to ask you to get to the Pierre around ten.''

"This is the worst sort of nightmare, isn't it, Rudy?''

"Not necessarily. It may be the best thing that's ever happened to you,'' he said cheerfully.

When she hung up, Kelly thought perhaps Rudy's cheeriness was put on. After all, Rudy Marchetta would lose a valuable client with the sale. Although successful attorneys always landed on their feet.

Which left her with a couple of hours to stew in. She phoned Gail and caught her about to leave her apartment. "I'm afraid I'll be in a little late today, Gail."

"I heard the news," Gail said.

"In the *Times*?"

"No, at the table last night. Mrs. Laurence was full of it—in more ways than one."

"Right," Kelly said, realizing she'd all but forgotten the party. Somehow it had faded into the background along with a concert in the park. "How'd everything go?"

"Well, except for Mrs. Laurence ruining my appetite, fine."

"If any calls come in, reporters from the media, et cetera, play dumb. Don't answer any questions. And that goes for customers and store employees, as well."

"No problem."

There was no point in trying to figure anything out, Kelly decided. Gregory had been lost in his own world since his wife's death. More than once he'd told her, "Things will never be the same." She should have taken his remark at more than face value.

Kelly killed some time rummaging through her clothes closet, knowing she had to feel in command when she appeared at the Pierre. A combat uniform, perhaps, complete with boots. Would the chairman of the board be there? And Gregory? Perhaps he'd been in New York all along, hiding out.

She chose a loosely fitted black cashmere jacket with a houndstooth skirt, all elegance and business when finished with a white silk blouse, intricately patterned scarf in gray, red and white and midheeled black pumps. The correct mood, she decided, not as austere as all black, but heavy on international chic and correct for facing the guillotine—or was it the hangman's noose the British favored?

Kelly looked at herself in the mirror, and a wave of memories washed over her. She thought of her mother's sweet, dreamy face and her father's rigid, self-righteous expression, that of a man who was absolutely certain of his opinions and his way of life. And she thought of the fear that gripped her family when her father was laid off from his job in the steel mill. It happened periodically, often enough for Kelly and her brothers to understand their father's ambitions for them. They must choose a field for themselves, excel in it and leave the Pennsylvania steel town far behind. No layoffs for the Aldrich kids. Cold showers, high marks in school and an obsessive need to get ahead.

Oh, Daddy, she thought, *it can happen anywhere. Except from the top you have a longer way to fall.*

THE HOTEL PIERRE, which Kelly had always thought of as a wedding cake of a building, looked unexpectedly forbidding. She'd been there dozens of times, but until now the circumstances were invariably pleasant and challenging. Now it seemed to her that she was entering alien territory. She had no idea what she would walk into and how things would be when she left. Her throat was dry, and even though the hotel lobby was cool, she felt clammy and warm.

She reached the tenth floor and walked down the carpeted corridor, wishing her heart would stop hammering so hard. The self-assured, ruggedly handsome man who opened the door to the Terro suite gave her a warm smile and looked faintly familiar. "Ah, Miss

Aldrich, right on the button in time-honored New York tradition. Never a moment to waste. I'm Sebastian Campbell." He put his hand out and shook hers, then drew her into the room. The chairman of Terro Limited was middle-aged and dressed in a Savile Row suit, and Kelly had the sudden impression he couldn't be budged by a tank if he didn't want to be. "Wonderful weather, too, wouldn't you say?"

"Today especially," Kelly said. "They say in New York there's one perfect day a year. This may be the day, although knowing New Yorkers, they're still arguing about it." She surprised even herself with the unexpected ease with which she was able to handle herself. But then she'd spent the past seven years in pressure cooker situations.

Around the long, narrow conference table were a dozen royal blue upholstered chairs. The scent of coffee and French cigarettes drifted in the air.

Although there were others in the room, Kelly's eye was drawn curiously to the broad-shouldered and unmoving figure at the window. Then Rudy Marchetta extricated himself from the small group of men standing at the conference table and came over to her. He bent to kiss her cheek. "Prepare yourself," he whispered in her ear, "the Redcoats are coming."

"I think they're already here," she whispered back.

As Campbell introduced her around, Kelly could tell by their surprised smiles that she wasn't quite what they expected. *Yes, fellas, I'm young,* she wanted to say, *but don't let that fool you.* She smiled sweetly and offered a strong handshake, always aware of the unmoving figure at the window.

The introductions were concluded, with Kelly easily committing names and faces to memory, except one—the quiet, waiting figure at the window.

"Come along, Tony. I think we can begin now," Sebastian Campbell said with a touch of impatience in his voice. At his words, all of Kelly's cool poise fell away, though she'd known this was coming from the moment she'd entered the room. "My brother, Anthony Campbell," Sebastian added, "president and chief executive officer of Terro International. He'll be headquartered in New York and will oversee the operation of Solow. That, of course, includes Lambs."

"We've already met," Tony said, moving rapidly toward her and extending his hand.

"So we have." Kelly let him take her hand and even shook his strongly, feeling the warmth of their palms touching. When she tried to pull away, he held on for a moment longer.

"Sleep well, Cinderella?"

"Cin—? Like a top."

"Strange. I was awake half the night. Fireworks kept going off in my head."

Kelly didn't even try to answer him, feeling unexpectedly trapped, as though the evening before had only been a rehearsal for this moment.

"I don't know what you're talking about," Sebastian said irritably. "But I think we can begin, Miss Aldrich. Oh, incidentally, coffee and biscuits are on the sideboard. Please help yourself." Kelly desperately wanted her fourth cup of coffee of the morning but merely shook her head, refusing the offer.

Sebastian took a seat at the head of the conference table with Kelly at his right, next to Rudy Marchetta.

Tony sat directly across the table, and when Kelly caught his amused expression, she returned it with the iciest, most lethal smile she could muster. Her mind rapidly flashed through the fashion show of the night before; he'd sat watching it, knowing he was the new owner of Lambs. From his very silence on the matter, she sensed trouble.

"I've explained the details of the sale to Mr. Marchetta," Sebastian began, "and we needn't go into that for the moment."

"If you don't mind," Kelly said, "I'd like to go into it right now. I've only got a couple of articles in the newspaper to go on. This whole thing has been the most tremendous surprise."

"Tony, I thought you were seeing Miss Aldrich for the specific purpose of—"

Tony raised his hands in a gesture of apology. "Blame it on the blue moon. I was getting around to it."

"Blue moon? What the devil does the blue moon have to do with anything?" Sebastian angrily shuffled the papers on the table, then smiled with assurance at Kelly. "My brother fancies himself a poet. I want to assure you, Miss Aldrich, we consider Lambs a viable institution that we have every intention of seeing into the twenty-first century." After a moment's pause, as though he anticipated a question from her, he went on. "We believe you're Lambs' number one asset and hope you'll stay on."

"I have a contract," she said coldly. But Kelly had something else on her mind. Surprises, for one. "I'm sorry," she said, deliberately directing her questions to Sebastian, "but I'm a little confused about some matters. I'm hoping to go back to the store to tell my employees that the transition is smooth and that nothing will be changed. I need your assurance on that matter, as well."

Sebastian cast a quick glance at his brother. Tony pushed his chair back and stood up. "I've been remiss," he said to Kelly. "This meeting was meant to introduce you to the executive staff of Terro. You should have come here fully aware of the sale and the terms of that sale beforehand. Come on, I detest the formality of conference rooms. Let's get out of here."

"Need I remind you that Lambs is only part of Solow," Sebastian said to him.

"And there's a long line of managers and CEOs waiting to pay their obeisances to the House of Campbell. Come on, Kelly, let's go."

Kelly turned to Rudy, who had put a warning hand on her arm. "Of course," she said to him, "I've got a very solipsistic point of view when it comes to Lambs. I really believe the sun rises and sets on it. But there are others in exactly the same position." She brushed her lips against Rudy's cheek. "I'll call you, when?"

"Better make it at home," he advised her. She understood. For Rudy, it was going to be a long day of phone calls from worried Solow executives and employees wondering just how safe their jobs were. And Rudy would have to sit through it all.

Once outside the conference room, however, Kelly stood her ground. "Just how involved are you that you can walk out on what is obviously something very important to a lot of people? Or are you president in name only?"

"Gregory told me you'd be a tough bundle to handle," Tony began on the way to the elevator, but Kelly finished the sentence for him.

"And decided it was better if he hid out for a while. Where is he, anyway?"

"Still in England. I haven't lied to you, Kelly."

"Except by omission."

The elevator door opened. "Let's go," Tony said, standing aside for her.

"Where have I heard that remark before?" she murmured.

Once they were in the street, Tony said, "You're not going to hold it against me that I took you for a picnic in the park and you fell asleep, are you?"

"And I thought you were the man from Manhattan Florists." She stood a distance away from him and regarded him curiously. The slanted morning light both paled his hair and shadowed his face, accenting its strong lines and planes. She squinted, trying to determine precisely what color his eyes were. Not quite green, not quite gray, not quite brown.

"What the devil are you staring at?" he asked.

"Hazel," she said, starting toward Fifty-seventh Street and Lambs. "Definitely hazel."

"I'll take your word for it," he said, and put a restraining hand on her arm. He gestured toward Central Park and the benches that lined the entrance. "If we're talking about hazelnut trees, let's find one and sit under it. Or how about sharing a bench with me for a half hour or so? I'll answer all your questions concerning Terro or hazel or anything else you want to know."

"I'll say that for you, Anthony Campbell. You really are either a poet or an odd sort of diplomat. Sure, why not? Park bench it is. And I've plenty of questions to ask and not about the color of your eyes."

Midmorning found several benches empty. Later, at noon, office workers would bring their lunches to the park. Now young mothers with their babies in strollers, people walking dogs and elderly retired couples made up most of the pedestrian traffic. A little farther into the park was the newly refurbished zoo. Lambs had featured a window when the zoo reopened to commemorate the event, but Kelly hadn't found the time to visit the place. Once again she had an extraordinary feeling of having lost precious moments, of having let something important slide away.

"Terro first," she said as soon as they were seated. "What is Terro doing here, and why? Why buy Solow out, just like that?"

"Kelly, Gregory Solow came to us with a proposition, not the other way around."

"Impossible," she burst out.

"Don't write the scenario. Just listen."

"He's a workaholic," she went on doggedly. "He loved the business world, loved the hustle, and he specially loved Lambs."

"I'm afraid you're right when you say he loved the hustle. The trouble is he overcommitted himself on a deal he turned in Great Britain." At Kelly's look of skepticism, he said, "Look the man suffered a deep loss when his wife died. Perhaps his judgment was impaired."

"Not Gregory. I know how he felt when Suzanne died, but you're trying to sell somebody to me I don't even know."

"He bought into a hotel in the Strand," Tony went on patiently, "and found himself without the money to turn it around, to make it a paying proposition. He went belly up and Terro bought him out."

"Oh, I see. You're scavengers, in other words."

"Not quite. Gregory learned that we were interested in buying up some New York real estate—"

"Isn't everybody," Kelly said.

"Just trying to get back what old George III let get away those many years ago. Usually a man like Gregory would easily rebound from the loss, but I don't think he really had the energy, the enthusiasm, the fire for the battle, and it took overextending his credit to teach him. When he came to us, he wanted out totally. We were willing. It was done on a handshake."

"In the best British tradition."

"Your boss is coming away from the deal a wealthy man. I wouldn't worry about him."

"I'm not worried about Gregory," Kelly said. But she felt betrayed and wondered if she could ever face him again. "I'm worried about Lambs, its employees and its future."

"Oh, it has a future, all right. Gregory considered it the ruby in the crown—an age-old tradition brought up-to-date by a very savvy chief operating officer. We see an unclouded horizon as far as Lambs is concerned."

Kelly got to her feet. "Come on, then, let me introduce you to your personnel. You can assure them their jobs are safe. It would be a very fitting gesture."

"Not yet. I'd like to buy you a cup of coffee, Kelly. I think you have a few questions you'd still like to ask me, and maybe I have a few of my own."

She glanced at her watch. "I've got a store to run."

"A half hour of your time."

"Fine, a half hour. And you're right—you still owe me a lot of answers."

"Fire away," Tony said when they were seated in the glass-enclosed atrium of the IBM building where they had gone for a coffee. The atrium was filled with leafy bamboo fronds and pots of flowering gloxinia. "Ask me all those questions that have been sitting at the tip of your tongue ever since we met." They were sharing some sweet buns on paper plates between them. Tony's invitation to breakfast had surprised her no more than his notion of a fast-food bar as an appropriate place to have it in.

"And to think the one question I asked you was whether you were with Manhattan Florists," she said.

"And I answered you honestly. I said no."

Then they just sat silently for a while. Kelly was amazed. There were dozens of questions she needed answered but couldn't form even one in her mind. At last in frustration she asked, "Where are you from in England?"

"Big house in a small hamlet in Cornwall, but I live in London. Sebastian will inherit the house, and so when I left it, I knew all I was taking with me was fond memories of an exalted boyhood. Next question."

"Married?"

"No more than you are."

"Ever been married?"

He shook his head. "No more than you've been."

"And you seem to know a lot about me," Kelly said. "Information not quite on my dossier."

"I'd be a fool not to."

"Gregory's been talking, then."

"He put it to me plainly enough. 'Woman's attached to her job,' he said. 'She has no social life that isn't tied to the store, and no hobbies.'"

"And Gregory's hobby is talking too much. And I imagine you've got all of the requisite British hobbies—shooting quail and quaffing ale, to make a poem of it."

"My hobby," he told her, "is examining bottom lines."

Kelly sat back in her chair and laughed. "Okay, I can believe it. You're telling me in your own way that I can relax, that nothing will change." She paused, waiting for agreement, but when none came she went on earnestly. "Nothing changing also means continuing our commitment to Job-Up."

"Hiring kids and paying them a decent wage for a job well done is a commitment I can live with."

"I think it's a little more expensive than that, Tony. I presume you've read those bottom lines carefully. We're taking some of the money out of the promotion budget to support our contribution to Job-Up."

"Job-Up, I gather, is Lambs' answer to the overindulgence the store specializes in."

The street darkened for a moment, and Kelly presumed that somewhere out of sight a cloud had passed over the morning sun. Although she wore a light jacket over a silk blouse, Kelly shivered at his remark. "The money Lambs makes, whether from five-thousand-dollar dresses or five-dollar lipsticks, is shared by a hundred employees from night watchmen to salespeople. It's money that goes back into the economy."

"Kelly," he said patiently, "we're both starting at ground zero, more or less. At the moment I'm more interested in Kelly Aldrich. Gregory told me you're from Pennsylvania, which makes it my favorite state from this moment on."

"I'm sure you'd like Pennsylvania a lot more than George III would have. After all, it's our cradle of liberty," she told him.

"And what town were you rocked to sleep in?"

"Bear Mills. No bears but plenty of mills." She paused, reluctant to go on, to talk about the town that thrived or failed from year to year on the variance of the steel industry, of her father whose livelihood depended on the price of steel in some faraway capital.

"Kelly?"

She found him watching her curiously and thought she must be frowning. "I grew up in a steel town," she said at last. "In a small house on a tiny tract of land. I haven't got too many exalted memories of my childhood. I had a paragon of a father who wanted us, my two brothers and me, to leave Bear Mills and never return. He wanted us not to have our lives run by the vagaries of the marketplace. He wanted us *in charge*. And we are in charge," she added hotly, as though Tony might challenge her on it. "I've got a lawyer brother in California and a doctor brother in Chicago." She reached over and broke a bun in half as though for emphasis, but knew she'd have trouble swallowing if she dared to take a bite. "Of course, on the other hand, I've never left the vagaries of the marketplace, have I?''

"We're back to that, are we?" he asked. "You've got a one-track mind."

"Why not? I've been on that track since I was a child."

"Maybe it's time you derailed for a while."

"My mother died when I was fourteen. She was the exact opposite of my father—a dreamer, a poet who floated around Bear Mills as if it were the near end of paradise, full of exquisite sunsets behind the giant smokestacks. Look," she said, breaking off, knowing she was getting too close to things she didn't want him to know, "how about coming back with me? I'll arrange a meeting with department heads. Perhaps you'd like to tell them what you've told me. I mean, not about growing up in Cornwall, but about Terro's promise to change nothing."

He regarded her for a moment. She realized almost at once that he wasn't being quite honest with her and that meeting Lambs' employees was the last thing he wanted to do. "I think I feel my brother's wrath all the way from the Pierre," he said. "My running out like that is sure to put him off his feed for the rest of the day. About visiting your bailiwick, I'll manage everything in time."

"Yes," she said, getting up and walking rapidly away, throwing her last words back at him, "I imagine you will."

CHAPTER FOUR

AT SEVEN O'CLOCK the next morning, New York wore a freshly washed air, particularly so in front of Lambs, where overnight a privately hired cleaners had scrubbed the pavement. The brass handles on the entrance doors were highly polished, and there wasn't a speck of city dust on the display windows.

Kelly, in a quick glance, took in the newly decorated front windows that flanked the main entrance. Long-haired mannequins in beige linen shorts and big dusty pink gazar shirts were posed on a dock, their empty eyes hidden behind sunglasses, the expressions on their pursed lips haughty and sophisticated. One could feel the summer sun, the waves beating against the dock, sense the yacht about to slide into port. She smiled. Lambs specialized in dreams.

The store occupied a forty-five-foot frontage on one of the most expensive streets in the world. The building, which was ornate, had been built at the turn of the century and was five stories high. Its exterior was Beaux-Arts, one of the few remaining examples in Manhattan of that earlier period in the city's architectural history.

The block upon which it stood was flanked by skyscrapers at either end. The small buildings in between, all very old and charming, seemed like little prisoners being kept alive for the time being only.

Kelly headed for the employees' entrance and pulled the door open. "Hi, Charlie," she said to the night watchman.

Charlie jumped to his feet, giving her a startled look. "What are you doing here this early, Miss Aldrich?"

"One of those nights I couldn't sleep, so I thought I'd just put the time to good use." When he quickly unlocked the door leading to the main part of the store, she added, "Don't bother with the elevator, I'll take the stairs."

"I read about Mr. Solow selling the place," he began.

"Now don't worry about a thing," she said. "The new owners have assured me Lambs is here to stay." When he gave her a relieved smile, she asked, "How long have you been with us, Charlie?"

"Almost a quarter of a century." He touched his hat as Kelly moved past him. "I'm sorry that Mr. Solow won't be with us anymore."

"So am I," Kelly said.

"Respectfully," Charlie said in an unexpectedly diffident manner, "what am I to do about the new owners? If they show up when I'm on duty, I mean."

"Good point," she remarked. "There's Mr. Sebastian Campbell and Mr. Tony Campbell so far. You're right. I'll get onto that."

Once she was alone on the main floor, Kelly stopped and experienced a sudden letdown. She was putting on a cheerful aspect, but she couldn't be sure of anything pertaining to the future, least of all Terro's real plans. The only thing she could count on was the certainty that they'd be around with magnifying glasses.

She glanced around the main floor, which had something of a bazaar in its atmosphere. A faint scent of perfume still lingered in the air. The store was in the midst of a promotion with Cabochard, a French fragrance that was floral without being cloying. Sprayed lightly in the front entrance between the outer and inner doors, a whiff escaped to the interior each time the door opened.

Kelly sometimes thought she liked Lambs best when it was empty of employees and customers and the counters still lay under their dust covers. She always felt like a little girl being given a chance to run amok in a toy store.

At Lambs, because of space considerations, one couldn't quite run amok. The aisles were narrower than in other stores and curved, resulting in a charming rabbit warren of small perfume and makeup counters and individual boutiques devoted to special themes: jewelry, handbags, hats, scarves. Many of the designers were area craftsmen with limited output. As with Job-Up, Kelly encouraged unknowns to submit samples of their work and placed trial orders as a sign of encouragement.

There were occasional disasters. And surprising successes, too, she thought, gazing smilingly at a counter of hand-painted baskets that weren't quite the store's look but sold remarkably well.

"Pays the rent," she said out loud. The manufacturer was the daughter of a valued Lambs customer. Kelly had agreed to show the line, believing it wouldn't last the week.

It had and several months besides.

Lambs was a model of true service. Operators in handsome uniforms still manned ancient, brass-ornamented elevators. The central curved stairway at the rear was of marble with two brass banisters at each side. Above was a huge crystal chandelier. Murals painted in the 1920s lined the walls of the stairway, depicting nostalgic New York scenes. The murals, like the chandelier, were valuable in their own right.

Kelly took the stairs quickly, stopping at the mezzanine, where a group of dresses by a young, innovative designer took up the central display space. She ran her fingers across a soft cashmere sweater dress, then stopped to retie a silk bow that didn't need her finishing touch. She was wasting time, doing anything to avoid thinking.

She went rapidly on her way after that, arriving on the fifth floor a little out of breath. She went directly into her office and over to the window, where she drew the curtains aside to let in the morning light. Fifty-seventh Street was one of the busiest in the city, but at that hour of the morning traffic was relatively sparse. The few brave souls out walking kept up a rapid pace, as though determined to get where they were going with no dawdling.

Dawdling along Fifty-seventh Street, on the other hand, was Kelly's favorite pastime. She knew every inch of the famous street, every window display from Henri Bendel's on the west side of Fifth Avenue to Tiffany's and Bonwit Teller's on the east side. She knew the antique shops and dress boutiques and the art galleries occupying the second floor of the venerable old Fuller Building on Madison Avenue. She

knew the man who sold hot dogs on the southeast
corner and the woman who begged from passersby on
the northeast corner.

And when she wasn't window gazing, she spent so
many hours in her gold-toned, antique-filled office
that it comprised a small universe more snugly comfortable than her apartment. She had narrowed her
world to center almost exclusively on Lambs.

Abruptly she thought about Gregory's office opposite hers. He'd seldom used the office, as Solow
Enterprises had main offices across town, but nevertheless, the mahogany-paneled suite had always been
at his disposal. She wondered whether Tony Campbell would take up residence there.

Perhaps if she moved quickly, she might comman-
deer the space for the advertising department, which
was now crowded into a small corner of the fourth
floor. Such a coup would open up much-needed selling space. A fantastic idea, she decided, and scribbled a note to talk to the advertising director and store
engineer first thing.

She'd had trouble getting to sleep the night before,
replaying over and over again her conversation with
Tony Campbell. He'd been more than pleasant. He'd
been mildly, charmingly interested in her. She'd been
flattered, but even without the flattery, her career, her
future were safe because of the contract she had with
Lambs. No one else in the store had the luxury of a
contract, however.

When she'd fallen asleep last night, her dreams had
been of Tony and his brother playing an impossible
three-sided game of chess with Gregory. Her father

was the referee, whipping them to a frenzy, telling them they all had to win.

"Look at me," Kelly kept crying. "Don't look at them. I've already won."

Yes, of course, she'd already won. Young, urban, competitive and successful—that was Kelly Aldrich all over. But now what?

That Terro was in full possession of Solow Enterprises and all its subsidiaries she had no doubt. What she wanted was further details of the deal from Rudy Marchetta. It was seven-thirty when she dialed him at home and found him ready to leave for his midtown office.

"You're an early bird, too," she commented dryly.

"Always was, but this business with Solow Enterprises is a nightmare waiting to materialize into the real thing."

"Should I be scared?"

"No, *you* don't have to worry. And, in any case, there's nothing we can do about it, Kelly. It's a fait accompli," Rudy said. "Gregory wanted out and Terro wanted in, period."

"Just like that," Kelly said. "You wake up one morning to find everything's the same, only different. What's your impression of the Campbell brothers? They sound like a vaudeville act, but somehow I don't believe they are."

"I've been trying to get hold of Gregory," Rudy said, "but no one seems to know when he's expected back. My guess is he knows he's left us dangling and is hiding out somewhere."

"It's hard for me to believe he's such a coward," Kelly threw in. "That's not the Gregory Solow I know."

"We'll hear his side of the story soon enough," Rudy said. "I'm afraid the only kind of advice I can give for the moment is to hang in there. Your contract is now owned by Terro, and there isn't too much you can do about it."

"What about you, Rudy?"

"I've been Gregory's personal lawyer for a long time and my loyalty still lies with him. Terro could have bulldozed right over me, but I don't believe they've come here to make trouble. They want the transition to be easy, believe me."

"Carry on. Wise words, Rudy, especially as I have no choice. Well, I'm used to making decisions on my own, but Gregory was available to back me up. I'm not quite certain how much input Anthony Campbell wants or if he knows anything about the business."

"Tony Campbell's a cool number, I'd say. His brother is a little easier to read."

"Is he? I thought Sebastian was levelheaded and businesslike but rather unapproachable."

"Maybe. I'd watch out for the droit du seigneur business. He looks like a man of appetites to me, one who means to have his way—maybe with you."

"Lovely," Kelly murmured. "I guess I'll have to watch myself at all times."

"As for the younger brother, I'd guess Tony's laid-back air masks steel where an ordinary man has nerves."

So far she'd been battling zero when it came to either brother. She'd been too disoriented by the turn of events to be anything but impressed by surface appearances. Kelly thanked Rudy and said goodbye. He told her to call him any time she had a question. She had a feeling she'd have any number of questions before the month was out.

Were they piranhas, the Campbell brothers? She wondered. Were her employees' jobs safe? Buy-outs inevitably meant shake-ups, and shake-ups meant employees who were considered redundant or too old could be put out to pasture. Yes, the Campbell brothers had come to town, and Kelly felt sick at heart.

Among the often consulted books on her desk was one containing the floor plans of the store. She picked it up, opened to the plans for the fourth floor and immediately became engrossed in a study of its layout. She had no idea how much time had passed before she heard a sudden noise outside her door. A quick glance at her desk clock told her it wasn't quite eight.

"That you, Charlie?"

The door opened and her heart took an unexpected little leap when she found Tony Campbell standing there. And yet when she recovered, Kelly realized she wasn't surprised at all. The man had a talent for showing up anywhere, anytime.

"May I come in?"

"Why not? You own the place."

He raised his eyebrows as though he hadn't expected so flip an answer. For the first time she noted the crease lines at his eyes and a small scar just above the corner of his lips. She found herself longing to ask about it and to be told some story about rugby and how he'd carried the ball for his public school in spite of a cut lip.

"You might want to mention to your watchman that I own the place. The only thing that impressed him was my British driver's license."

"Oh, I already told him to expect you."

"Described me to a T?" he asked, advancing into the room.

"Oh, yes, all the way down to that scar on the corner of your lip."

"That," he said with a deprecating grin. "Playing rugby."

She laughed. "I told him that, too. Incidentally, Charlie's been with us for a quarter of a century."

"Must be something about the place, then."

"I think it's called loyalty."

Tony looked around the office as if surprised to find it filled with elegant, old pieces and of a respectable size.

"Come for an early-morning white glove inspection?" she asked.

"Yes, as a matter of fact."

She slammed the floor plan book shut. Perhaps he'd come to take over Gregory's office, in which case she'd just lost the opportunity of a lifetime.

"Do you always buy companies off the rack, so to speak? You know," she said, "without examining the seams and buttons?"

"Not always, but when you buy a bag of Crackerjacks, you know there's going to be a prize in it. You don't know exactly what the prize is, but you can be pretty certain of its value in relation to the whole."

"And you like Crackerjacks."

"Love them. And the prize, as well."

"Somehow I don't quite believe you."

"The truth of the matter is," he said, coming over to her desk and leaning across it, "my brother Sebastian is a pretty cagey man. He's had a vested interest in New York real estate for a long time. And Lambs, after all, is real estate."

She stared once more at the scar and then decided he'd won it in the War of the Roses. "Let's go, then," she said abruptly, slipping into her shoes. "Perhaps you know more about Lambs than I do. Still, I'm going to give you the special ten-dollar tour—pay at the door as you go out."

THE FOURTH FLOOR WAS given over to women's sportswear, with the advertising department squeezed along a narrow back corridor. Kelly hadn't shown Tony the top-floor offices, figuring on giving him a pitch about tight space first.

"We keep up floor displays for two weeks," she explained, particularly proud of the current display with an Italian garden theme.

"Nice," Tony commented.

"Of course, our display personnel is unionized," Kelly threw in.

"We'll have to take a look at their contracts."

"Ironclad."

"Well, from the appearance of things, they know their job. How many in the department?"

Kelly laughed. "Three. We're not Macy's." She deliberately led him back to the advertising department. "We're using valuable selling space for the ad department because we have no choice," she said.

"Every square inch counts, in other words."

"I've decided to carve space out of the fifth-floor executive offices," she added. "We'll all have to give up something."

"Never thought of putting a refreshment counter in Lambs?"

"No space," she told him after a moment of shocked silence, "not even for an executive dining room. I hope you're not thinking of it."

"Cost per square inch," he reminded her, "so many plates of soup, so many cups of coffee per hour."

"You *are* joking."

"Maybe, maybe not," he said, making no attempt to hide a smile.

"I'm not crazy about interference in the way we run the store, especially when that interference has no basis in fact. We're not a general store, not a food emporium, and decidedly not a museum."

She headed for the third floor without giving him a chance to answer her. "Coming?" She looked back up to find him at the top of the stairs, gazing down at her. She experienced the oddest feeling of being wrong somehow, disapproved of—a new experience that made her falter at the next step.

He caught up. "Soundly trounced. The problem is I could use a good cup of coffee at this juncture."

"I'll take you out for a cup as soon as we finish the tour," she told him. She was being hard—that was it—the cool, snappy businesswoman, and the trouble was she had no idea how to be otherwise. "Look," she began, "I appreciate change, and God knows we need to make plenty of adjustments for the 1990s, but we've found our market and our market doesn't need a bowl of soup at noon. They're all on diets, and the largest size we carry is fourteen. Now, would you like to see our third floor? Incidentally, it features the most expensive, outré and original clothes to be found in the city."

"Just how much will one of these gowns sink your customer?" he asked, gesturing at a display of intricately embroidered evening gowns that greeted them when they stepped off onto the third floor.

Kelly felt the heat rise to her face. "The annual budget for a small country."

"And how many do you sell?"

"You'd be surprised."

He caught her arm in a strong grip. "I can bear it. Tell me."

"The emerald, five thousand dollars plus tax. The shocking pink, seven thousand. The embroidery is handmade. I believe the sales figures are something like ten in the space of two weeks. You have a disapproving look on your face," she added. "The women who wear these dresses can easily afford them." She let out a sigh. "I'm not going to apologize about stocking gowns our customers want to buy."

"I haven't said a word," he stated, going past her to the stairwell, where he took the stairs down two at a time. Watching him, she told herself that he was a businessman, and he only needed to be convinced. Still, she couldn't help feeling something had subtly changed in the way she was viewing her job—something that had begun in her brain even before she'd discovered the news about Terro.

Suddenly she felt stifled by the tight, busy, enclosed world in which she spent too many of her wak-

ing hours. For a moment, standing at the top of the
stairs, she experienced an attack of dizziness. She
reached out and grabbed the handrail. A couple of
customers went past her, chattering on the way up. In
a moment she was back to normal, telling herself that
at this late date it would do no good to question what
she was doing and why she was doing it.

WHEN TONY LET himself into the suite at the Hotel
Carlyle later that day, he expected to order in a light
supper and then spend the rest of the evening knee-
deep in computer printouts. His brother, however, had
other plans, plans that spilled from the salon into
Tony's bedroom. Dark suits among the men
abounded. In contrast the women were a brilliant array of color, and Tony found himself wondering how
many of the dresses could be had for four figures at
Lambs.

Sebastian was having one of his power cocktail
parties: a spontaneous affair in Tony's suite—not his
own—meant to bring friends and important acquaintances together for an hour or two before they went on
to other engagements. He had, of course, carefully
neglected to tell Tony about it. Which meant Tony
would have to smile and make small talk with members of the British upper classes who found themselves in Manhattan at the same time as Sebastian, as
well as with any number of American millionaires.
Easy work for some, perhaps, but Tony was in no
mood for bantering.

"Damn," he said to his brother, pulling him aside.
"Couldn't you have arranged this somewhere else?
Your room, for instance?"

"Don't be an ass, Tony. And it'll take an hour and a half of your time, no more and possibly less. Lighten up. We're doing precisely what we said we'd do—conquering New York."

Tony threw out a bitter laugh. "Conquering New York? I've a feeling it's easier to conquer Mars."

Sebastian pulled on his cigarette. "They call this networking. Where in hell have you been, anyway? I've had the *Times* on the phone wanting an interview. Also a fashion magazine, W something. They want to know where Lambs stands. I told them where it always has. No use stirring anything up until the moment of truth."

Tony felt a sudden desire to grab his brother by his collar and give him a good shaking as he had when they were younger. Although Sebastian was the elder brother, it seemed that Tony had spent a lifetime rescuing him from one misadventure or another.

"Your work with Terro International is finished here. The operation is my baby from now on," Tony reminded him. "Incidentally, when's your flight out?"

Sebastian laughed. "We're all one big happy family, baby brother, don't try to turn our differences about Solow into an intramural war. As the Americans put it, everything's going to be A-okay. So lighten up. You look as if you've been told you have two minutes to live. Ah, here she is, my little assistant." Sebastian turned with delight to the young brunette who came toward him, smiling and holding out a drink.

Little assistant, Tony thought, a euphemism for the sort of woman a man—or, this man—picked up when he left his wife and children back home in England.

Tony went over to the well-stocked bar for a stiff drink, but had scarcely wet his lips when he was confronted by a slender, overdressed blonde who offered him a wide, sexy smile. "You a married man, Tony?"

She was dressed in a white silk dress with great puffed sleeves. Her plunging neckline was emphasized by a huge emerald-encrusted pin. While he gazed at her as might a bird-watcher confronting a nightingale where it ought not to be, she laughed. "We met in London. I had reddish-brown hair then. Mariette Powell."

"Yes, yes, of course," he said hastily, extending a hand. He vaguely remembered her blue eyes and smile.

"I asked, are you a married man? It's not quite the question I'd have asked in London, but then you didn't own Lambs at the time. I believe we talked about music."

"What's being married got to do with owning Lambs?"

She trilled a laugh. "Good heavens, you need a woman around you singing its praises."

"I'm not married," he told her. "Am I in trouble?"

"I should say so. You won't be able to trust your hired employees so much as a wife. What do you think of the place?"

"Earning its keep, I should think."

She let loose another laugh. "Earning its keep. There you are. My dear," she went on, tucking her arm through his and drawing him over to the window, "if that's all you think of the store, you might just as well own ... Macy's."

"Might not be a bad idea, at all."

"You see," she began in earnest, "a woman wants a shop that's perfect, that offers her a small, exclusive array of tasteful clothes, a look tailored to her lifestyle, and friendly employees who know her by name and pamper her."

Tony remembered hearing something similar from Diane Bourne. Yet what this woman now told him interested him anew, although he had no idea what fashion entailed, what was tasteful, what not. He nodded at the dress she was wearing. "Lambs?" He wasn't certain he liked the style.

"This?" She smiled and hid her face behind her hands for a moment. "I'm sorry, but I must confess. I bought this in Paris. You see, I have to have so many things. We go so many places. We're expected to buy in Paris, Milan, London. You understand."

"Nevertheless, we must order something quite like it," he said in a very polite way.

"No, no, no, you mustn't," she said. "You see what I mean? I'm going to tell you just what your wife would say. Never tinker with perfection. Never, never, never tinker with perfection."

At that moment her husband tapped her arm, and after throwing a greeting at Tony, told her they had to leave for another engagement. "Oh, darling, you remember Tony Campbell. He owns Lambs now," she said.

Tony shook the man's hand, remembering him as the chief operating officer of a stock brokerage firm.

Powell smiled and quipped, "I wish you'd order your doorman to keep my wife out of the place."

She giggled, and as they walked away, called back, "Remember—never, never, never."

Sebastian came up to him. "Never what?" he asked.

"Curious," Tony said, looking after the woman. "She's apparently been caught by the spell of Lambs. Seems to be worried we might change its image."

Sebastian laughed. "You assured her we'd never tinker with perfection."

"I assured her nothing," Tony said. "I'm surprised at the interest everyone seems to show in a rather small enterprise catering to upscale customers who could easily take their business elsewhere."

"They may have to yet," Sebastian said, wandering away to greet another guest with a clap on the shoulder.

A week before Tony might have agreed with his brother; perhaps disposing of Lambs would have been one of the few areas they agreed about. But the stakes had changed for Tony. And all because of Kelly Aldrich. She was making him see things in a new way, and she was curling into his mind in a way that might be impossible to dislodge.

CHAPTER FIVE

"KELLY!"

The cheerful telephone voice was familiar, but Kelly, just coming out of a deep sleep, failed to recognize it. "Who is this?"

"Out of sight, out of mind, is that it?"

Her heart skipped a beat at the sound of the faint foreign accent that hinted at mysterious origins—origins that had never been clearly explained. "Gregory Solow," she said, smiling now but unable to resist a little dig. "Well, well, well, out of hiding, are you?"

"Was I in hiding? That's news to me."

"Exactly what do you call not being around to tell me about the most momentous event of my life?"

He laughed. "If that's the most momentous event, you're in big trouble, Kelly."

"Wonderful," she said. "Not back a minute and you're already handing me a lecture. You *are* back, aren't you? Not calling me from London."

"Landed at Kennedy at an ungodly hour, got to my apartment at an ungodly hour and flopped into bed."

"And it's still an ungodly hour." She glanced at her bedside clock. The alarm was about to go off. "I gather you're operating on your usual four hours' sleep with no time off for jet lag."

"You're right, as usual. Well, I'm waiting to be creamed. Go ahead. I deserve it."

"You do," she said, but couldn't help smiling at the sound of his endearing voice. "I'll want the truth, Gregory. You owe me that much. When can we meet?"

"Has Tony Campbell moved into my old office yet?"

"No. I didn't even bother introducing it to him. I've decided that advertising needs the space more than he does."

"Ouch. Is that what you've wanted to do all along? Never mind. Don't answer. I'll be at Lambs at ten. Hold breakfast for me, although I can't give you much time. I've got a busy schedule."

"Apologizing for bad behavior all over the place, I'll bet."

He laughed. "Don't try that smartass stuff on the Campbell brothers. They may not have my easy ways. Coffee and a Danish. See you then."

Damn, she thought, hanging up. He was still Gregory Solow and she still loved the old buzzard, but his excuses had better be good ones. As far as she was concerned, the man had a lot to make up for.

WHEN HE CAME BURSTING into her office precisely at ten, Gregory Solow appeared the picture of health. He was tanned and rested and had grown a salt-and-pepper beard that gave him the look of a professor at an Ivy League college.

Kelly rushed to greet him. "A beard. Really, Gregory, I hardly know you." She felt the feathery tickle against her lips and wondered if his looks weren't all that had changed. She stood back and examined him. "You've lost weight, too."

He was dressed, as always, in his meticulous manner but the slight paunch had disappeared. Something else about him had also changed. The sad, haunted look in his eyes was replaced by something a little more satisfied and yet harder, more determined.

"Yes, I've changed," he said, as though reading her mind.

"So you have."

"For the better?" The question was a little boyishly asked.

"Decidedly." Then she added as she exhaled, "I heard about the troubles in London."

"Troubles? Oh, the hotel." He shrugged it off. "No problems, Kelly. I'm remarkably solvent. All right," he added as he noted the frown on Kelly's face, "my incompetence hit me square in the face. I bought a white elephant, believing I could make a butterfly out of it. Once I added in the costs of renovation plus inflation, I realized what I'd done. You want to know why I threw in the towel on Solow Enterprises."

Kelly nodded.

He went over to the sideboard where she had coffee and pastry waiting for him and helped himself. "I loved my wife as much after forty years of marriage," he said quietly, "as when I first saw her. Well, you know what happened. She died."

"Come sit next to me," Kelly said, going over to the sofa and patting the cushion next to her.

"A lot of the stuffing was taken out of me," he continued, joining her. "But *carry on* was the medicine everyone from my doctor to the doorman advised me to take. Fill up the time, keep busy and make no changes just yet. So," he added, "I carried on. But you can't run a marathon if you haven't any reason to get to the finish line. There was no longer anything at the finish line that interested me."

"Oh, Gregory." She took up his hand and patted it. "You don't have to say any more."

"I couldn't trust my business instincts anymore," he told her. "When I learned Terro was shopping the States for some properties, I approached them—plain and simple."

And fast and secretly, she wanted to say, but held back. She was trying to decide just how sorry she should really feel for him when her intercom went off. She got up reluctantly to answer it. "Gail, I'm busy right now," she began.

"Mrs. Sorenson," her assistant said in a terse tone.

Kelly looked over at Gregory and mouthed Mrs. Sorenson's name. "Where is she?" she asked Gail.

"Mezzanine, security office."

"All right. I hope somebody brought her a cup of tea and those dried biscuits she likes. I'll be right down. Call her daughter." She hung up and couldn't resist a smile.

"Mrs. Sorenson," Gregory said.

"We haven't seen her around here lately. Her visit was overdue."

"Ah. Our millionaire kleptomaniac. Come on, I'll go with you," Gregory said as Kelly headed for the door.

She stopped and gaped at him in surprise. "Gregory, you're out of it. You don't work here anymore."

"You mean I don't boss here anymore," he said with a smile. "I think Terro expects to benefit for the next couple of weeks from my expertise. We concluded the deal on a handshake, but there's a lot more to a handshake than just saying goodbye."

"I never wanted you to say goodbye. Oh, Gregory," Kelly said, "I hope you haven't made a mistake."

"No." He shook his head. "No, it's just that old habits die hard."

"I'm happy to hear that," Kelly said, "but your office is being emptied out today. No discussions, no reprieve."

"Your mind goes a million miles a minute," he said. "I'm still coming with you."

"Come along then. Mrs. Sorenson adores you. If we can't find her daughter, you're going to escort her home."

They grabbed a crowded elevator down to the mezzanine and went immediately to the office occupied by the chief of security. There they found the small chic blonde who'd been a popular movie actress in the fifties. She had come to New York after her third divorce and for a while had appeared in a soap opera. Her kleptomania was her only vice, one tolerated by the upscale stores in which she practiced it.

"Mrs. Sorenson," Kelly said, going up to the actress and planting a kiss on her cheek. "How are you doing?" She exchanged a glance with the chief of security, an ex-policeman who shook his head slightly, meaning the stolen object had been retrieved and no harm had been done. When he caught sight of Gregory, his face exploded in a wide, pleased smile.

"They seem to think I walked out of the store with a perfume atomizer," Mrs. Sorenson said in a very resonant, reasonable voice.

"Perhaps you forgot you had it in your hands," Kelly said soothingly. "Would you like to buy it?" The offending article was sitting on the desk, a small hand-etched antique jar taken from a corner booth that held expensive items for the boudoir.

"Good heavens, no, what would I need it for?" Mrs. Sorenson stared at the atomizer with distaste. "I must own a dozen like it." Then she spotted Gregory. "Darling," she said, getting up and greeting him with open arms, "I came here merely to see you."

"Well, here I am, then."

"I've been trying to find a particular shade of lipstick, but no one seems to have it and I can't quite remember the name."

"Suppose we have the cosmetics buyer help you," he said.

Kelly took the security chief aside. "Is her daughter on her way?"

"She'll be here in ten minutes."

"Okay, keep Mrs. Sorenson comfy. I'll ask the cosmetics buyer to bag a couple of sample lipsticks for her. No other big problems?"

"It's too early in the morning for the big ones, Ms Aldrich. The little ones are taking care of themselves."

Kelly went over to the woman and picked up her hand. "Wonderful to see you again, Mrs. Sorenson. Your daughter's coming by for you."

Her face lit up. "Marvelous. I haven't seen her since breakfast this morning."

Gregory shook her hand vigorously. "Wonderful to see you again, my love." He caught up to Kelly at the elevator. She had been cornered there by the lingerie buyer, who greeted him with a shrill little cry.

The elevator door opened and Kelly stepped in, waiting for Gregory, but he waved her on. "I'll be in tomorrow about the office."

Kelly understood how emotional his return to the store was and that he had to assure his ex-employees that their jobs were safe. "How about dinner tonight?" she called. "I'll cook."

"The Russian Tea Room," he said, referring to one of the most popular restaurants in New York. "I'll pick you up at eight."

"We've got a lot to talk about."

"I know."

The elevator door closed.

Good, she thought. She'd order the usual, a Russian pancake made of cottage cheese called *syrniki*.

WHILE NEW YORK POSSESSED thousands of restaurants catering to every ethnic taste, very few remained popular over a long period, but for reasons that had little to do with cuisine. The Russian Tea Room was an exception. From morning till night it was crowded with business people, celebrities and tourists eager to return home with stories of having seen Yoko Ono at the next table or Diane Keaton. Like Mortimer's, farther east, the famous regulars were bound to meet each other over and over again. That evening the restaurant was crowded and noisy. When Kelly arrived, she found Gregory seated at a round banquette for four. She wondered aloud about the extra seating.

"I asked Tony Campbell and his date to join us. Sebastian wasn't available." Gregory's tone was matter-of-fact, and he clearly failed to note Kelly's reaction. It struck her that Gregory wanted to avoid talking about business and his "treachery"—which was how Kelly couldn't resist thinking of it. But worse than that was knowing he had invited Tony Campbell. Although they hadn't talked since his white glove inspection of the store the morning before, he'd never been far from her mind. She'd found herself too often having mental arguments with him—about Lambs and Job-Up—and about why he should leave them both alone.

"Nice to see you on good terms with Terro's principals," she managed at last. "Somehow I imagined you'd be in an adversarial position with them."

"Whatever for?" he asked, fixing her with a look of genuine surprise. "They did me a favor."

"Perhaps it's the last favor they'll ever do anybody."

Gregory frowned. "What don't you trust about them?"

"Nothing specific," she said. "They're not you."

He shook his head. "I'm beginning to see a different Kelly Aldrich, one faintly paranoid."

"Not paranoid, protective—of our, I mean my, no I mean *their* employees. The world is littered with the bodies of victims of corporate takeovers."

He reached out and patted her hand. "Lambs is a New York institution. If the Brits know anything, it's how to preserve the past. Ah." His face brightened and he got quickly to his feet.

"You're right," Tony said, coming up behind Kelly, whose view was away from the entrance to the restaurant. "We certainly know how to preserve the past. It's the future we need a little practice with. Kelly Aldrich, Gregory Solow, meet Diane Bourne," he said of the tall, beautiful woman with him. "First names all," Tony suggested, sitting down opposite Kelly after touching her briefly on the shoulder. "Let's be extremely American."

"That's what I adore about Americans most of all," Diane said, smiling across at Kelly. "You hold nothing back. You tell perfect strangers about your jobs, your salaries, how much your houses cost and how naughty your children are, all in one breath."

"I know," Kelly said. "We're remarkably non-judgmental and very gossipy."

"Diane's in the States on an interesting errand," Tony said after the waiter had departed with the drink order. "My brother Sebastian, in his infinite wisdom, has decided that what the world needs is a history of Terro, neatly done up in a four-color illustrated, leather-bound volume. Diane, who has handled public relations for us, is writing and producing this earth-shattering epic."

Diane threw him a look of disgust. "You make it sound so self-serving, Tony. There's no earthly reason why Terro shouldn't explain its origins to the curious world at large."

He laughed. "The curious world at large. My brother has certainly brainwashed you, Diane."

"I'm curious," Kelly said.

"There, you see," Diane said triumphantly.

"What I like is an employee who takes her job seriously," he went on. "Don't let me discourage you for a minute, as if I had a choice in the matter."

Kelly examined Tony's companion. She had, in a moment, caught something between them and, in a flash of intuition, believed it was Diane Bourne Tony had rushed to the night of the Job-Up benefit at the Met.

"Terro was begun by my grandfather as a real estate venture," Tony explained to Kelly. "With some very unsavory characters, incidentally. However, he managed to break himself free of them just as the bailiff arrived at the front door. By the time my father took over the reins some thirty years ago, Terro was as pure as apple blossoms in spring. When he handed the same reins to my brother, the only missing item in our reputation was a Nobel prize for purity. End of story."

"I wonder why I don't believe a word you've said," Kelly remarked. "I mean, about the purity."

He cast her a startled glance. "Do you know something I don't know?"

"The expression on your face at this moment tells me everything." They exchanged a long look that held something conspiratorial to it, as if neither could be rid of the memory of that moment when she had fallen asleep in his arms.

She was thankful for the arrival of their drink order, after which Gregory held up his glass and said to Diane, "You'll have to reserve a chapter for Lambs."

"Oh, more than a chapter. You'll have to fill me in on the history of Solow. Your accent," Diane remarked. "I'm not sure..."

"I was born in Budapest," he said, "and arrived on these shores when I was eighteen."

"And he cultivates his accent carefully," Kelly added, offering him a grin. "That's part of the Solow image. Mystery, castles in the mountains of Hungary lost to the Russians. A forebear known as the Black Prince or something equally dangerous."

"The woman has a wild imagination," Gregory said, keeping his eyes on Diane.

"Well, we need color." Diane rested her chin on her hand, regarding Gregory in an interested way from across the table, as though the possibility of a Black Prince in his background intrigued *her* a great deal. "A prince—especially a black one—would fit in very well with the history of Terro, in spite of everything Tony said. After all, the senior Campbell is a viscount."

Kelly turned to Tony. "A viscount?"

"The Campbells of Cornwall," Diane said.

Tony smiled sheepishly at Kelly. "My father. I had nothing to do with it."

"If we could but name our parents," Gregory murmured.

Kelly thought of her mother and those books full of poems waiting for a publisher and an eager audience. And she thought of her taciturn father and his relentless ambition for his children. "Americans don't believe in that sort of thing," she said, a little too sharply. "Titles, I mean."

"Of course not," Tony said in an even voice. "Why would you?"

In an extraordinary moment of understanding she realized that the whole notion irritated him, too; that there was something about his relationship with his brother and perhaps even his father that was unresolved.

"What's a Campbell doing in Cornwall?" she asked. "I always thought the name was Scottish."

"Family legend has it that our Campbell ancestor acted as a spy for King Richard the Lionhearted—or one of the Richards, anyway," Tony told her, warming to the subject. "For which act of treason he was booted out of Scotland, fortunately for him—and for me—with his head still attached to his body. The English crown promptly rewarded him for his zeal with a title and a very pretty portion of Cornwall. Of course it may all be hearsay, one of our romantic, albeit seditious, grand family sagas, but I always thought it had the ring of truth."

"Oh, we'll have to add that to the legend I'm preparing about Terro," Diane said, smiling.

"Go right ahead," Tony told her. "You have my blessing, although Sebastian may take a different view of things."

Kelly, listening to their banter, felt an unexpected ache tug at her heart. The conversation had quickly dispelled the notion that she and Tony might share common ground. The differences between them were clearly never wider.

Later, after dinner, Kelly excused herself and went to the ladies' room. She was surprised when Diane followed her in and sat down at the vanity mirror where Kelly was combing her hair.

"I wanted to thank you for putting Tony in his place about the book."

Kelly looked at her curiously through the mirror. She had expressed some interest in learning the company's history, but that was all. She didn't believe her remark influenced Tony at all. No, Diane had followed her merely to satisfy some inner curiosity, although Tony was certainly at the bottom of it all. "Did I set him straight?" she asked. "I don't remember."

"He hates pretense, and he thinks a promotional book is all pretense and vanity. The project is an interesting one, however, no matter how hard he's trying to sabotage it."

"Good heavens," Kelly said. "Lambs makes mailings to its customers all the time, bragging about its abilities in the image department. We can make you beautiful. Count on us. Image. That's our stock-in-trade, and we want to make certain our customers know it."

Diane gave her a grateful smile. "What do you think of the boss?" she asked unexpectedly, bending forward to apply some lipstick and catching Kelly's eye in the vanity mirror.

Kelly was surprised by the openness of the question. Did Diane really expect an honest answer? She doubted it. "I think of him," she lied easily, "in only one way, that he regards Lambs as the jewel it is, to be left untouched."

"He seems to talk an inordinate amount about you. I've been awfully curious to meet you."

Kelly began to comb her thick hair furiously, paying careful attention to the way it curled under. She hoped the long, slow burning of her face didn't show. "I imagine it's easy to talk about someone you've just met,'' she said carefully, ''and whose career you hold in your hands, just as it's hard to reveal one's deepest, most private thoughts.''

''He said you run your store with an iron fist and with charm and diplomacy. I see what he meant.''

The lump that formed at the back of Kelly's throat prevented an immediate answer.

''You can stop combing now,'' Diane said, getting to her feet. ''Your hair is really very beautiful, and I've got the oddest feeling it's never out of shape.''

Kelly forced a laugh as she followed her out.

''Teasel's,'' Gregory suggested when they reached the table. ''I'm for continuing the party.'' He referred to a popular new after-dinner club.

''Wonderful,'' Diane breathed, clapping her hands with delight. ''Tony?''

''That's that, then,'' Gregory said without waiting for an answer from either Tony or Kelly.

Kelly didn't even bother telling them she wasn't going until they were outside the restaurant. ''I'm sorry,'' she began in an apologetic tone, ''but I've had one of those long, insane days. If you'll excuse me, I'll just grab a cab and head home.''

''Since when have you let long, insane days stop you before?'' Gregory said in a playful tone that was new to him.

''I'm getting old,'' she said, offering him a placating grin. ''Unlike you, who have shed a few years since I last saw you.'' She held out her hand to Diane. ''Come visit me. I'll give you a behind-the-scenes tour.''

Diane shook her hand warmly. ''It's a date.''

Kelly gave Tony a quick smile before running into the street to hail a cab. She was astonished to find Tony right behind her. "I'm not going," she told him.

"I know. I'm seeing you home," he said, bundling her into the cab and closing the door firmly behind him.

"You needn't," she began.

"Where to?" the cabbie asked.

"I'm quite safe," Kelly said. "My building has both a doorman and an elevator operator."

"Where to?" the cabbie asked once more.

"I wasn't thinking about safe," Tony said. "Windows on the World," he told the driver, referring to the restaurant café at the top of the World Trade Center in lower Manhattan.

"I'm sorry, driver," Kelly said, "but stop first at Second Avenue and Forty-fourth Street."

"World Trade Center," Tony said.

The driver twisted around to look at Kelly, then at Tony. "Which is it, ma'am?"

A taxi pulled up ahead of them. Gregory and Diane climbed in, but not before Diane glanced briefly over at them.

"I said I'd catch up," Tony told her.

"After you see me back to my apartment."

"Precisely."

"Windows on the World," Kelly said to the driver. "I don't know what you think you're doing," she said to Tony when the cab started up.

"I know what you were doing," he remarked. "You were trying to escape a situation you thought of as mildly uncomfortable."

"What?" She stared at him, astonished. She was tired, and it had nothing to do with Tony and Diane Bourne.

"She's a good friend," he said, as if he had not only read her mind but guided her thinking.

"Does she agree with that assessment?"

"Yes, though I don't think we've signed a contract on the matter."

"And you thought I'd care one way or the other about you and Diane. You have an ego the size of... the size of the World Trade Center."

"Both towers?"

"Laid end to end," she said.

"Laid end to end they'd reach the moon."

"Good, climb them and land there."

He laughed. "Kelly Aldrich, chief executive officer of Lambs and petulant kid. I like the combination."

"Nobody ever said I had to act my age. All I have to do is get the job done," she told him, "and I need my sleep."

"Gregory said you're a workaholic and don't need a lot of sleep."

He'd been discussing her with both Gregory and Diane. The notion infuriated her. "For one, I don't like the club scene," she said, squeezing into the farthest corner of the cab and crossing her arms.

"And two?" His voice had a soft, almost curious undertone, as if he wanted the truth but didn't expect to hear it.

"Two, you came in with Diane and it was awfully rude to leave her on a spurious excuse."

"She knows I'd want to see you safely tucked into bed."

"It didn't bother Gregory one bit to let me go along on my own."

"I slipped him a dollar bill."

"You're impossible."

The cab turned left at Eleventh Avenue, which at that hour of the night was nearly empty of traffic. Kelly tried to push deeper into the corner. Tony Campbell had a way of running off with her. The last time he'd pretended there was nothing amiss. She wondered what wasn't amiss this time.

ONE HUNDRED AND SEVEN STORIES above the city, pushing at the sky and hemmed in by two rivers below, Windows on the World turned Wall Street and indeed all of the city into a field of fireflies. The café in which Tony and Kelly sat was more intimate than the restaurant, more softly lit. The city below was all the sparkle they needed.

"The first time I was here," Tony said, "the whole place was closed in by clouds leaning against the window, and they never let up. My view was of white woollies. Then, just before we left, there was a slight parting, like a curtain opening briefly on a stage. And there she was, a gray, wet, gleaming New York—revealed only to disappear again before I had a chance to size her up."

"And did you own a piece of Manhattan, then?"

He smiled and shook his head. "The lady wasn't even a gleam in my brother Sebastian's eye."

She leaned back, fingering the stem of her wineglass. "You mean Terro's coming here wasn't your idea at all?"

"No, I didn't say that, Kelly. My father headed the company at the time and Sebastian was in charge of development. I was just out of university, seeing the world."

"And when you came back you joined them."

He shook his head. "I was trained for the law and had settled down nicely in a job I liked. That's when the call came. My father retired, Sebastian took over and I was expected to do my share."

"You don't seem like a man who'd toe the mark, no matter who told you to."

"I thought Americans put great store in the family," he said, the expression on his face one of surprise.

She let out a quick breath. "We do."

He bent his head as if waiting for more. "And..."

"And, nothing. We put great store in the family." Her father giving marching orders, her mother dreaming in her room with a Do Not Disturb sign on the door, Poet in Residence. And Kelly and her two brothers running the house like a boot camp with her father the sergeant. *This is all you have to know, kids. Hard work never hurt anybody.* Hard work, cold showers, good marks, ambition, Kelly treated no different from her brothers.

"Kelly?"

She looked up, startled, and realized she'd been staring into her untouched glass of pale wine as though it were a window on the past. "I was thinking of my mother. She was a poet," Kelly said at last.

"Do I know her?"

She shook her head. "No, she was never published. I mean, I don't think she ever even tried."

"Have you committed some of her poetry to memory?" His question was gently asked.

"Lines here and there. My brother has all her work with him in California. We figured we'd divide it up, but so far it hasn't happened. I thought perhaps I'd try to find a publisher one day. She wrote poems for us on our birthdays. They'd arrive in large envelopes through the mail. She'd illustrate them with pictures cut out of magazines."

Tony took up his glass as if to salute her and then to her surprise, began to recite a poem she recognized at once as "Intimations of Immortality," an ode to early childhood by Wordsworth.

"There was a time when meadow, grove and stream,
The earth, and every common sight
To me did seem
Apparelled in celestial light,
The glory and the freshness of a dream.
It is not now as it hath been of yore;—
Turn wheresoe'er I may,
By night or day,
The things which I have seen I now can see no more."

"You like poetry, I see," she said. *The things which I have seen I now can see no more.* Would she ever tell him she had been glad to see the end of her childhood and was happy she could see them no more?

"Oh, we had poetry drummed into us. But you're right," he added, "quoting poetry is very much an

English hobby. I'd like to hear your mother's poetry sometime."

"You may, just," she said. "When we can fly to California."

"It's a date." He smiled directly into her eyes. She thought on a barely perceptible intake of breath that his smile was magnetic and that it would take very little for her to fly with him anywhere he liked. "You might manage a few choice sentences before then," he added.

"I will. When the occasion arises."

"Which isn't now," he said. "Pity."

"Oh, the occasion would have to be Halloween or Christmas or my birthday."

"I'll have to stick around then."

"I'm afraid you will, anyway," she said with a smile. "I've got a feeling Lambs is going to see a lot of you."

"Perhaps more than you'll consider good for it," he added after a moment's hesitation and with a slight darkening of his eyes. But then, as though he read the curious look on her face, he said, "Shop talk isn't poetry and is definitely disallowed on a night like tonight."

"A thousand apologies," Kelly said. "As long as we're talking about the past, tell me that all your memories of your childhood are good ones."

"*Most* were," he said with a wry smile. "I was younger than Sebastian and bigger than he. It gave me great pleasure to knock him to the ground on occasion and sit on him."

"Are you still knocking him to the ground?"

His expression grew serious. "No," he said at last. "Not that you'd notice. I've taken on other opponents now, and they're a lot tougher to beat."

"Which," she said, wondering if at last they had arrived at the reason why he had followed her, "makes me happy you're on our side. I'd hate like hell to be knocked to the ground."

He reached over and put his hand on hers. "You think I've knocked you to the ground by taking over Lambs, don't you? I gather you don't like change very much."

"Talking about business not allowed," she said, aware of his touch and not moving her hand from under his. "But since you want an answer, change isn't always for the better."

"Improving dividends for our investors is."

"Are we on dangerous ground, then?" she asked quietly.

"Not unless you consider the bottom line dangerous."

Their eyes held. She tried hard to read just what it was he expected of her. "I'll consider your bottom line dangerous if it dictates a change in policy."

"We're not going to lose you, Kelly. You and I aren't going to cross swords. You can go just as far as your ambition takes you."

Somehow his remark, flattering as it was meant to be, sent a long, icy shudder down her back. She pulled her hand away. "The view out there is a little too overwhelming," she said. "And I don't think you should keep Diane or Gregory waiting. Shall we go?"

"You're going to make absolutely certain our differences stay alive and well, aren't you?" he asked, gesturing for the waiter.

"No. But you took me by surprise once. I'd be a fool not to be wary after that." She got up and went out to the elevator and waited for him to catch up.

"Kelly."

She turned. He stood very close to her. She felt her heart begin to race as he reached out and put his hands on her arms. "Look," she said, "Gregory and I had a good, serious working partnership. I keep thinking you're handling things on a more personal level. I mean the magnetic, Tony Campbell level. The charm level is meant to catch me off guard. I can't afford to fall for it," she added abruptly. "My life, my career, everything I've worked hard for is on the line, and I don't want you to hand me a bill of goods." The elevator door opened. It emptied of its passengers and Kelly pulled away and stepped inside quickly.

CHAPTER SIX

DURING THE NIGHT and through the following morning, Friday, even in the midst of work, Kelly often found herself replaying her conversation with Tony. By midmorning, however, some of her anger began naturally to wear off. At last she reached the conclusion that she'd reacted a little too harshly even to Tony's simplest remarks. Perhaps she was jittery because the other shoe had to drop eventually, and waiting for it was nerve-racking.

With each ring of the telephone, she expected to hear from Tony. Each time she picked up the receiver, forcing herself to keep her voice calm, and each time she experienced a disappointment she didn't want to question. If Tony wanted to scramble her brains and her emotions, he was certainly succeeding.

Late that morning the telephone rang once more. The voice she heard at the other end this time filled her with relief.

"You're back," she said to Warren Bedford.

"Not for long, I'm afraid."

Warren, an executive with a large international corporation, spent a lot of time abroad. When he was in town, Kelly and he saw a lot of each other, although almost from the beginning he'd been more serious about their relationship than she. He'd heard of the sale of Lambs and commiserated with Kelly, then asked to meet her for dinner. She checked her calendar. Friday evenings were usually taken up with concerts of one kind or another, often charity events, as was the one penciled in at eight. She agreed with alacrity, deciding the concert could easily be missed.

At midday, after a tour of the store, she returned to her office, feeling restless, aware of time taking on a new dimension. When she was among people the hours raced along but stalled when she was alone. When she heard a light, familiar knock at the door, she called out, "Come on in, Gail."

Her assistant opened the door halfway and peered in. "Your pet project, Isabella, is a pain in the you-know-what."

Kelly put her pen down. "What now?"

"We've got three other kids from Job-Up working in the store, but only Isabella acts like the brat she really is."

"Talented brat. Come in, let's talk about it."

"I was hoping you'd come down to the fitting room and talk to her."

Kelly was only too glad to get away from paperwork. "Want to clue me in?"

"She was late again and they're shorthanded in fitting," Gail said as they headed for the back stairway. "She said she hates hemming, hates hawing, too, come to think of it."

"Ha-ha," Kelly said. "Let's see if we can't convince her that donkey's work is what seniors in high school do before they become full-fledged famous designers."

The fitting room was divided into tiny workrooms. In a cubicle off to the right Kelly found Isabella bent over a bright red ruffled dress with the bottom ruffle half removed.

When Kelly saw the girl, she gave a low moan and an almost imperceptible shake of her head that sent Gail bowing away with a mouthed "Good luck." The teenager had cut her luxurious black hair into short, up-ended spikes. She was outfitted in black leather from a very short skirt that rode her hips, to an over-size, wide-shouldered jacket that couldn't possibly be comfortable in the warm cubicle. Even as she fixed a smile on her face to show the girl she wasn't impressed, Kelly made a mental note to ask the store engineer to check out the air-conditioning.

"Isabella?"

The girl looked up belligerently. Her makeup was exaggerated, her carmine lipstick carefully applied. "Oh, hi," she said truculently, staring at Kelly as if daring her to make a remark. "This stupid ruffle."

"Why is it stupid? Looks perfectly smart to me. A plus. Should go on to college."

Isabella didn't crack a smile. "Take it off, then turn the dumb hem part up *and* the dumb lining. The customer wants it even shorter and she doesn't have the legs for it."

"Ours not to question why, once in a while," Kelly said. "Put the dress down for a minute. Let's talk about what's bugging you."

Isabella kept the dress on her lap and released a heavy sigh. "She needs it this evening."

Kelly had long before decided that Isabella had an innate shyness that made her seem sullen, but now wondered. It was obvious the hairdo and clothing were meant to irritate her and everyone else in the store, but Kelly refused to make an issue of it. She pulled up a chair, knowing nothing about Isabella was ever going to be easy. "I don't understand you, Isabella. What's bugging you? The minute you're offered help, you back away. It would be wonderful if you could skip all the boring parts like hemming, but you *are* getting paid for it, you know."

"That."

"That. Or you could work at a checkout counter in a supermarket and not be anywhere near clothes, if you'd like. Look," she went on earnestly when she saw Isabella frown, "if you'd toe the mark, you'd have your whole career neatly laid out for you. We're willing to back you, but you have to give something, as well."

"You don't know what it's like, Miss Aldrich," Isabella burst out. "I mean, you were born rich. You don't have to go home every day to—"

"To what, Isabella? To a house that isn't a palace? You have it all wrong about me. I *wasn't* born rich. I don't believe my life at your age was very different from yours. And you know what?" She reached out and took the girl's hands between hers. "I didn't have half your talent. I once thought maybe I'd be a poet or a writer or something, but I had no one to help me release my creative self, no Job-Up and no Kelly Aldrich."

Isabella gave her a sharp, reluctantly interested look.

"I learned something, though, that only one person was responsible for how I managed my life."

"You," Isabella said.

"That's right. You're expected to work hard, but for your own sake, not ours."

There was a slight rustle at the door. Isabella looked up past her and then down at the dress still in her lap, gently extricating her hands from Kelly's.

Kelly turned. Tony stood in the doorframe, leaning against it, hands dug into his pockets. She blanched, wondering just how much he had heard. Damn, he had a way of appearing when least expected. She turned back to Isabella, ignoring him. "You know what? Let me come to see you at home, meet your mom and your family. We can talk more then." She knew Isabella's father had died and that her mother worked.

"But—" Isabella began.

"No buts." She thought quickly of her calendar and wondered how her Sunday schedule looked. Probably too busy by far. "Sunday," she said, getting to her feet. "I'll have Gail stop by and get directions." Staten Island, as she remembered. The quiet, unknown borough, the island reached from Manhattan by ferry. She had always wanted to take a ride on the ferry to Staten Island.

"But—" Isabella said once again.

"Sunday."

"What time?"

Kelly had to conceal a slight smile. She didn't know of any other member of her staff who'd reveal such reluctance to entertain the boss. "I'll check my calendar and let you know, okay?"

"Okay."

The last was given grudgingly, but Kelly didn't care. It was time she met and discussed her daughter's future with Mrs. Sanchez. She went past Tony, tossing over her shoulder as he followed her out, "Anything I can do for you?"

"Gregory was telling me something about an office."

She was going to have to have a word with Gregory. Advertising had made the move overnight into his office, and he knew it.

"We're enlarging the selling space on the fourth floor, but we could probably manage something near the window," she told him. "I'll have a talk with our engineer. He doubles as architect on the matter of temporary office space. Gregory hardly ever used his office," she added.

"Gregory was hands-off. I'm hands-on."

"Gregory was interested, helpful, enthusiastic. Come on, I'll call the engineer. Meanwhile, if you have some things you want to do, you can use my office and telephone."

"Very generous of you," he said. "What will you do while I'm using your telephone?"

She preceded him to the stairs, but before opening the door to her office she took a quick glance at her watch. Suddenly she wanted him to know about Warren Bedford and the fact that she was seeing him for dinner.

"Oh, you can use it now and all evening. I've got a date at, um, seven, and meanwhile I'm expected in the display department right about now."

"A date at seven?" He raised his eyebrows as if the possibility hadn't occurred to him, but then he wouldn't have given a thought to the heavy schedule she was forced to maintain. She imagined him checking her calendar without the least embarrassment. "I was hoping we'd manage dinner together."

"Sorry, an old friend just came back to town. As a matter of fact," she said, giving him a smile of inspiration, "I've given up my ticket to a charity affair so that I could be with him. A concert at the Town Hall with supper afterward. Oh, and cocktails before. Perhaps you—? No, forget I said that. It wouldn't be your speed at all. There won't be a fashion show, and it isn't anywhere near Central Park."

Perhaps he'd call Diane Bourne and see the evening out with her. Kelly didn't dare speculate. As she let him into her office, however, she couldn't help feeling she'd won something, although uncertain of what exactly she'd won.

THE CLOCK WAS SET for nine. Kelly lay in bed Sunday morning staring at the minute hand and waiting for the alarm to go off. The telephone rang in unison with the alarm. She reached over, hit the alarm button and picked up the receiver all in one swooping motion.

"What time's your Staten Island date?" It was Tony, cheerful and unexpected.

A shiver that required no explanation ran along her arms. It seemed to her that Tony was never far from her thoughts. "I said I'd be there at eleven-thirty. Why do you ask?"

"The grumpy little creature works for me, doesn't she?"

"Yes, of course." Kelly pulled herself up and plumped the pillow behind her with one hand. "You're not planning to come along, are you?"

"It's a beautiful Sunday," he said. "Nothing I'd like better than a ferry ride to Staten Island."

"Have a nice day and I'll see you another time," Kelly said. "Tony," she added when he didn't answer, "Isabella's a kid in trouble. She'll shut up like a clam with you along."

"Willing to make a bet on it?"

"I don't bet when I know the outcome."

"What time shall I pick you up?"

"If you mess this up for me," she began, then threw in the towel. "Oh, damn, come along, then. I've ordered a cab for ten."

"I'll go you one better, Kelly. I've got a convertible with its top down. See you."

She replaced the receiver, wondering if Isabella would have any idea who he was. Probably not. She fiddled with the idea of acting as if Tony were her date, then decided against it. She hadn't any doubt that Tony had his own agenda, and experience had already taught her he played by rules that could change at any minute.

THE STREET WAS LINED on both sides by small, unprepossessing houses held together by care and hard work, and the home owners were an ethnic mix, as evidenced by children playing together in the street. The small patch of grass in front of a white stucco house was piled with objects on card tables. Evidently someone was having a garage sale.

Halfway down the block, Kelly spied Isabella standing on the front porch of a graying house badly in need of paint. She was wearing the same short leather skirt, the same spiked hairdo and an overlarge T-shirt that was splattered with an abstract design.

"Make that yourself?" Kelly asked, coming up the path and stepping over a pair of abandoned skates and a doll minus an arm.

"It's nothing," Isabella said, staring at Tony.

"This is Mr. Campbell, Isabella Sanchez."

Isabella carefully wiped her hand on her skirt. "How do you do, Mr. Campbell," she said in an excessively polite manner, holding out her hand to be shaken.

"Pleased to meet you, Miss Sanchez."

Kelly noted the dark circles under the girl's eyes and reflected that her skin seemed dull and lifeless. "Mr. Campbell is the new owner of Lambs," Kelly began.

"I know," Isabella said, still watching him.

"And you're Job-Up's best hope for the future," Tony said, flashing a smile at her.

A slow red blush suffused Isabella's face. Kelly at that moment thought she could easily throw her arms around Tony and hug him. "Well," she said, wondering whether they were going to be invited in. She looked around. "This is a fine day, isn't it?"

"I guess you want to come in and meet my mom," Isabella said, going over to the door and opening it reluctantly.

Inside, the television set was blaring, a small child in a playpen greedily sucked at a bottle of milk, and two youngsters sat on the floor in front of the television set playing with an Erector set. A pleasant scent of cooking drifted in the air—onions fried in olive oil and something else, as well, that Kelly couldn't quite identify.

"That's my baby sister Ayline in the playpen. She gets into everything. That's my brother Luis and his best friend on the floor," Isabella said, leading the way through the small living room crowded with furniture. Kelly, in a quick glance, took in the fact that the place was clean if disarranged. She found touches that were obviously Isabella's in a couple of needle-point pillows on a worn couch, and a club chair that had been newly reupholstered.

Just then a small woman, her bronze face framed by a flowered blue scarf wrapped tightly around her head, came into the room, wiping her hands on her apron. The signs of what she had once been still lingered in her attractive eyes and soft features, but Kelly suspected she was at least ten years younger than she appeared to be.

"Miss Aldrich? I thought I heard voices," she said in a deep Southern accent. "I told her to do something about her hair before you came, but she wouldn't. It's the latest style, she tells me. I can't fight the latest style, now can I? Although if her father were alive, she wouldn't have dared show up looking like that." The woman stopped when she caught sight of Tony, who was crouching beside the youngsters playing with the Erector set. "Oh, I'm sorry," she said.

"Mrs. Sanchez, this is Mr. Campbell. He's the new owner of Lambs and he's very interested in the Job-Up program."

Tony put out his hand and shook hers vigorously. "Miss Aldrich tells me your daughter is very talented."

Mrs. Sanchez grinned. "Oh, well, that. Gets it from her grandmother, I suppose. Not from me, I can tell you. From when she was a wee thing, the child could sew two bits of fabric together and come up with something most amazing. There's been no stopping her. Will you have something to drink? Coffee, tea?''

"As a matter of fact, I wanted to invite you and Isabella to lunch," Kelly said. "But with the children here..."

Mrs. Sanchez leaned over the playpen and picked up the child. "This is Ayline," she said. "Luis say hello," she added to the youngster struggling with the Erector set. He barely looked up. *"Luis."* She shrugged, and as Ayline was struggling in her arms, Mrs. Sanchez put her back in the playpen, handing her a teddy bear to play with.

"I've made lunch," she said, turning a shy smile on Kelly. "A Creole dish from my home in Louisiana."

"Ah, that's the scent," Kelly said, now recognizing bay leaf and okra mixed in with the onions.

"Chicken and okra gumbo. I've got enough for everybody."

Isabella, who had stood in the open doorway during their exchange, dashed into the house, slamming the door shut when the phone rang. "I'll get it. It's for me."

"Check your grandfather and see if he's all right," Mrs. Sanchez called and then shook her head. "I've got an in-between child who's more responsible than Isabella. She's off baby-sitting now. My father lives with us, but he isn't feeling too well lately. He's in bed. Isabella, you hear? You will stay for lunch, Miss Aldrich?''

Kelly looked at Tony, who nodded. "Yes, of course, we'd be happy to, if it's no bother. I did want to talk to you about your daughter," Kelly said.

Tony, as if on cue, bent over the youngsters on the floor and made a quiet remark, which sent them scurrying for a few more pieces.

"How's her schoolwork?" Kelly asked.

Mrs. Sanchez beckoned her into the kitchen, where she busied herself with the cooking. "All right, I guess. No failing marks, although she complains all the time. Graduating next week, that's all I care about. The only class the girl likes is art. Miss Aldrich," she said, turning from the stove and facing Kelly with a harried expression. "It's not that Isabella isn't treated right here or at school. I hold down a night job. I'm a practical nurse. I admit I can't keep an eye on her the way I want to. If my father weren't sick—" She broke off and turned back to her cooking. "No, it's that gang she hangs around with. Not one of them has her brains or talent. Isabella! Is that Robbie you're talking to? Get off the phone and come set the table."

"I'll take care of it," Kelly said, glancing helplessly around the small, cluttered kitchen, which was dominated by a large center table.

"Isabella!"

"I'll take care of the table, Mrs. Sanchez. It's all right."

"And see about your grandfather at once!"

A cramped house and a harried woman with an infant in arms and an all-night job, Kelly reflected. And Job-Up had dropped Isabella into Lambs, which catered to some of the wealthiest women in the world.

Well, now Kelly had come face-to-face with the source of some of the girl's problems.

THE MUSIC of the ship's horn filled the sky as the ferry pulled out of its slip. On this warm late spring day the water was clear and calm. The fog that had dimmed the far shore on their way out had dissipated. Children scurried between the cars on the front deck to get a good view of the bay and skyline. Kelly suggested the top deck, which had a clear, open view of the Manhattan skyline. As the ferry picked up steam, the breeze whipped Kelly's hair around her face.

"We'll also get a good look at the Statue of Liberty," she remarked.

"I see the Statue of Liberty every time I fly into Kennedy," Tony said.

"It's not the same. From the air it hasn't got the same majesty."

"Oh, by all means, then, we must see the majestic lady." He took her hand and led her through the crowds to a spot that held a good view of the bay. "Well, there she is," he said, pointing across the waves to the imposing statue guarding the gateway to the States.

"I know it sounds sentimental and wacky," Kelly said, "but I really get a rush seeing her out there. Symbols really do mean something. Although," she added, "I suppose she's a symbol more of what was than what is. I mean, with all these foreign businessmen invading our shores. Poor, tired, huddled masses you're not."

"I told you that we're simply trying to get back what our beloved George III lost during your War of Independence. You don't blame us, do you? But," he added, looking seriously into her eyes, "I don't think the lady in the bay is what's on our minds, Kelly. Answer just one question. Accomplish what you came for?"

"Yes, as a matter of fact, I did," Kelly said, aware of being put on the defensive. "I learned that Isabella's a defiant teenager with an overworked and overtired mother trying to keep her family together."

"And in you walk, the fairy godmother in blue silk, dispensing charm and good cheer when Isabella could have throttled you for stepping into her territory."

"That's patently unfair, Tony." She felt her gorge rise. "Why did you come along, then? To watch me make a fool of myself?"

"No," he said. "To make sure you didn't make a fool of Isabella."

"I don't know what you're talking about," she said. "Half the time you were building the Brooklyn Bridge with a couple of seven-year-olds and the other half you were ODing on chicken gumbo."

He laughed. "Worth dying for. Lighten up, lady. All I want to know is what you think you accomplished visiting a kid at home where chaos is king."

"Damn it," she said quietly. "I'd like to do something. She obviously needs help. I'll get personnel on it."

"Kelly, the woman is a marvel, and she's managing her life. Stay out of it. She doesn't want charity. Not from you, not from anyone. At the moment she's in possession of a bright, rebellious teenager who's cut her hair into spikes and spends too much time on the phone with a boyfriend called Robbie. It's not your business. Your business is only to see that she gets to work on time and performs up to par while she's there. I take it you weren't a rebellious teenager.''

''I wore my hair long and parted in the middle, with thick waves that stood out three yards on either side,'' Kelly said, ''but I wasn't rebellious.''

''You also had an intact home with a father and a mother.''

''Oh, that I had,'' Kelly said hotly, ''quite intact. I happen to understand Isabella a lot more than you think. And with your privileged childhood you haven't got a clue what a real struggle is.''

''I understand one thing, Kelly. Step back from personal involvement with your employees. They don't appreciate it, and they could begin to expect more from you than you can afford to give.''

''That's a callous remark, and I feel sorry for the employees of Terro if that's what you really believe.''

''Need I remind you that you're an employee of Terro?''

''No,'' she said, stung. ''You don't have to. I'm aware of it every minute.''

He glanced over at her and then said in a softened voice. ''Let's not get away from the subject of Isabella. That statue out in the bay represents poor people, disenfranchised in their own countries who came to America, worked their tails off so their kids could join the mainstream. Mrs. Sanchez came up from Louisiana. Maybe she didn't have to pass the lady on her way here, but she represents the good people who want their children to succeed. Give Isabella some space. Don't interfere. Just set the ground rules. Obey or get out.''

"Is that your credo? Obey or get out?"

"My credo is the bottom line. I've got a passel of investors to worry about who want a return on investment. I believe in running a tight organization, rewarding my employees for the good work they do, and I obey the law. Kelly," he went on, "you're the kid from the mill town. Isabella represents a whole new chance to get out from under the sunless sky and make it happen all over again."

"Really? You think I'm trying to relive my teenage years? Dr. Freud, you've got it all wrong."

"Maybe." He turned to her and unexpectedly brushed his hand through her hair. "Out three yards on either side?"

She laughed. "Maybe four. What are you getting at?"

"Father let you get away with it?"

She shook her head. "I had a little more sense than Isabella. I wore my hair tied back when he was around."

He pushed her hair back and examined her carefully. "Gives you the schoolmarm look. But nice." He released her hair, and in another moment bent over and quickly brushed his lips against hers. "I imagine you were the properest little girl in town."

"In our house we towed the mark, if only to avoid further marching orders." She spoke a little breathlessly, still feeling the faint brush of his lips against hers, as though the kiss had actually deepened and deepened again.

"Poor Kelly," he said. "To be deprived of rebellion at so early an age."

"Oh, I wouldn't worry about me," she said. "Rebellion isn't the private preserve of the very young."

"Are you giving me a warning?"

Her smile was a level one. "Is there something I have to warn you about? No, don't answer that," she added. "We both know the dangers ahead."

"So we do." He paused. "Mind if I ask you a question that's none of my business?"

"Go ahead. I'm not required to answer it."

"Tell me about you and Gregory Solow."

She regarded him with astonishment. She thought he'd asked the question a little clumsily, as though he'd thought about it long and hard. Kelly wasn't certain whether to be annoyed or flattered.

"I'm not certain what you mean by that. Gregory was my boss and my mentor."

"Okay," he said. "Older, wealthy man. Young, beautiful protégé."

"I'm trying to figure out whether I should be insulted or not," she said. "If you mean did I get to the top by sleeping with the boss, then I am insulted."

"I'm sorry," he told her. "I didn't mean my question to sound so crude. I was wondering whether you're free, that's all."

"Whether or not I'm free doesn't enter into our discussion. But I will tell you about Gregory and me, anyway. He's like—no, he *was* a father to me. He loved Suzanne passionately and her death was a terrible blow. He's changed," she added, looking off into the distance and thinking of how quickly Gregory had broken the tie between them once he sold everything to Terro. She promised herself to call him that evening and have a long talk with the man. "He was a benign father figure to his entire staff," she said. "Surely you must see that. Not only with me, but with everyone. He allowed us space in which to be creative, and he believed in us. Any other questions?"

He shook his head, watching her with an intently serious expression that Kelly couldn't interpret. She felt his touch, however, and the warmth of his flesh against hers sent startling little chills down her spine. "Since we're sharing confidences," she said, "you might tell me something about Diane Bourne."

"Diane and I go back a long way. She works for Terro."

"Ah. Is that a habit you have? Extracurricular activities with your employees?"

"We've always known we can count on each other," he said. "For support, encouragement, comfort during trying times."

"Meaning you have an occasional on-again, off-again affair as the whim strikes?"

He whistled in admiration. "You're wrong, but you don't beat about the bush, do you?"

"You opened the door to all this sharing of information."

"So I did. There's nothing between Diane and me. And as far as I can see, she's developing an interest in Gregory Solow. You don't mind sharing your old friend with her, do you?"

"He was never mine to share," she said quietly, creasing her brow in a frown. And now when she most needed Gregory's advice, she thought, he was as elusive as a firefly in daylight. "And we're talking about Diane."

"As a final word on the subject," he told her. "There is nothing between us. The truth is, Kelly, I broke with Diane the night I met you."

She closed her eyes for a moment, remembering how she had run away from him after the concert. She saw the museum lit up and the fountains playing. It even seemed to her that remnants of the fireworks still lay against the night air. She had run away rather than listen to the opening of her creaky old heart.

CHAPTER SEVEN

THE WINDOWS OF LAMBS had been closed to public view on Wednesday, the time traditionally set aside for changing displays. At seven that evening Kelly stepped outside to watch the unveiling of the new windows. With her was her display director, Eric Linden, fresh out of art school, brash and innovative. Hers was the only store in Manhattan that could have put up with his daring and verve.

"Darling Kelly," he'd say as he presented her with each new idea, "this will make headlines in the *New York Times*."

"And a summons to appear before a judge," Kelly would invariably respond.

This time his idea was witty, if expensive. "And," he'd added, "we can splatter the scent of beer and sawdust all over the entrance."

"If I believed you meant it," Kelly answered with a laugh, "I'd sent you to Bellevue for observation."

Several passersby were standing in front of the windows when Kelly came down with Eric. The scent of Mary Chess's Tuberose filled the air, a warm scent with a floral topnote.

"Well?" he asked of the display.

"It'll do," Kelly said solemnly, hiding her smile of approval. "Of course, the new owners might not be quite as easygoing as Mr. Solow when it comes to picking up the tab." The made-to-order mannequins alone had cost a bundle.

"The new owners will *love* it," he squealed.

The display was of a saloon—straight out of a wild West movie. It carried from the left- to the right-hand window as though the entrance break didn't exist. The scene was a copy of one featured in an old James Stewart cowboy film, *Destry Rides Again*. A mannequin with an uncanny resemblance to Marlene Dietrich wore a short, sexy, ruffled dress by a young, new talent Kelly thought worthy of promotion.

The mannequin's mouth was open in song, and she stood at a table, her foot in a sequined shoe balanced on a saloon chair. Kelly had been with the display from its conception as a quick sketch to the ordering of the props, but she hadn't expected such a dynamic or amusing re-creation.

Mannequins ranged along the bar, insouciant, cheeks heavily rouged, long, thick hair combed into elaborate curls. They wore colorful dance dresses with dipped hems and poufed shoulders. Drifting from the front entrance, with the scent of perfume, was the sound of Marlene Dietrich singing "See What the Boys in the Back Room Will Have."

Kelly heard the comments of passersby with something amounting to glee.

"Fantastic window. Sensational. *Destry Rides Again*, my all-time favorite movie."

Eric nudged her. "See?" he whispered.

"Do you suppose the clothes are for sale?" someone asked. "I mean, they look like costumes."

"They're for sale, but I never heard of the designer," her companion answered, pointing to the discreet sign to the right of the window.

"Now all I need is someplace to wear it."

"At home with your favorite lover," Kelly said gaily. She waved goodbye to Eric and ran out to hail a cab. She was on her way to the Carlyle to see Sebastian Campbell, at his invitation. The displays at Lambs always stirred interest, and she intended to invite him to view this one.

On the way to the hotel she reflected on Tony and wondered whether he'd be at the meeting. Since their visit to Staten Island, she hadn't seen Tony nor had much time to think about him. Her schedule was always tight; she was forever manipulating appointments to squeeze in yet one more. In fact, she'd crowded Sebastian into an already overflowing day.

Sebastian, however, wasn't at the bar as planned when Kelly arrived at the hotel. She was directed instead to the suite he occupied on one of the upper floors.

When Sebastian opened his door, he invited her in with an immediate apology. "Sorry to have you come up here, but a call came in from England, and it was one I wanted to take."

"Of course, I understand perfectly," she said, smiling and shaking his hand, not quite believing his excuse, although she couldn't have said why.

Sebastian was well groomed, attractive, and his manner was charming, if a little vapid as evidenced by a weak handshake. He wore a well-fitted double-breasted suit. His tie bore a crest she was curious about, a dragon she thought, which she didn't dare examine too closely. She remembered Tony talking about knocking him to the ground when they were young and sitting on him.

"I took the liberty of ordering a light dinner," he told her, taking her arm in an intimate manner and leading her over to the sofa.

"Thank you," she said, "but you shouldn't have. As a matter of fact, I've got an engagement." She found the atmosphere cloying and wanted out of there as quickly as possible. She glanced around the suite and through the door into the bedroom. They were alone, and Tony had obviously not been invited to the meeting.

Something about Sebastian was decidedly off-putting. His eyes were cold, she decided. They were nocturnal, careful eyes. She reflected on how different the brothers were. At first meeting Sebastian might possess all the charm, but he wouldn't wear well.

"And what would you like to drink?" he asked, going over to the bar.

"Oh, I think white wine. That'll be fine."

When he came over to her with the wine, he raised his own glass of Scotch. His mouth creased into a smile as he handed her the glass. His breath smelled of whisky. Kelly couldn't believe he'd be crude enough to make a pass at her, but then she realized he'd been drinking before her arrival.

"You're a smart girl," he said, sitting down next to her.

Kelly decided not to take on the word *girl*. She gave him a cool smile. "I'd better be," she remarked.

"What would you say to taking Lambs nation-wide?"

"I'm sorry," she began as though she were deaf, although she understood precisely what he'd said. She'd discussed establishing clone stores in other cities with Gregory, and their decision had been a negative one; the ambience of Lambs defied duplication.

"Gregory and I have discussed the idea," she told him, aware of the constraint in her voice, "and we decided it couldn't be done."

"Perhaps it was an idea whose time hadn't quite come," he suggested.

She stared at him for a long moment. He'd been drinking, but it hadn't made him dumb. And he wouldn't make a pass, either, at least not quite yet. "I assure you," she said at last, "the time still hasn't come to expand into copycat stores."

"A refusal to go national?" He shook his head as though there were something certifiably wrong with her. "Gregory says you're bright and ambitious, but refusing to see the next logical step in your operation strikes me as being a bit odd."

"Odd? The next logical step isn't always the correct step."

"You'll never know unless you lift one foot and put it down in front of the other."

"And sometimes that can throw you off balance." Her mind was working furiously. She didn't like the tone of the conversation. Sebastian wasn't asking her to consider the possibility of expansion; he was ordering her.

"Mr. Campbell," she began in a formal way, "you can't clone spontaneity. We depend on small suppliers, on bright kids who walk in off the street with a clever design idea but no facilities for producing in large quantities. We nurture them along. We don't exploit them before they've barely begun. Incidentally, have you even been to Lambs?''

He shook his head. ''I buy black ink as opposed to red. Believe it or not, I don't have to visit the factory that makes the ink.''

''I don't think your brother would agree with you about going national,'' she said.

''Ah, Tony. He has a way of catching one off guard. Just when you think you know him, he turns around and presents you with another face entirely. My dear Kelly,'' Sebastian said, taking up her glass of wine, which she hadn't touched, ''suppose I refill this.''

She waited with an unexpected feeling of dread while he filled another glass with chilled wine for her. When he came back, he sat down again. ''Tony was the one who suggested both possibilities.''

''Suggested what possibilities?'' The voice that interrupted their conversation was frosty.

Kelly turned to find Tony advancing on them, his face devoid of expression. His glance quickly took in Kelly and then his brother.

Kelly carefully put her glass down and got to her feet. ''Expansion,'' she said. ''Taking Lambs national. You might have discussed it with me, but then you have a habit of letting everyone else know what's on your mind concerning my operation and letting me find out from a notice in the *Times*.''

''Sebastian spoke a little prematurely,'' Tony said. He turned to his brother. ''I thought we were meeting downstairs.''

''We were,'' Sebastian said. ''A call came in for me. I had to handle it.''

"Kelly, sit down." Tony gestured her to a chair. "We've just floated something into the air, that's all."

She shook her head. "If you want my input, you'll have to warn me ahead so that I can come armed with facts and figures. If you intend to proceed whether I agree or not, I'd appreciate notice before the event so that I can prepare my public smile. And now if you'll excuse me . . ."

She offered a shaky smile to both brothers and went quickly to the door without turning around. Not until she was back in the street hailing a cab did she relax. By then she had made up her mind to fight them every inch of the way.

THE URGENT MESSAGE on Kelly's answering machine at home was from Rudy Marchetta.

He didn't waste time with preliminaries. "What's this I hear about Terro shopping a new location for Lambs?"

"You have it wrong, Rudy. They're talking about expansion, not selling the store," Kelly said tiredly. "Taking on new spaces, I suppose, although it would surprise me if they're that far ahead in their thinking. No," she said, shaking her head, "you've got it all wrong."

"Kelly, one of my clients was asked to shop around for a flagship space for Lambs."

Kelly felt the perspiration begin to form along her forehead. "I'm sorry. Maybe I'm a little dense. Or aren't we on the same wavelength? I've just come back from a meeting with the Campbells. They're talking about taking the store national."

"And I'm passing on information that's about as good as you can get. Or maybe you don't know that Terro has picked up the real estate on either side of Lambs. I can see them applying the wrecking ball to all three buildings. I can also see a tall glass building overshadowing Fifty-seventh Street."

She took so long in gathering her senses that Rudy called her name softly. "Kelly, are you all right?"

"I've just been punched in both ears, but sure, I'm all right. Let me call you back."

Kelly replaced the receiver and sat very still. What was it her mother had once written in a birthday poem? Kelly had turned thirteen. A fragment came back to her. *Be sweet, like a soft sea of violets in a summer field.* Being sweet wasn't the way to handle Terro. She wasn't her mother's child so much as her father's.

The number at the Hotel Carlyle was familiar to her; valued customers and friends stayed there and a few called it home. She was just about to ask the operator for Tony's room when she slammed the receiver down. It wasn't quite the time to confront him. He was the enemy now and, she believed, a formidable one.

What she wanted was a long freezing shower and a battle plan. But then Kelly recalled she was due for a dinner meeting with the Job-Up executive committee. She rushed into the shower. She'd be late, but she could make it.

A STOREWIDE SALE had been scheduled for Thursday. It began badly with a fire scare in the basement. A shipment of blouses from Hong Kong hadn't arrived. Then Gail called in sick. To cap the morning panic, a fur coat was reported stolen from the stockroom before a security tag had been placed on it. By noon Kelly was certain she was on a nonstop merry-go-round with no brass ring in sight.

Tony called three times, and she didn't take or return any of them. She told her secretary to tell Mr. Campbell—in fact, either Mr. Campbell—that she was busy and couldn't be paged. The sale brought in many more customers than usual, and she wanted to move all the spring stock out and much of the summer stock that hadn't been selling as well as expected.

She tried half a dozen times to phone Gregory Solow and at last found him in the temporary office Terro had lent him at his old headquarters.

"I've got to see you," she said tersely.

"Can it wait until after lunch?"

"Certainly. Come here about five," she said, glancing automatically at her calendar and remembering that she had kept the late afternoon clear because of the sale.

"Five on a sale day? Sounds bad."

"It is."

"Wouldn't want to give me a hint?" he asked in a jocular fashion.

"You know what the hint is." She glanced up to find Tony coming into her office bearing a suspicious box that looked as if it contained a pizza. "Five at my apartment." She hung up and glared at her visitor. "What are you doing here?"

"Five at your apartment," he said. "Sounds inviting.

"You bastard," she said, advancing on him. "You're going to sell the building out from under us. Going national. Just a smoke screen to get my attention, with the Campbell brothers playing good cop, bad cop. And get that thing out of my office. I prefer the scent of roses to garlic."

He grinned at her. "Finished?"

"With you, yes."

"Great. Sit down. Or better yet, order in some coffee. Mushrooms, cheese, the works, and heavy on the mozzarella."

"Tony," she said, "if I could tell you to get out of my life for good, this would be the moment I'd do it."

He set the pizza down on the cocktail table, then went over to her desk, picked up the telephone and politely asked her secretary if she might order some coffee for them. He added that she should hold Kelly's calls for a while.

"Mushrooms and cheese," Kelly said, looking at the pizza. "It's a wonder that it isn't filled with sausage, since you're such a cannibal."

"Cannibal? I don't get your reasoning, Kelly. When it comes to the way I do business, I'm a virtual vegetarian. Plates?"

"In the cabinet. I'm not hungry, but I want to see you work." She watched from her desk, tapping her fingers on the mahogany surface as he went over to the cabinet. He'd been at the back of her mind all week—not the man who held her future in his hands, but the man with the magnetic smile and overt sexuality who, with just a look could send her pulse racing. But now they were enemies and, for that, she'd have the rest of her life to wallow in regret.

He turned to her triumphantly, holding up two elegant porcelain dishes. "Pizza on porcelain."

"Don't bother bringing a dish for me."

"Let's not draw swords over a friendly slice of pizza." He carefully lifted out a serving and, with a flourish, placed it on the plate. But when her secretary knocked on the door and came in with coffee, Tony solemnly handed her the pizza instead. Kelly noted that for all his aristocratic ways the man was essentially decent—at least on a personal level. Too bad decency didn't square with his actions on a grander scale.

"Have some," he told Kelly when they were alone, fetching another plate. "Might sweeten your mood and make you able to deal with the possibility of change."

"You're a snake in the grass, and nothing's going to change my mood except your backing away from Lambs all the way across the Atlantic. Do you understand what you're trying to do? You're trying to sell the land from under me. Nothing you do or say is going to charm me into telling you to go ahead or say that it's a wonderful idea. In fact, I may take out a large ad in the *New York Times* telling you to take Terro and go back where you came from."

He gave a hearty laugh. "I'm here to stay, Aldrich, and I'm going to make you eat your words, along with the pizza."

"Why have you put the real estate up for sale? Lambs and the building are a duo, like Romeo and Juliet, Pelléas and Mélisande."

"Doomed lovers, all of them," he remarked. "We're talking about a change of venue, not the end

of life. The most valuable part of the Lambs operation, as it stands now, is the real estate," he said, regarding her steadily, almost daring her to disagree.

"Do you really mean that?" she asked quietly.

"I'm afraid so."

"Then we have nothing to discuss." She felt tears
start inexplicably at the back of her eyes. It was unfair. Her nerves, like her backbone, were steel. She
wasn't supposed to break down into sobs at the possibility of change. She was supposed to present her
arguments forcibly and with whatever facts she had at
hand. "Tony, you can't split Lambs like an atom."
She caught the slight break in her voice and turned it
into a laugh. "If you do, the explosion might just destroy everything."

"I'm sorry," he told her. "We have to slice away the
excesses of our purchase. They call what we're doing
profit over loss. We can't afford to be sentimental.
Some things are going to go down for the count."

"It's what you planned all along, isn't it?"

He stood up and drew his lips together tightly. "I
wanted to see you," he said, "to apologize for what I
can imagine was Sebastian's friendly way of giving you
a karate chop. Kelly." He came quickly over and drew
her to her feet. "Lambs isn't going out of business. If
anything, it'll be bigger and better than ever. Pretend
I'm a Hollywood mogul. I'm going to make you a
star." He took her chin in his hand and briefly pressed
his lips against hers.

"Sure," she said. "I know just how those moguls
operate. Thanks, but no thanks. And now, if you'll
excuse me, I'll go about the business of running my
operation." She moved past him but turned at the

open door. "Coming? Or do you still need office space?"

He picked up the pizza and followed her out, depositing the box on her secretary's desk. "There's enough here for a midafternoon snack," he told her with a wink.

Kelly didn't stay to hear her answer. She wanted to fade into the middle of the sale crowd and forget about Terro and Tony Campbell.

"DON'T TELL ME this is all new to you, Gregory."

Sitting on the sofa in her office late that afternoon and facing Kelly behind her desk, Gregory sniffed. "Tomatoes and garlic? Odd scent for your office, Kelly."

"Pizza," she said. "I can't imagine how it could linger this long. Forget that, you old malingerer. We're not here to discuss fragrances. What do you know and why haven't you told me?"

"It's not a problem," he said, watching her evenly. "Terro knows you have a contract with Lambs, not an address. All they're trying to do is expand the operation."

"Destroying a landmark building and dumping Lambs somewhere else isn't a problem?" She came around her desk and bent down, pretending to look in his ear. "You don't mind, do you? Just want to discover if it's hollow inside. The trouble with you, Gregory, is that all this leisure isn't good for you." She flopped down beside him on the sofa. "Except that you are looking quite wonderful, better than I've seen you in...in *years*. Which brings me back to my point.

You have to help me show the Campbell brothers the door, now, before they do any further damage."

"Kelly," he said, taking up both her hands, "stop running around like a chicken without a head. Times change, life changes, the world goes round and you're not being asked to give up anything."

"Aren't I?"

"You're the Lambs image. Don't worry about anything else."

"Benedict Arnold," she sputtered. "Why are you defending them? I know what happens in these takeovers, these expansions. The first thing to go are the old employees. Charlie the night watchman—they'll replace him with a robot. No." She shook her head emphatically. "Uh-uh, it's not going to happen. And they're not going to bulldoze the building, either!"

"Not with the employees in it, I hope," he said in mock horror.

"Stop joking, Gregory. Haven't you any sense of history?"

"A one-hundred-year-old building isn't history. It's old age, that's all."

"My mother had a very clever poem about old age."

"Spare me," Gregory said with a roll of his eyes.

"Something about green leaves turning yellow and being more beautiful for it. Something like that. I'll remember it after a while."

"Forget the poetry," Gregory said. "Just how do you intend to fight Terro? Lie down in front of the bulldozer?"

"If I have to."

He gave an impatient sigh. "Kelly, Terro means business. All you're being asked to do is go along with their expansion plans. Good Lord, anyone else in your position would be shopping Park Avenue co-ops and houses in the Hamptons. You're asking to stay small. That's like asking to have your salary reduced because you can't stand what money can buy."

"In this case, small is good and big is bad, in my opinion."

"Do you really know what you've just said, my dear?" He asked the question with good humor, as though she were just kidding him along.

"The store," she said quietly, aware of having used the words before and knowing she would undoubtedly use them many more times, "is the sum of its parts. It's unique because of its location in the heart of the Silk Stocking district and because the building is old and has nooks and crannies, small corners and hidden places, an intimate, cozy atmosphere. It can't be copied. It can only be phonied up. You may quote me on the evening news."

"Kelly, if you really want to stay small, I can think of a dozen operations that would trip over themselves to hire you. But that isn't what you want," he told her.

"Certainly I can get another job," she said. "Make more money, have a lot of power. I can let Lambs fall on its face going national. But I'm not going to. They're out to desiccate Lambs, take it apart until there's nothing left but a—*bah*."

"And I can't argue the pros and cons, at least not at this hour," he said impatiently. "I'm no longer involved with the operation, and I've got a date with a lady, who, incidentally, promised to meet me here."

Surprise lit Kelly's face, but before she could recover, he said, "Diane."

"Bourne?"

"Bourne, bred and quite beautiful."

"Gregory!" Kelly couldn't quite take in the information. Was he trying to tell her he'd fallen for Diane Bourne right under Tony's nose? "Let me catch my breath. Well," she added after a moment, "you *are* an artful old dodger. So this is where your leisure time is leading you. Good heavens." She began to pace her office. "I'm beginning to feel a hundred years old. No wonder you have that ruddy color and air of self-satisfaction. My, my, my. It almost makes me forget you're a viper, Gregory."

He gave a broad laugh but was stopped from answering her by the intercom and Diane Bourne's arrival.

"Am I disturbing anything?" Diane asked on the threshold to Kelly's office. She was dressed in a bright red suit, which Kelly recognized as a Lambs exclusive.

"You've disturbed nothing," Kelly said, smiling at her. "We leave that to Gregory. Good to see you and good to see you've been prowling our Young Designer Shop."

"Mmm, and parting with a pretty bundle." Diane shook Kelly's hand warmly before offering a cheek to be kissed by Gregory. From the gesture Kelly couldn't quite read the woman's true feelings. One thing Kelly herself felt; she had been shunted off to a quiet corner of Gregory's life. The idea was a hard one to swallow.

"We're off to a cocktail party," Gregory told her, tucking his arm through Diane's and beaming possessively. "And the theater afterward."

A brand-new Gregory, pleased about going out to dinner and plays—this required getting used to. Kelly had known him through all the years of his wife's illness, and now she was seeing a part of him she'd never known existed.

"Wonderful," she managed. "What are you seeing?"

"*The Phantom of the Opera*," Diane said. "Gregory's been a genius at acquiring tickets to everything worthwhile in New York."

"We saw that a year ago, didn't we?" Kelly said.

"No, my dear," Gregory said softly. "You saw it, and my body was present on the occasion, of course, but *I* wasn't."

"Oh, Gregory, of course," Kelly said, contrite. "How could I have been so stupid?"

"Goodbye, my dear. We'll talk soon," he told her quite cheerfully as she ushered them to the door. Gregory spontaneously turned and kissed her on the cheek. "Have some fun, too," he told her. "That's what we're here for, after all, isn't it?"

She exchanged a glance with Diane, whose expression was completely noncommittal. "Yes, now that you mention it," Kelly said.

When they were gone, she spent several minutes wondering just what kind of game Diane was playing and where Tony fitted in. That Gregory was smitten was written all over his face. She couldn't help thinking of Suzanne and his devotion to her. But evidently this was a new Gregory, and the new Gregory hadn't been a help about Lambs. He'd been inordinately flip over the danger the building was in of being torn down. After a while, Kelly began to wonder why she was being so sentimental about Gregory when he'd cast her out to drift alone.

It was only later that evening, when the store had closed its doors and Kelly once more stood outside Lambs and gazed up at the building, that she understood precisely what she had to do. The Lambs building traced back to the turn of the century, and Kelly was going to stop Tony Campbell at the pass with the Landmarks Commission to help her.

CHAPTER EIGHT

DAMN IT, he'd been ringing Sebastian's room for twenty minutes and still no answer. There was no earthly reason for his brother to be out so early in the morning, nor for him to be late for a ten o'clock appointment, especially since their suites at the Hotel Carlyle were only two floors apart. Except that when it came to Sebastian, reason took a holiday. Slamming the receiver down, Tony proceeded to pace the floor, slipping back in memory to a time in Cornwall when his father called him down from London.

Tony gladly arranged a weekend visit, wondering idly but without worry what sort of family business required his help. He came home in a relaxed mood, only to discover his father on the offensive from the beginning.

"Can't afford your so-called independent streak any longer, Tony. The fact is, Sebastian can't handle Terro by himself. He's overwhelmed and needs your help."

"And how are you feeling this evening?" Tony asked. But his father, who had no sense of humor, was intent upon getting his point across.

"I'm afraid my invitation for you to join Terro is non-negotiable."

What his father didn't say was that, of the two brothers, Tony was the more reliable, a quicker study.

As the second son of a viscount, he'd ultimately receive a small share of the estate, while Sebastian would ultimately have everything—the title, the lands and the directorship of Terro. That had been fine with Tony. It allowed him to follow his own agenda.

"I'm happy where I am," Tony pointed out to his father, knowing his argument was fruitless but wanting to score a point, anyway.

"You'll be happier at Terro."

"Perhaps you'd like to rename it Terror."

His father didn't laugh. But he did promise Sebastian would shape up and that Tony would have an option to get out later. He even hinted the rewards would be greater than any Tony could manage on his own.

"I don't need bribes," Tony had said angrily. But his father's appeal had touched him. The rights of primogeniture were embedded in English history. His father, Sebastian and he were all slaves to that history.

Now, in a flash of insight that troubled him, Tony realized he'd always thought his real life would begin when he was free of Sebastian and Terro, but in spite of his father's promises he wondered if he'd ever really expected to be free. So why had he been playing this waiting game? Even believing that, if the venture in the states worked out well, he might walk away.

He stopped his restless pacing and gazed out the hotel window to the avenue below. For a moment he forgot his irritation with his brother. There was a purposeful mood to the early-morning throngs on their way to work, an air of well-being, and it infected him. He couldn't shake the sense that something precious was about to turn the corner. He felt expectancy and renewal and didn't want to examine why.

New York was an ideal city for observing contrasts: across the avenue, in front of a store that specialized in Tiffany lamps, a derelict doffed his hat and performed a little jig as part of his panhandling act. Tony almost opened the hotel window to toss him some money, but realized it was a physical impossibility.

Job-Up. The thought came to him involuntarily. Look a problem in the face and it becomes more than an abstract notion, whether a derelict doing a jig or a kid trying to climb out of poverty.

Abruptly he returned to the phone and dialed his brother's room, but again there was no answer. He checked his watch. A minute or two had passed. He decided to wait ten more minutes, giving Sebastian the benefit of the doubt.

His mind slipped to Kelly, who would already be in the store that meant so much to her. He wondered what she was doing and thinking. He hadn't been able to get her out of his mind, her infectious laugh, the wind blowing through her hair in the salt breeze as they stood on the ferry and, not the least of it, her kindness, no matter how ill-guided, to both Isabella and her mother.

Kelly Aldrich was a design in contradiction, like Manhattan itself. One part of her was hard-edged and single-minded. He amused himself thinking that if she were to remain an adversary, he'd be up against someone who just might best him. In the middle of a business negotiation he'd want to touch her more than to get her to sign on the dotted line.

But she possessed another side, a vulnerable one. The day before he'd had to stop himself more than once from pulling her close and assuring her that everything would be all right.

Just as well, because it wouldn't be all right. Terro's plans for Lambs and Kelly's intent to keep everything the same was a built-in explosion waiting to be released.

At the end of ten minutes Tony dialed Sebastian's room and got a busy signal. He slammed the receiver down and wasted no time in getting to his brother's room. He rapped quickly on the door and heard a rustling sound from within, then complete silence. He raised his fist and pounded on the door, knowing he was nursing an anger far out of proportion to Sebastian's tardiness. The lock clicked at last and the door opened.

"What's all the noise about?" Sebastian, unshaven, wearing a loosely belted robe, seemed slightly dazed.

Tony tried for a calm tone. "We had an appointment a half hour ago. When did you get in last night? Never mind," he said with a wave of his hand. "I can see it's business as usual, with a bottle in one hand and a woman in the other."

"Sobersides Tony, isn't that what we called you as a kid? Try not to lecture me at this time of the morning." Sebastian went over to the bar and poured himself a drink. "It's a little early for your hypocritical moralizing."

Was he moralizing and was it hypocritical? Perhaps if his thoughts about Kelly were put into action, his brother would have a point. "We're in this city on business," Tony said wearily, and not for the first time. "And you're going to keep your mind clear because you don't have a choice." He stopped at a sudden noise and turned to find a young woman standing at the bedroom door, wrapped in a towel and smiling vapidly.

"Get back in the bedroom," Sebastian ordered.

"But, Sebastian—" she began.

He fixed her with a hard smile, and she went docilely back into the room, quietly closing the door. "All right," he said to Tony, "speak your piece. Have done with it."

"Your wife should have thrown you out years ago."

Sebastian downed his drink. "She thinks the world of me."

"She likes the big house, the promise of a title and the charge account at Harrods. That's about what she thinks of you, and she still should have thrown you out."

"That what you set up this little meeting for, to tell me what my wife should or shouldn't do?"

"Get rid of your friend," Tony said, going over to the door. "I'm going to the office. I want you there exactly fifteen minutes from now. I need your signature on some papers." He opened the door and let himself out without turning back.

An hour later his office door opened and Sebastian strolled in, dressed in a double-breasted gray suit, a cravat at his throat.

"Really playing the country squire," Tony remarked, throwing down his pen and stretching his legs out.

"Where are the papers I have to sign?" Sebastian asked, a hint of uncertainty in his tone.

Studying him, Tony felt drained of any feelings for the man. He reached for a folder on his desk, withdrew some papers and said tersely, "Sign them."

Neither talked as Sebastian scribbled his signature without glancing at the contents. "Now, if that's all you want of me," he said, finishing the last with a flourish, "I've got an appointment."

"Sit down." Sebastian let out a sigh and sat down. "Your unbridled arrogance is becoming a problem," Tony said. "Manhattan is a town where gossip is second only to tourism as a source of profit. I don't want Terro on the defensive because your name is in all the columns."

"Let them say what they want," Sebastian answered carelessly. He reached into his jacket pocket and extracted a cigarette case. "You're talking apples and pears. Americans like success. They don't even care how you achieve it."

"You wouldn't be the first hustler they've ridden out of town on the rails or, in this case, on British Airways."

"You've been reading too many cowboy stories. What I do and with whom is my business. As long as I show up when needed and act the part of elder statesman, you haven't got a thing to say."

"What we do in the next couple of months is entirely my business. We're heavy into New York real estate, a market that's gone a little soft. That footage along Fifty-seventh Street is all of a piece now, thanks to the acquisition of Lambs."

His brother was slumped in his chair with his eyes closed, a lit cigarette in his hand. Tony plodded on, although he knew Sebastian was perfectly capable of falling asleep then and there.

"We're getting rid of deadwood," he went on, believing in a way that he was talking more for himself than for his brother. "I've got a buyer interested in Lambs. They'd plan on taking it national. Meanwhile, we're to keep our noses clean, just as we do everywhere else. I've already booked a flight home for you."

Tony had the satisfaction of seeing Sebastian sit straight up. "You've what?"

"You're the titular head of Terro. They need you in London."

"You're not dealing me anything I haven't already planned," Sebastian said, trying to move onto the offensive, trying to save face, as Tony had expected.

"Then I don't think we have anything more to say to each other."

"So long as you remember that I'm the head of Terro."

"Believe me, it's impossible to forget."

Sebastian stubbed out his cigarette and wordlessly left the office.

Tony didn't move for several seconds. Then, without knowing he was going to do it, he dialed Kelly's number, realizing with a shock that he'd memorized it.

"You ever get depressed and need a friendly face?" he asked when she came on the line.

"Sure."

"Well, I'm depressed. I need a friendly face. Meet me at that little restaurant that's catercornered to the store."

"Is that an order, boss?"

"I always knew rank had its privileges," he said, feeling better already.

THE WAITRESS EYED Tony as she placed a basket of bread on the table. He smiled at her. His relationship with women had always been easy, possibly because he never really lost his head or his heart to any of them. Until Kelly had appeared on the scene, anyway. It was a long time since a challenging woman had piqued his interest as well as his libido. He'd positioned himself at a restaurant window with a clear view of the front entrance to Lambs, not wanting to miss a moment of Kelly. Something undefinable about the woman was hauling him in. He wanted to see her leave the store and cross the street, wanted to watch her when she didn't know she was being observed.

He'd known women who were more beautiful, more available, certainly more amenable. But to Tony, Kelly was a combination of intangibles that had intrigued him from the first.

There she was. He leaned back and narrowed his eyes, watching as she crossed the wide street at a rapid pace. Her gait was lovely and sexy; she wore something short, revealing long, shapely legs. Her hair swung about her face, and her smile was sweet and, he thought, a little dreamy.

He felt an ache in his loins that was decidedly sexual, and more. It was the *more* he wanted to possess. She came into the restaurant and he rose, reaching for

her. For a moment they didn't speak but stood holding hands.

"I was surprised you called me when you needed a
friend," she said in a breathy voice as though she'd
run all the way. "After all, between your brother, your
business associates and Diane Bourne..." She stopped
and looked at him shrewdly. "Unless, of course, it has
something to do with Lambs?"

"You're the only thing that isn't depressing me," he
told her.

She smiled, gently extricated her hands and sat
down. "Okay, I'm Dr. Aldrich, on call at all hours.
What's your problem, Mr. Campbell?"

Her remark surprised him, and he threw back his
head and laughed. He was happy, actually happy.
"You're quick and you're clever, Doc."

"You have a funny way of acting depressed," she
commented.

"And you have a marvelous way of making me feel
my problems are solved just by being with you."

"I can think of a hundred different ways of taking
advantage of your mood," she said.

"Nothing would please me more."

She shook her head. "Uh-uh, not quite yet. I'd
better test you first to see if you won't break."

The waitress came by and asked if they wished to
order drinks.

"Drunk already," Tony said.

The waitress's eyes slid quickly to Kelly and back.
"Would you like to see the menu?"

"I'll have the fruit salad," Kelly said quickly. She
ate frequently at the restaurant. "My patient will have

something substantial," she went on. "Pastrami on rye. He has to keep up his level of energy."

"French fries?" The question was asked of Tony.

"Certainly," Kelly said.

"Keep it up," Tony said. "I like a beautiful woman to take my life in her hands."

"I haf decided," Kelly said, once the waitress was gone, and in a fake Viennese accent, "zat you're not in too fragile a state of mind, my freund. Or should I zay my Freud? Be zat as it may, I wish you to look across the street and, when you have finished looking, describe to me ze scene."

He willingly obliged, already certain of the game they'd have to play out. "I see a five-story building decked out with certain stone embellishments, Beaux-Arts, I believe. I see a couple of women going in. No one coming out. Perhaps they are led down to a secret chamber where they're fed to the god Mammon. I believe he holds sway over credit cards." He turned his eyes on Kelly, noting the amused sparkle in her eyes, then returned to his perusal of the scene. "No, that's not what I see at all. I see a tall, glass skyscraper taking up a hundred feet or so of frontage. Inside is a leafy court filled with flowers in which ordinary citizens may take their weary ease without it costing them a cent."

"Low body blow, patient," Kelly said. "The doctor is going to mark up your card with a C minus, which means go back to England, carrying your ambitions with you. Take a look at that building, sir, a real close look. Are you seriously thinking of destroying it?"

"Not personally, no."

"Ah, you'll pay some wrecker to come in the middle of the night to smash it to smithereens. In the morning you'll say, 'Who me? Innocent, I'm innocent. I'll fire the man and see that he never does another dishonest day's work in his life. Tut, tut, so old Lambs is gone. Well, never mind. We'll share the wealth, make a national chain of it and imitate every teensy-weensy Beaux-Arts part of it in plastic. Oh, they do wonderful things in plastic these days.'"

"Have you finished?" he asked calmly.

"No. Nature is red in tooth and claw. And I'm seeing red. How I'm seeing red."

What a fool he'd been, believing she'd hurried on the wind just to be with him. "Always wear a chip on your shoulder the size of Boulder Dam?"

Kelly shook her head. "Is your mood blackening?"

He gave her a grim smile. "Kelly, you have it in you to color it anything you like." He thought briefly of Sebastian and the quiet battle they'd had not less than an hour before.

"Build your skyscraper if you must, but build it around Lambs."

He shook his head. "Kelly, when you signed aboard with Solow Enterprises, the one guarantee you never had is that the store would remain the same until the twenty-fifth century."

"I'll settle for the twenty-fourth."

He picked up his sandwich and took a bite but had trouble chewing and swallowing. Damn, if she could do this over a minor point she'd never win, he hated to think of what would happen over major ones.

"The twenty-third century, maybe?" she asked. She toyed with the salad, spearing a piece of fruit and then pushing it off the fork, only to spear another.

"Funny lady."

"You never did tell me what was depressing you. It obviously has nothing to do with real estate. That aspect of your life seems totally under control."

Gazing at her, he knew he detected determination in her eyes. She was far from accepting his opinion of things. Somewhere along the line their battle might get bloody, and he was sorry about it. Losing wouldn't make the lady happy at all.

"The doctor is waiting," she said. "And there are half a dozen patients in my outer office with problems I can guarantee are worse than yours."

He laughed and put the sandwich down. "Just some family stuff," he told her. "Easily handled, but it leaves a sour taste in the mouth."

"Great. We have that out of the way, then. Which leaves us at the impasse where our audience last saw us. A store you expect to demolish and a name and idea you want to plaster all over the country."

"Kelly, don't interfere. Just do your job and leave the high finance to us."

She put her fork down carefully and reached for her cup of coffee. "How can anyone function properly when there's a possibility of a bunch of pink slips coming down the road?"

"Where'd you get that idea?" he snapped.

"Pink slips happen when it's perceived that a store's image has to change or be enlarged or whatever. Suddenly old and valued employees begin to look just old. Go national and the human element is removed. All you've got is plastic—plastic buildings, plastic ideas, plastic clothes.''

"Plastic," he reminded her, "used to mean malleable."

"Don't change the subject. I'm talking about the malleable stuff that hardens into replicas of the real thing, except something gets lost in the translation. And now," she said, moving her chair back, "I've got a date at one. I set aside a couple of hours every week to see the work of young new designers, and I don't want to be late. As a matter of fact, you should come along and see how Lambs' reputation was built.''

"More Isabellas?" he remarked.

"If we're lucky, they're a little more stable. These are young or maybe not-so-young people who have ideas, some good, some bad, some silly, some adorable. If we—or better our customers—can help them on the road to success, so be it. Come on. Doctor's orders.''

He had a deskful of work and a full calendar, but he was curious. "You're on.''

IN THE RABBIT WARREN of rooms on the fifth floor of Lambs was a small area set aside for conferences, and it was there that Kelly and the head buyers of each department met with their vendors every Tuesday afternoon. The room was painted a soothing, neutral taupe. A narrow conference table took up the center, and along the left wall was a long clothing rack, now empty. Sometimes it seemed to Kelly that every artisan in New York with a commercial product to sell showed up on Lambs' doorstep sooner or later. Some could be refused with a shake of the head and a kind word; others made a sale on the spot. Certain ideas needed developing; others required smoothing down. The encouraging word for all who came to Lambs and were refused was not to be discouraged.

When Kelly arrived at the conference room with Tony in tow, the narrow corridor outside was already filled.

"A good dozen," Kelly said when they were seated inside with her buyers. "About average." She referred to her appointments list. "Sandy Allemain, sportswear."

The young man who came ebulliently into the room with a friend, both carrying brown garment bags, wore a gold earring in one ear, and shaggy hair that looked as if it had been carefully combed into a careless tumble. It struck Tony that he displayed an appealing boyish enthusiasm.

"Where'd you go to school?" Kelly inquired as the two young men opened the garment bags.

"Parsons School of Design. Graduated last year. We set up this little manufacturing place in a loft downtown. We're calling it Allemain Sports."

"Nice," Kelly said.

Tony admired her patience and the air of ease in the room.

"Parsons really has a gung-ho design department," she went on.

"Right," he said. "I learned a lot." He pulled the first garment off the rack, an emerald-green silk jumpsuit with a complicated wrapping at the waist.

"Nice," Kelly said again, getting up and examining the garment with her Young Designers buyer.

As they ran through the dozen garments shown, Tony, who had no idea whether they were saleable or not, sat back in his chair watching Kelly at work. As far as he was concerned, she was narrowing her talents. She should be leaving this work to subordinates.

By the time the young man left, he'd extracted a promise from the buyer to visit his showroom. "It's probably a go for him," Kelly explained to Tony. "He's serious, and he's already selling some of his garments downtown where most of the avant-garde clothes make their appearance in New York. What he showed us was beautifully constructed and elegant enough for our customers. In other words, he understands the kind of thing we're likely to buy. I'd say he's clever and seems ambitious, just the sort of person we put the Lambs name behind. I'm glad you're here," Kelly added with a smile. "Maybe you're a lucky talisman. We don't always start out so well."

The next half-dozen artisans, however, belied her enthusiasm. They were turned away with words of encouragement, but were, nevertheless, turned away.

A hat designer showing felt bowlers in bright colors was given an order on the spot and promised to deliver for an August display window. When she booked the young woman's designs for a fall display, Kelly turned quickly to Tony. She was telling him in a glance that Lambs was going ahead as always.

He said nothing. The quarrel they had wasn't about whether to keep the store intact but about whether to make it bigger.

At the end of two hours, Tony got to his feet and took Kelly aside. "I've got an appointment I can't cancel," he told her. "I get your point, but I'm still not sold on why you think the Lambs model has nothing to do with the way the rest of the country lives."

"I told you—" she began.

"Not now," he said, shaking his head.

"No, of course not." She bit her lower lip and turned away. "Who's next?"

Tony went to the door, opened it and gave a quick backward glance. Kelly quickly looked down, leafing determinedly through her papers. He wondered as he went rapidly down the stairs if she'd be avoiding his looks more and more.

KELLY STOOD at her office window late that afternoon, feeling an unexpected loss of energy. Then she remembered she hadn't had lunch. She'd sat with Tony in the restaurant across the street and toyed with her food while they discussed the fate of the store. He could look her straight in the eye and let the smoothest lies flow off his tongue, while preparing to slam Lambs into the ground.

I'm depressed. I need a friendly face. She'd fallen for his words and hurried to meet Tony, her heart pounding in her chest. He'd risen to greet her, grasping her hands in his, and for a long moment there in the crowded restaurant, Kelly had believed they could fall in love. Perhaps they had already.

If only you'd do exactly what I want you to, then everything would be all right between us. She suspected those were the words Tony wanted to say to her. They hovered in the air each time the subject of Lambs came up, ruining everything.

She stared out her window at the familiar street. Buildings that should stand for centuries seemed to be daily falling to the wrecker's ball, and perhaps the microcosm across the way that represented the best parts of the city would disappear before the year was out.

She knew the five-story buildings on either side of Lambs were of no particular architectural value and that Terro would destroy them without a thought. But somehow if Lambs could stand as a last holdout, whatever other charming buildings there were left in New York, might also survive "progress."

She turned back to her desk and ran quickly through her Rolodex for Francine Marshall's number. Francine was a member of the New York Preservation Committee and might still be in her office. They had gone to school together and lunched occasionally, met for dinner or a play every so often and talked about how they'd like to get away to Tahiti one day.

"It's Kelly," she said when Francine came on the line. "Anything new on declaring Lambs a landmark?"

"Takes time," Francine said at once. "You're dealing with the bureaucracy here, not a vendor desperate to please."

"Can't you light a firecracker under them?"

"Sure, but then we'd have nothing left and then what would happen?"

Kelly laughed. She could count on Francine to keep things light, even when the preservation of New York's landmarks was uppermost in her mind. "What I'd like," Kelly said, "is the names of some powerful people who might put in the right word for me."

"The New York Preservation Committee hates to be nudged by powerful people," Francine told her. "They've got a tough job to do and they want to be fair about it. Yours is a beautiful Beaux-Arts building, but the determination has to be whether it's unique in the city—"

"It's unique, damn it!" Kelly burst in.

"That's what everybody says. Kelly, the best thing you can do is get Terro to agree to hold off for a while. Take the pressure off while we go quietly and sanely about our business. Meanwhile, I've heard that Mr. Tony Campbell is a gorgeous bit of goods and absolutely single. What you want to do, my girl, is have him fall for you hook, line and wrecker's ball. Then, when he wants to give you a diamond necklace from Cartier's, you say, 'No, my darling. I want Lambs wrapped up in gold foil with a shiny blue ribbon.'"

"Thanks," Kelly said. "I knew I could count on you. I may try blackmailing the committee instead. Everybody has a deep, dark secret, maybe even you. I'll have to find a gumshoe who'll do a little undercover work for me, and I do mean undercover."

"Stick to Tony Campbell," Francine said. "Go the direct route. Think of the way it could pay off."

"If only it were so easy," Kelly said just before hanging up.

CHAPTER NINE

A NIGHT WIND rustled the curtains as splatters of moonlight played tag on the patterned carpet. Tony sat in the darkness, tie off, shirt open at the collar, a glass of Scotch in his hand. He swirled the amber liquid around the ice, taking in the pleasant tinkle and staring at the play of light along the floor.

Sebastian, with barely a word, had departed earlier that day for England. Tony figured his brother would nurse his hurt all the way across the Atlantic. Matters had worsened between them with this trip. Sebastian resented Tony's control of the international operation, his vision of running the American branch from London with frequent forays to New York having been shot down. Sooner or later their differences would have to be handled, but at that point their father would enter the picture, and if there was anything the senior Campbell disliked, it was confrontation. However, too many of Sebastian's peccadilloes had been pushed under the rug for too long. Bailing him out was rapidly becoming too costly.

But it wasn't Sebastian who kept Tony sitting alone, communing with the darkness. It was Kelly Aldrich. He wasn't used to being under anyone's power. And he didn't like it. He especially didn't like being under the spell of a determined American woman whose entire life was woven around her career. But he hadn't been able to get her out of his mind.

When he first encountered her in the shadow of the Temple of Dendur, she'd been buzzing around the flowers and place cards with the energy of a whole hive of bees.

Are you from Manhattan Florists? The question had tickled him then and did so now. The remark had certainly put him in his place, head of an international real estate corporation mistaken for an arranger of orchids and assorted weeds.

Orchids and weeds, an apt metaphor perhaps for Kelly herself, a contradiction of sorts: the vulnerable product of a mill town who had turned into something glamorous and sexy.

There was something about her eyes, as if the light in them led the way to her soul.

He'd wanted to touch her from the very beginning, trying clumsily with the orchid. She'd allowed his gallantry, although Tony guessed she hadn't quite known how to handle it.

There had been women in Tony's life whom he'd admired; whom he'd even figured on loving, but true intimacy had never developed and he hadn't cared a whit. With Kelly it was different, and that frightened him. She could, with no effort at all, reach into the dark where all his secrets were hidden. Maybe she sensed it, too. He hoped so. Maybe she wanted to follow that thread as delicate as a spider's silk, which led to the hidden emotions, thoughts, desires he'd always kept to himself.

He closed his eyes and saw her as he had never seen her in real life, wearing something white, diaphanous and floating. Her hair was loose, wrapping around her face as she moved toward him. Her smile was soft, unlike any smile she had yet offered him, beckoning, calling, whispering to him.

He let the dream go on, even though he knew quite well where it would lead him. He moved in the chair, crossed and then uncrossed his legs. She was coming closer, her breasts almost visible through the swaying material. The outline of her body was shapely and inviting. He reached for her. She was soft, her flesh smooth as satin. Her perfume was light, tantalizing. She drew her arms around his neck.

DON'T WASTE YOUR TIME dating men who can't give you everything you'd ever want in this life. Her father's words, laying out her life for her. *Remember that old bromide: it's as easy to fall in love with a rich man as a poor one.* The men who traveled in Mrs. Laurence's circle would have made her father's wish list, but not necessarily Kelly's.

For this party Kelly selected a long, black, body-hugging dress with a plunging neckline emphasized by a white satin collar, the kind of dress that made her look both sophisticated and yet a little wild, like a tiger on the prowl. Perhaps that's what she was. Something about Tony Campbell had brought out the desire to act sexy. Although she didn't expect to meet him at the dinner party.

Just before she left home, she stopped to look at herself in the long hall mirror. The light was good, and upon closer examination Kelly thought she saw right through the woman in the mirror, the woman she was supposed to be.

She had a momentary glimpse of a little girl sitting on her mother's lap, listening to a soft warm voice reciting poetry. And then her father appeared, calling it nonsense. There had been no room in his life for flowers, trips to the woods and words that rhyme. He'd had his agenda as far as his children was concerned. And the agenda had succeeded: they were successful, they made money, and they showed the world their mettle.

Kelly sighed at her reflection, trying to understand just what was bothering her. She'd succeeded and she'd had fun along the way. Hard work had never hurt anybody, her father had said, and he'd been right.

The rewards are worth it, he'd told her. And he'd been right again. She was passing on his message to the kids in Job-Up. Nose to the grindstone, stake out your ambition, follow the yellow brick road. If it happened to me, it could happen to you. She'd become an elegant young model of success, invited to parties in the best penthouses. Arriving alone and thoroughly in charge of her life.

The Laurence apartment occupied the penthouse of a large prewar building on Central Park South, one of the many classic gems that edged the park. Its antique and flower-filled marble lobby and heavily carpeted floors were a public preview of the precious apartments above, one to a floor.

The elevator door opened directly into a small foyer leading into the Laurence apartment. The butler greeted Kelly and took her wrap. The sound of music and laughter filtered out as Kelly headed toward the main salon. She knew Mrs. Laurence's apartment well, and her parties. Usually they attracted an eclectic mix of people in the arts and business. One was as likely to meet a filmmaker as an ex-secretary of state. While entertaining, the energetic woman managed to push forward the various charitable causes in which she had an interest.

Kelly had thought of calling Warren Bedford and asking him to come along, but her conscience told her it would be unfair to him. She had no fears about arriving alone at parties. In fact, there was a certain amount of adventure attached to it. Mrs. Laurence's acquaintance was wide and varied, and Kelly had met a number of interesting men at her apartment at one time or another.

She was absolutely in charge of her life, she thought, squaring her shoulders and heading for the circular entrance hall that led to the main salon.

Centered in the hall was one of Mrs. Laurence's wilder decorating feats—a shallow tide pool filled with lighted candles on floating lilacs and goldfish, which the woman had declared were very rare and old. Kelly carefully walked around it, having been regaled by stories of inebriated guests who had fallen in and some not so inebriated, too.

At the entrance to the salon, Kelly was met with a hug and a kiss puffed into the air by her smiling hostess. "Darling, I want you to meet someone who's new to the city," she said without preliminaries. "She's been talking about volunteering for the UN, but I'm trying to convince her that Job-Up could use her just as much. Talk up Isabella's success story, won't you?"

"I'm going to have to," Kelly said. "This afternoon I received a couple of calls inquiring about whether the dress is for sale. I hemmed and hawed, but it's a possibility. And this, mind you, two weeks after the fashion show.''

''Marvelous,'' Mrs. Laurence said. ''You don't suppose Isabella was up to anything?''

''About the dresses?'' Kelly shook her head. ''Not a chance. Both calls came directly to me from good customers. Think positive, Mrs. Laurence. Besides, I don't believe Isabella is quite that canny.''

''Some of her friends might be.''

Kelly thought of the house on Staten Island, of the harried mother who ran the place to the best of her abilities, and of a sullen Isabella who wanted to travel the ladder of success by elevator. ''I trust Isabella. She's fixed on her career. Maybe she's in too much of a hurry, but we'll tame her.'' Kelly wondered if she didn't sound too pompous.

Mrs. Laurence, however, laughed indulgently, patting her arm. ''Come along, Kelly. Meet my friend. You realize Job-Up is such a new concept that sometimes I fall for my own skepticism. Sometimes I expect things to fail rather than to succeed.''

''Bite your tongue,'' Kelly said, drawing her arm through the older woman's. ''Let's go to work.''

A string quartet playing Vivaldi was tucked into a small alcove, the music a pleasant background to Kelly's pitch for the program. The room was spacious, high-ceilinged and filled with antique furniture and masses of flowers in huge vases.

Their quarry, with almost as much enthusiasm as Kelly suspected she had money, had almost agreed to attend the next committee meeting when Kelly felt a light kiss on the top of her head. She found Gregory Solow grinning at her.

"How wonderful," she said with delight, and was able to complete her pitch successfully by introducing Gregory as a partisan for the program.

"Nice of you to help," Kelly whispered to him afterward when their quarry excused herself and hurried off to tell the news to her husband.

"Mrs. Laurence has nominated me for the board of directors," he said.

"Well, well, well, just see what retirement can do."

Gregory whisked two glasses of champagne from a tray being carried by a white-coated waiter and handed her one, saying jovially, "I don't abandon old friends or old projects."

"So nice of you to remind me how obliging you are. You might just talk to the Campbell brothers about their plans for the building and save everybody a lot of trouble."

Gregory shook his head. "I'm afraid you can't expect much help from me there, Kelly. The fate of Lambs is out of my hands, but your job is safe, no matter what happens."

"I'm surprised at you," Kelly said. "You have employees in the store who are nearing retirement." She spoke the words without animosity, believing that Gregory only needed his memory shaken. "And the building's a landmark."

Gregory continued to shake his head while he spoke. "Kelly, if you're unhappy, you could let them buy you out of your contract."

"What?" She realized her reaction was loud enough to cause a sudden lull in the talk around her. "How can you say such a callous thing?" she asked in a lowered voice.

"Any prestigious organization from here to the coast would be happy to have you remodel their image," he remarked, his manner completely unruffled.

"Gregory, if I let Terro destroy Lambs by taking it national and on top of that pull the building to the ground, it would be like . . . like giving them a part of me to destroy. Come on, Gregory," she said, brushing her hand across his bearded cheek, "help me. You have some clout with Terro. After all, they must owe you the moon."

"Maybe I didn't handle the sale the way I should have," Gregory conceded. "I was anxious to get out from under. Perhaps I might have managed to preserve the building. But," he added with a shrug, "there's nothing I can do now. Oh, there's Diane." His face brightened, and Kelly was amazed to see a genuine look of happiness sparkle in his eyes. "Come along, my dear."

But she was stopped by the sound of her name shrieked out across the room. "Kelleee." She turned to find a handsome dark-skinned man hurrying toward her. He grabbed her in a tight hug.

"Raju," she managed as he squeezed her once more.

"Kelleee, my dearest, how are you? It's been much too long. How long has it been? But, of course, I've been in India. Have you seen my latest?"

"Wife? Film? Which are you talking about?" Raju was an Indian film star whose production company had used Lambs for a shoot two years previously.

"You are hilarious. I'm afraid it's the same wife. She's much too beautiful and clever to part with, especially since she writes my scripts. I heard some scoundrels are going to demolish Lambs. Who are they? I'll kill them. Wasn't that Gregory I just saw? Doesn't he have anything to say about it?''

"Splendid, Raju. You ask him yourself." Kelly looked around and found Gregory with Diane Bourne. "Come along. How'd you hear about Lambs, anyway? I didn't think the news had spread worldwide— at least not yet."

"My wife's favorite saleswoman, of course. Have you seen my latest film?''

"I was just about to," she said, coming up to Gregory and Diane and smiling at them. She remembered the way the store had been turned upside down for the film shoot and how furious Gregory had been over the whole affair, although the story had been featured on the six o'clock news.

Kelly was curious about Diane being with Gregory, about the sparkle in Gregory's eyes and about where Tony stood in all this, but she was diverted from further speculation when she saw Mrs. Laurence step out onto the terrace. As she recalled, Mrs. Laurence also contributed heavily to the upkeep of city parks and sat on a private preservation committee. It was time to put in a good word about the building. Mrs. Laurence, she figured, owed her one.

She found the woman engaged in a conversation with her nephew, and so she waited politely at the far side of the terrace, trying to work out the details of her pitch. The terrace had an inviting view north across the great expanse of the park, and in the distance she could see the band shell lit up. Beyond that lay the great museum bathed in a kind of green light, signaling some fashionable event. She remembered now—a wedding party for the scions of two wealthy families. She'd been annoyed to hear that the bride had been fitted for her dress in Paris. Taking Lambs personally, again, she thought with a smile.

"Looking for a blue moon?"

Kelly whipped around, already knowing who stood behind her, whispering the words in her ears. She realized that Mrs. Laurence was no longer on the terrace and that they were alone. She was aware of every nerve ending in her body. "No," she said, wondering if he could hear the unexpected rattling of her heart, "I don't expect a rare event to come sailing over the horizon, not for a long time."

Tony smiled at her, seemed about to say something, but with a light shake of his head, stepped to the terrace wall and looked out at the park. "What do you suppose is happening at the band shell?"

"Oh, they have lots of free events in the park all summer long. Or so I hear. We sponsor one every August. Dance, as a matter of fact. A week-long festival. We usually get a full house. Oh, damn," she said, casting a sideways glance at him. "We're booked this summer, too. I hope you're not going to renege. I mean, I hope they won't be dancing to the sound of a landmark being exploded."

He took her arms in a strong grip. "Knock it off. Isn't that what you Americans say?"

"I certainly don't say it. Knock what off? I'm just bringing you up-to-date—"

"You're sticking the knife in and turning it 360 degrees."

"I didn't think you could feel pain."

"You don't know anything about me," he snapped.

"Really?" She looked away at the distant scene, at the lighted museum, of the happiness within. It was true; she was trying to bait him, so deep was her anger and yet so confused her emotions. "I'd say you're a classic case of wannabe. That's an American term, too. You wannabe top dog and can't settle for less, can you?"

"Kelly," he said tiredly, "I've got stockholders who keep prodding me to do more, but right now I don't want to go into it. Not with you and not tonight. It's ten o'clock, and even I think it's time to let go and forget our differences. How about it?"

"Oh, you're right," she said. And why not? He wouldn't change his mind. It would take a tank to make him change it, or the strong arm of the preservation law, and she'd already put that into motion. "I surrender."

"Well, we can offer thanks to the night for some things," he told her.

"What are you doing here, anyway? No, I won't ask. You know our hostess with the mostess from way back. You came with Diane and Gregory." She suddenly wanted to ask about the light in Gregory's eyes and found herself envying Diane.

"We've become quite a threesome," he remarked. "I think your friend Gregory has met his match in Diane."

"Really? How so?"

"Ah, who can tell what sparks the heart and libido?" He turned to the terrace view again, resting his arms along the marble balustrade. "I think they call it love at first sight."

"Love at—" She stopped and flushed, remembering her reaction to Tony that first night. Alone in her apartment, she had wondered whether such things could happen. Aeons ago. The thought had occurred aeons ago when he was the magical creature who'd materialized in the Temple of Dendur and whisked her away. Now, of course, she knew better.

"First sight," he finished for her. "It happens, you know."

"The foolishness of dreamers," Kelly said, trying to recover herself. "You fall in love with an idea, knowing nothing about the reality. You may not even like the same toothpaste."

"Spearmint," he said.

"Oh, cinnamon at all costs."

"I'll have to try cinnamon, then."

"That's easily solved," she said, "but life still isn't that way. You leave hairs in the wash basin, your socks on the floor, come home late for dinner, flirt with your secretary, vote Democratic—"

"Tory."

"Or Republican when it should be the other way around. You drive too fast and overdraw your bank account. Forget I said that," she added. "I believe you own the bank. But then we're not talking about you. We're talking about the problems of getting to know you. I mean, the one you fall in love with at first sight."

"Did you?" he asked, still gazing out over the park.

"Did I what?" she asked, knowing precisely what he meant.

"Want me to spell it out for you?" He turned toward her, his expression serious.

She shook her head. She heard the music start up again, some sprightly air. She heard the sound of the dinner bell and thought of how she was being saved by it.

Or almost saved. Tony took her in his arms and put his lips to hers in a long, soft kiss. How welcome the touch of his lips was, she thought, responding to it tentatively as though exploring new, unfamiliar territory.

Then Tony pulled away and for a long moment stood gazing at her. "I don't think I want that answer quite yet," he said. He reached out, and in a gesture she began to think was characteristic, drew his fingers through her hair, pulling it back, away from her face. He seemed about to say something more, but then took her arm and said, "That dinner bell sounds a little impatient."

She let out a breath she thought she'd been holding forever.

The tables were set for ten, and Kelly found Gregory and Diane already seated. Gregory sat opposite Kelly, with Diane at his side, Tony next to Kelly.

They were halfway through dinner when an attractive blonde named Cybil French, sitting on Gregory's left, directed a remark to him that reached clearly over the other conversations taking place around the wide table.

"I can't believe you're going to close Lambs," she said in her soft Southern accent. "Such a beautiful store."

Kelly sensed rather than heard Tony's quick, annoyed intake of breath. Cybil was a jewelry designer who owned an exclusive shop on Madison Avenue and gave generously to Job-Up. "Close Lambs?" Diane asked the question. "Where in the world did you get that notion?"

"But the store," Cybil began.

"We won't be closing Lambs," Tony said smoothly. "On the contrary. If anything, Lambs could be a household name in a few years, with a store in every big-city mall throughout the country."

"You might have to step over a few dead bodies on your way there," Kelly remarked, addressing herself carefully to the remains of the squab on her plate.

"Dead bodies. Good Lord," Diane said, looking astonished. "What in the world's wrong with expanding?"

"Nothing, if you want to play the fat man in the circus."

"Kelly." Gregory was frowning at her from across the table. She made a small moue, holding herself back from sticking her tongue out at him. Suddenly, for the first time, Kelly felt as if Gregory, her old boss and mentor, was a stranger, and more than that, a stranger not on her side. She glanced around the table and wondered just how alone she was. She was palpably aware of Tony next to her and of his disapproval. The taste of his kiss, which had lingered on her lips until that moment, faded.

"I'm not sure I know what you're all talking about," Cybil said. "I was talking about the store, the *building*, that lovely Beaux-Arts masterpiece. I think your plans are wonderful," she went on, addressing Kelly. "The building is a historic one and deserves to be given landmark status. Wish I could be as lucky with mine. It's just an old rat trap waiting to be baited by some real estate mogul.''

Gregory looked astonished. "Landmark status?" Kelly caught a glance between him and Tony. "That's news to me."

"Well, so I've heard," Cybil said, looking at Kelly, who shook her head quickly to tell her the subject shouldn't be discussed. "Or maybe I've just heard some wishful thinking. I guess that's it. Right, Kelly?"

"Right," Kelly said. Her dessert had lost all taste, and even the coffee seemed to have a bitter edge. It was time to make a hasty exit. She carefully put down her fork and knife and excused herself. She didn't want any questions from Tony just then.

She escaped into the drawing room and spun on her heels for a moment, trying to work out a graceful exit line. Then Mrs. Laurence flagged her down. "How are the other youngsters working out?"

For a moment Kelly looked at her nonplussed. "Youngsters?"

"The ones we sent you from Job-Up."

"Oh, yes, of course. Fine." Only Isabella was a tinderbox, but then she was easily the most talented.

"Can we plan on a couple more?"

"I'll have to check with my CEO," Kelly said.

"Check what?" Tony came up behind her, and Kelly saw that she couldn't make a clean escape, not quite yet.

"Adding more part-timers to the payroll. We could use a couple more."

Tony pointed to his watch. "Midnight," he said. "I thought we'd agreed earlier not to talk business after ten o'clock."

Kelly backed away immediately. "Sorry, boss. I got carried away." She must learn to play, she told herself. To take notice of a world out there that had nothing to do with the tiny piece of earth she was in danger of losing. Perhaps somewhere in the city someone was teaching a course on how to relax after office hours, how to laugh, flirt, fall in love and stay in love.

Mrs. Laurence was gazing at her, wearing an expression of bafflement. "Want to call me, Kelly? We can discuss it."

Discuss what? Kelly wondered for a split second. Oh, yes, of course, jobs. "Yes," she said in a relieved voice. "I'll call you."

Their hostess returned to the dining room, shaking her head. "Young people."

Kelly went past Tony through the drawing room and into the entrance hall. He caught up with her at the pool that took up the central portion. "You can't get away quite so easily," he said. "I want an explanation and I want it now."

"About what?" she asked him innocently. "At midnight I presume we're talking about the weather."

"It's been a long, hard journey, pulling the real estate together," he said. "You know perfectly well what I'm talking about. There's going to be no petitioning of preservation societies about hundred-year-old buildings of no architectural value whatsoever. Good Lord, I think I know something about preserving age-old monuments, and Lambs is neither age-old nor a monument."

"This isn't Britain, and we've lost enough of our history as it is. I'm sorry, Tony, but this is one battle I'm going to win if I can."

"Call your friends off, Kelly."

"I couldn't if I wanted to. It's midnight."

"If you continue trying to fight me, I'll personally take a crane and wrecking ball and knock Lambs from here to kingdom come. And if you think I don't mean what I say, just try me."

His anger was so complete that Kelly could only stand there shaking her head. "You really aren't used to being crossed, are you?"

"Not where it matters."

"And it matters that much? I really feel sorry for you, then. Somehow I thought that under your tough exterior was a human being. I think you can have my resignation right now, right here, Mr. Campbell. See you." She smiled brightly at him and began to walk around the pool.

"Sorry," he said, coming up behind her. "You have a contract."

She turned to him. "Mr. Campbell, you are a bastard!" With one swift, surprising movement to which she gave no thought whatsoever, she splayed her fingers against his chest and pushed him backward into the pool among the goldfish and lily pads. She should have done that long before, she thought, in the pool facing the Temple of Dendur. She went quickly into the foyer where she retrieved her cape from a startled butler, not even turning around when she heard the curse that turned into a roaring laugh.

When she reached the street, she found it brightly lit and busy, even for that time of night. She was exhilarated and decided to walk east, possibly all the way home without benefit of a cab.

Pushing Tony into Mrs. Laurence's pool hadn't solved anything at all, not about her resignation nor about the building. He'd be soaking wet, feeling the fool and having every beautiful woman at the party fussing over him.

Let them, she decided, walking quickly past doormen hailing cabs or helping people out of cabs and limousines, past couples walking arm in arm and a group of women laughing together, past some conventioneers who whistled at her, and a couple of night cleaning women ambling slowly toward the subway.

She stopped when she got to the corner. She remembered his curse and laugh. Tony Campbell would know how to recover from a dunking. She thought of Diane Bourne ministering to him. And Gregory standing there helpless, wondering what had gotten into his prize pupil, Kelly Aldrich.

And Tony Campbell standing there wet. Standing there wet with someone shoving a drink at him. Someone, a woman, maybe Diane Bourne helping him out of his wet jacket. The goldfish, for heaven's sake, those rare, aged creatures. Suppose he'd crushed one?

And those women offering him succor, drinks, words of encouragement or praise or whatever one offered under such circumstances. Offers to take him home and dry him out, maybe?

She turned around and went back past the trudging cleaning ladies and the conventioneers who whistled at her and the laughing women and couples walking hand in hand, past doormen whistling for taxis or opening the doors of taxis or limousines. Finally, when she reached the beautiful old building that contained the Laurence apartment, she stopped in front of the doorman, who looked at her curiously.

"Forgot something," she said as he escorted her to the elevator. She rode up, tapping her foot with no thoughts about what would happen once she arrived back at the apartment. When the elevator door opened, she smiled at the butler and didn't remove her cape but went quickly around the pool where the lilies appeared slightly askew. She couldn't see any dead goldfish. She continued into the main salon, which was oddly quiet when she entered, and everyone stared at her.

Tony wasn't there.

"In the kitchen, I think," someone whispered to her. She left the drawing room and went down a long corridor to the kitchen, where she found Tony, dripping wet, talking rather calmly to an agitated Gregory Solow. Mrs. Laurence was standing with a servant who held out a large towel. Diane Bourne held his jacket in her hand.

Tony whipped around when she came in and grinned as if he were glad to see her and it was all a big joke. "I was just telling them how I lost my balance and fell into the pool. Imagine that."

"Tony fall into a pool?" Diane remarked. "Impossible."

"That pool is going to go," Mrs. Laurence said.

Kelly came over to him and held out her hand. "Come on, I'll take you home and dry you out."

"Perhaps the back elevator," Mrs. Laurence suggested.

"Suits me fine," Tony said. "Oh, and incidentally, send any bills to me."

"Don't be foolish."

"What happened to the goldfish?" Kelly asked.

"Swam for their lives," Tony said.

"Of course. They'd know a shark when they saw one."

He pulled her through the kitchen and to the service entrance. The door closed behind them, and Tony punched the elevator button before turning to her and offering her a quirky grin. "Thought you got me, didn't you?"

"Not at all. I felt sorry for the goldfish, that's all. Came back to see if I could offer artificial respiration."

"You didn't care whether I drowned or not?"

"Drowned? The pool's only a foot deep."

"I don't swim. Remember Jim Thorpe? He drowned in only an inch of water."

"He was drunk."

"I think I was, too," he said. The elevator stopped, and when they got in it, he pulled her close. "I haven't heard the word sorry yet." His mouth hovered close to hers.

She felt the chill of his damp suit but decided she deserved it. "But I'm not sorry," she said. "You deserved a good dousing and a lot more besides."

"Saints preserve us, will the woman never shut up?" He put his mouth to hers, and Kelly knew she was where she had wanted to be all that night—in his arms.

His lips were softly on hers at first. Then his arms tightened as he pulled her closer, the kiss deepening.

He prodded her lips with his tongue, and she opened her mouth to him. He touched her tongue with his, claiming his due. His mouth was soft, his breath heated and winey. A funny tingle began climbing along her back, spreading its warmth until an all-enveloping flame coursed through her, leaving her breathless. She felt his body tense and knew he was aroused, as she was.

The elevator came to a stop and they drew quickly apart. The back doorman peered in at them, his expression immobile. "May I get you a cab?"

CHAPTER TEN

KELLY SUPPRESSED a smile at the doorman's question, squaring her shoulders and marching straight ahead as though it were a perfectly normal event to be seen walking out of an elevator with a man in a wet tuxedo.

"I think we'll walk for a bit," Tony said, carefully adjusting his tie in a mirror on the side wall. "It's a fine night for ducks and fishes."

"Yes, *sir*," said the doorman, rushing to open the service door that led directly to Central Park South.

"He'll have some story to tell his wife when he gets home," Kelly said as soon as they were clear of the apartment house and heading toward Fifth Avenue. The activity on the street had changed little: conventioneers, couples hand in hand, doormen whistling for taxis. It was a fine night, indeed, she thought, tentatively touching her lips for the feel of his kiss, which hadn't gone away. She was still intoxicated by the aftershock. Her blood was hot and surging.

"I'm happy to know we've made his day," Tony remarked. "Gives me one more reason to be glad I got up this morning."

"Think we'll ever be asked back again to the Laurence premises? Our hostess looked properly horrified."

"She's a stout woman, and I suspect she's seen a lot more in her life than she admits to."

"Does she know about us?" Kelly asked. "I mean, about our quarrel? I mean, the fact that I pushed you into her goldfish pond?"

Tony pulled up short, unconsciously letting the flow of late-night traffic move around them. "Kelly, are we talking just to keep from facing what happened back there between us? And I don't mean our contretemps."

"I know you don't," Kelly murmured. It was true, she thought, the weightiness of that shared kiss hung between them: a fire had been ignited that could take forever to quench.

"I'd hate like hell to leave it unfinished. I'm not talking about the contretemps. That will certainly continue in another time and another place, perhaps a boxing ring, perhaps the park, with seconds holding pistols. I'm talking about that kiss, Ms Aldrich. The one you responded to with a hint of everything you've got."

"Tony, it shouldn't have happened. And for every reason in the world."

"Kelly, Kelly," he said, shaking his head, "I have no intention of selling you anything, not the Empire State Building and not the fact that you belong in my arms. Oh, baby," he added, reaching out and cupping her chin in his hand, "that kiss happened because it was just sitting there waiting for us."

She tried to look away. Meeting his gaze was too dangerous an admission. All she wanted to do was keep her tone lighter than his, let him know it was a mistake, a spontaneous aberration not to be repeated. "Of course, all elevators contain kisses just waiting to happen. Perched on the Down button, no doubt. Or maybe the Close Door button. You've got a funny view of life."

"Have I? I don't think so. In some ways I have a scientific turn of mind. I know, for instance, that when a certain person's flesh touches a certain other person's, sparks fly." He bent his face to hers and once again touched his lips to hers.

"Taxi?" A yellow cab slid to a halt with a screech, and the driver grinned at them.

"You're a lifesaver," Tony called out, tucking his arm through Kelly's. "Let's go. I've got a sudden desire to get out of these wet clothes."

"Fall in the lake over at the park?" the driver asked.

"You might say that." Tony pulled the door open and made an exaggerated bow to Kelly. *"Madam."*

"You're a clown," she said, stepping into the cab. She knew the smile on her face held more than just amusement. Tony Campbell was the most exciting man she'd ever met. She might not trust him from one moment to the next, but he was a man to be loved and the thought frightened her.

"Where to?" the cabdriver asked.

Tony didn't stop for her opinion. "Hotel Carlyle."

Kelly drew in a breath. "But I thought maybe—" she began, then stopped. What had she thought? That she'd take him back to her apartment? Have him strip there and towel himself dry? She passed a hand along her brow, uncertain how to finish her sentence.

"You thought nothing, Kelly."

He was right. She'd had one mindless idea, returning to the Laurence apartment and pulling him away,
as if she owned him. The kiss had been as inevitable as
their sitting together in a taxi going east on Sixtieth
Street toward the Hotel Carlyle.

Tony relaxed against the seat as though he were in
his own, private, air-conditioned paradise. Kelly, on
the other hand, remained with her back rigid, staring
straight ahead, hoping her posture might somehow
hide the fact that she was floating on air.

Suddenly some invisible string that had been holding her together, making everything come out the way
it should, snapped. She owed no explanations to departed ghosts. The shadows that danced in the corri-
dors of her life were silent. There could be no clacking
of tongues, no disapproving frowns, not now, not with
the way she felt. All memory of the way she had been
instructed to live her life miraculously departed.

"Driver's not going to be too happy about being left
with a sopping wet seat," Tony said as the cab cut up
Madison Avenue toward the Carlyle.

Kelly turned to him and laughed, almost a little too
brightly, wondering if her eyes told of the longing
welling up in her. "You can always solve wet seats with
a generous tip." Her voice didn't sound quite right,
either, as though a lump had formed in her throat,
preventing her usual speech.

"Clever lady, you've absolved me of all guilt, which
is perfectly suitable because right now all I want to do
is touch you, hold you and kiss you."

Perhaps words have a volition of their own, she
thought. He shouldn't want to touch her, hold her,
kiss her. They had too much separating them; there

would be an end to the evening, and she'd have to return alone to her apartment and to all the tomorrows she needed to face.

"Tony," she began once again, but in a voice that wavered with uncertainty, "I think you ought to tell the driver to take me home after he drops you off. After you pay him the generous tip."

"Anybody ever hint you talk too much?"

"I always thought of myself as the soul of discretion."

His voice was almost a whisper. He didn't touch her but sat regarding her with an expression of total seriousness. "You know what happened back there. You're not going home, not now."

She refused to look at him. Yes, she knew and knew as well the inevitability of the next act to be played out.

He reached across the seat and took her hand in his. "It began with a blue moon," he told her, "not tonight, not in an elevator, but when I was the man from Manhattan Florists."

"Perhaps," she murmured. "Perhaps you're right."

The lobby of the Hotel Carlyle was busy, even at that time of night. Kelly thought there must have been a party somewhere. She smelled a heady mix of perfumes in the air and took in the sound of laughing voices. But it was all a backdrop; she and Tony were alone in a strange space where time wasn't measured by the usual standards.

He held her hand as though it might be necessary to coax her into the elevator, entwining his fingers with hers. But she went willingly along. There was no need for coaxing, for talking about the future, for wondering about the heated beckonings of her body.

But when the door closed on the crowded elevator, Kelly felt a moment of panic. She stared straight ahead, hiding any clues from the other passengers that she was holding a wild excitement in check by only a thin thread. She was with the man who paid her salary, the man she must pretend never to have kissed or loved or entwined her body with. In the world of business they were doing battle. Reason told her to run away when the elevator stopped on his floor. It stopped. He tugged at her hand and they stepped off into a quiet corridor. Tony drew his hand to the back of her neck and paused only once to kiss her.

They entered the suite, into a darkness where slivers of moonlight cast shadows in eerie, fragmented murals across the walls and carpeted floor. There was a faint scent in the air of the after-shave he wore. Without turning on the light, Tony closed the door in a movement so swift and wild that Kelly felt a frisson of fear. In a moment he had her in a tight grip, pinned against the wall by his hard, insistent body. But then he hesitated, as if admitting he were being too quick, too careless.

"Kelly." Her name came out in a whisper as he released his grip and cupped her face between his hands. "Do you feel it, too?"

She closed her eyes for a second before opening them. His face was caught in the errant light, and she could see him quite clearly examining her. For the space of a heartbeat a heated message full of meaning passed between them. He bent and sought her mouth in a long, drawn-out kiss that began with a light dance of his lips against hers, ending in a deeper pressure meant to convey without misunderstanding that there could be only one ending to this moment.

Her desire for him was so intense that it surpassed any objection that lingered at the back of her mind. She ran her hand down the length of his back, down the still-damp fabric, before reaching up to grip his shoulders and pull him closer. His mouth ground against hers as she opened to him. His tongue darted in, touching, exploring, taking possession. She could feel the hard muscles of his thighs against hers and his rising desire that filled and warmed her with inexplicable happiness.

The molten heat flowing through her robbed her of all thought. She heard a cry from some far-off place and then realized it had come from deep within her. In a moment he had gathered her up and carried her to his bed.

He slowly undressed her, his gaze drifting over her body as each piece of clothing dropped to the floor. Then he removed his own clothes. She watched, unashamed, wanting only to know him, to see all of him. His body, in the moonlight coming through the window, was bronzed and strong. Everything about him was taut, precise and commanding.

He bent over her and, with his kiss, pressed her into the downy softness of the bed. She felt his weight as he lay over her and his soft, gentle touch. He began to caress her lightly until her nipples flushed and stiffened. His hand drifted across her bare stomach, skirting her thighs and passing over the warm center of her being.

And then his mouth, like fire on her breast, pulled at its tip. She reached out for him, scarcely aware of crying his name.

He raised himself and gazed into her eyes for a long moment. She heard in the distance the long, low wail of a police car, the shuddering sound of an airplane overhead—Manhattan's ceaseless mumbling. The city never changed, love or the opposite of love could happen and it went ceaselessly on, the sounds emanating from somewhere, from anywhere, going on, forever. He touched her breast, leaning on one hand.

"I want it to start slow," he said, "and to go on into the next millenium. Agreed?"

"With no time out for good behavior."

"Good behavior has nothing to do with the way I feel now, Kelly. Slowly, everything slowly, so I can commit it to memory."

Their mouths met urgently with suppressed longing. She knew that she wanted him far more quickly than she'd have him know. Every cell in her body cried for release from the fever that consumed her at his touch.

He stroked her breasts, then nuzzled the hard, tender buds. His lips took hers once again, and every seed of doubt or fear vanished.

His hands played over her back and her thighs, and then he slowly rubbed the triangular mound of her womanhood. Her heart pounded, her breath coming in short gasps as she slid her hands across his back and down. She reveled in his warm, firm flesh. He moved against her, and the rock hardness of his manhood crushed against her hip. She reached for him, feeling that every move she made was brand-new, and after a light, tentative touch, which forced a soft cry from him, she tightened her grip, sensing the thrill that rode through him.

"Slowly," he murmured, "to last forever."

But his mouth was on her throat, her breasts, her stomach. He whispered her name as his hands soothed her flesh. She moaned at the tender invasion of his fingers and arched, ready to receive him.

He lowered his body, easing his weight over her, stroking her rib cage, her hips, sliding his fingers over her thighs and tracing a path upward to where their bodies would join. Kelly instinctively angled to meet him. Then slowly, slowly, he filled her and was still. She felt herself melt with the honeyed, liquid sweetness of him, the warmth deep within her as she moved against him.

"Shh, be still," he said, "or it'll be over too quickly."

"I know—slowly," she said in a thick voice, feeling as if her happiness might spill over. His mouth hovered above hers. She tilted her chin, barely touching her lips to his, then tracing it with her tongue.

He laughed.

Her tongue found his, playing tentatively at first, then joining in a slow, consuming rhythm. When he leisurely began the primeval motion, she wrapped her legs around him, pulling him in deeply and riding the crest of a tidal wave, bracing herself for the final, raging thunderstorm.

When it came, it was like nothing she'd ever experienced before—raging, roaring, almost painful. Clinging to him as if to a lifeline, she thought she was hurtling into space.

An instant or a century passed before he lifted himself and looked down into her face. His eyes were soft, smudged with spent passion.

"I can't believe it happened that way," she said after a while, touching his damp chest with her fingers.

"I'm not surprised in the least." He bent to her lips. "I knew from the moment I first saw you just how it would happen."

"Was I that easy a mark?"

He cupped her chin. "Not an easy mark. Not by a long shot. Not even a short shot. I knew, that's all. Bided my time and waited."

"Waited? You could've fooled me." She wrapped her arms around him.

"It was good, Kelly, wasn't it?"

"Yes," she confessed. "Very good."

THE FIRST TENTACLES of light crept between the half-open curtains. Kelly, nestling in the crook of Tony's arm, her head upon his chest, came awake quickly.

Ah, it was because of the dream lying at the edge of her mind that she'd awakened so abruptly.

In the clear light of morning the events of the previous night took on a slightly different cast, and somehow her dream explained it to her, although she couldn't quite understand its meaning.

In her dream she was clinging to a raft in rough seas. A huge ship festooned with lights plowed through the waters, a crowd of glittering people at the railing. They pointed at her and laughed before the ship swept majestically past and out of sight. She was left alone, holding on to the raft, waiting for rescue.

Kelly moved out of the circle of Tony's arms and raised herself on one elbow. His breathing was soft and rhythmic. His face in repose was boyish and without that sharp look of self-possession. She thought with the most intense happiness that he had with a whisper and a touch raised her to heights of passion past imagining. He was intense, caring and practiced, wanting her to reach the same complete fulfillment as he.

Then what, she wondered, was the small warning in the pit of her stomach? It required no searching for an answer. She sensed that as soon as real life intruded she and Tony would be back as always, with Terro and Lambs stubbornly between them. "What am I going to do about you, about this?" she whispered. He moved. A lock of hair fell over his eyes, and she pushed it lightly back.

But if nothing in the world mattered, and only she and he inhabited the planet, she knew that the love they had made would sear her to him and complete her life. *Slowly,* he had said, and he'd made every touch stretch out the heated moments. He had laid claim to her, and even if he didn't know how successful he had been, she knew. She was his. Now and forever.

She lay back against her pillow and covered herself with the blanket. I don't regret it, she told herself. I don't and I won't. She didn't know what to make of her headlong rush into his arms. It paralleled the same strange, floating, unreal feeling when they'd first met and wandered into Central Park hand in hand.

It had to stop. She had to take control again.

She allowed herself a small smile and stretched luxuriously. Spontaneously she bent over Tony and lightly kissed his lips. Perhaps taking control could wait a little while longer.

He stirred. "What time is it?"

She touched his nose. "I don't think I'm going to tell you."

He opened his eyes and squinted at her. "Obviously you're an early riser, the kind who wakes with a smile on her lips." He yawned. "I'm usually slow and in a vile mood."

"You have it all wrong, Tony. Are you in a bad mood?"

He shook his head, grinning at her out of his half-closed eyes. "Not with you in my sights."

"I have to go home, change and get to work."

"You don't have to do any of those things, Kelly. I'm declaring a national holiday, flags raised and cannons booming. Fireworks, too, come to think of it, and drinks all around." He reached for her and pulled her close. "How come you're as beautiful in the morning as you were last night?"

"Fish oil salesman."

"You wouldn't mean snake oil?"

"That, too." She lay over him, feeling his body respond, and put her lips to his.

"Snake oil's good for you," he said between his lips.

She collapsed against him, feeling his arms grip her tightly, letting him catch her yet again in that erotic net that tangled her emotions and knotted her mind.

Later, when he had drifted off to sleep, Kelly rose and picked up their clothes that had been so carelessly tossed onto the floor the night before. Her dress would need some hanging out in the moist heat of the shower.

Soon, fully awake after a long, leisurely shower, she came back into the bedroom wrapped in a white terry robe. She found Tony propped up in bed, the television set tuned to a mindless morning show.

"I love American telly," he told her.

"Hooray, you've finally told me something about your likes and dislikes. What's your favorite program?"

"*Sesame Street.*"

"Of course, it would be." There was a light knock at the door. "Company?"

"I rang for breakfast while you were in the shower."

"Tony, I have to go home, change and go to work in that order," she reiterated. "Lambs waits for no one."

"Have breakfast with me."

She went through the bedroom into the salon and opened the door. The waiter wheeled in a cart heavy with steaming silver servers.

"I like the cool with which he greeted me," Kelly remarked, coming into the bedroom once the waiter was gone. "Does he find you in such a position often?"

"Never," Tony told her, stepping nude out of bed.

"Liar."

"I liked *your* cool answering the door."

"I see. The others hide behind the sofa."

"Pour me a cup of tea," he said. "I take quick showers before I attempt to answer smart-aleck remarks." He grabbed a silk paisley robe from his closet and went into the bedroom.

Pour him a cup of tea, indeed. He took tea for breakfast, she coffee. And he did, indeed, say *tomah-toes* when she said *tomaytoes*. But Kelly didn't want to call the whole thing off. She smiled with the most incandescent happiness, hugging her arms. And yet, at the height of her happiness, her dream returned and, with it, a curious understanding of its symbols.

The ship was on a pleasure cruise with the passengers enjoying its gaiety and opulence. Kelly was distanced, hanging on to a raft and waiting for rescue. Her dreams were never complicated.

"Be ready when your ship comes in," her father had often told them. He'd produced clichés for every occasion. And there she was in the water, watching her ship disappear. She wasn't awaiting rescue; she was just letting it go by. She wanted, quite simply, to thumb her nose at her father, and what easier way than to tread water and watch her future float away?

She looked up to find Tony in the room, smelling of after-shave, his hair wet and slicked down.

"From the expression on your face I'd say you were communing with a very tough guru."

"The toughest. The kind who tells you what to do with your life or else. Tea with milk and sugar?" She held her hand poised over the teapot. No sense in taking him into her dreams. He might, in fact, place an entirely different interpretation on a luxury ship sailing through strange waters.

"Might as well get used to the way I take tea," Tony said. "Milk and plenty of sugar." He sat down at the table and helped himself to bacon and eggs. After slathering butter on his toast, he looked up to find

Kelly, her elbows on the table, leaning forward in her seat and smiling at him.

"Did I do that?" he asked, reaching over and touching her lips.

"Uh-huh."

"I like your smile. The wattage has gone up considerably since we first met."

"I wasn't about to smile at the man from Manhattan Florists. After all, he owed me three hundred stalks of freesia."

"Did you check the invoice when it came in?" he asked.

"Yes. And they billed me. But I told them they'd see payment when hell freesias over."

Tony laughed. "Lady, you deserve a promotion for that remark." He broke off a bit of the bread, added a dollop of eggs to it and offered it to her. She shook her head. Happiness of the sort she was feeling left no room for an appetite.

"Stay with me today," he said.

"Uh-uh. I never take time off. The last time it happened was when I was laid low with a one hundred four temperature."

"I think with a little prodding I could raise your temperature a bit. Come on." He reached across the table and put his hand on hers. "Stay. Say to hell with it all. We can handle anything urgent right here."

"Urgent?" She laughed.

"We could stay here for weeks," he went on, refusing to smile. "They can slip papers under the door for us to sign and we can slip them right back out."

"Oh, persuasive, persuasive, Campbell. That's your stock-in-trade."

"Having second thoughts in the proverbial cold light of day?" he asked her suddenly, watching her closely over the rim of his cup.

She shook her head. "About last night, no."

"And now?"

"Your mentioning giving me a promotion did it. I remembered I was married to my job."

"Perhaps we ought to do something about that."

"Not with my contract you won't."

They regarded each other levelly. In the cold light of day reality wore a sleepy, satiated face, one that said the fun couldn't go on forever. "I have to go to work," she said simply.

"Sure you're not showing off for the bossman?"

She got up and went around to him. She tilted his chin and placed her lips squarely on his. "I can think of a nice way to show off, but this isn't the time to put it into action." He reached for her, but she danced away, disappearing into the bedroom. There she quickly dressed in her long gown, wondering just how she'd look going out through the lobby and hailing a cab. In a moment the jokes had soured and the memory of their lovemaking faded ever so slightly. When she came back, she was fully dressed and Tony was finishing up the last of the eggs.

He looked up at her. "Kelly, sit down. I'll need a good reason about why you're leaving and I want it in triplicate."

"I'll fax it to you. We'll talk later." She released a sigh, like a little explosion. "I'm not good at mornings after, I guess."

He stood up and came over to her, but instead of kissing her he placed his lips against her hair. "What do you want me to say?"

"Nothing. Or perhaps, go slow, danger zone ahead."

He brushed his hand along her cheek. "One thing I can say about you is that you'll never bore me. You might infuriate me, but you'll never bore me. I want you to call your friend at the historical preservation society, incidentally, and tell her it was all a mistake, the building has no value as a monument, and that you acted in haste."

"Oh! I don't believe what I just heard," she said, pulling out of his grip. "The least you could have done is wait until I got into the office and faxed me a memo."

"Kelly, do it. Make the call. And remember this. Whatever happens between you and me is separate and apart from Terro and Lambs."

"You consider this separate and apart? Bringing this up now? Goodbye, Tony." She turned and walked swiftly to the door, pulling it open without looking back.

"Hey!" He was at her side, his hand over hers as she grasped the handle. "All it takes is a sentence to send you running off as if nothing had happened between us."

"Perhaps nothing has," she told him. She felt an unexpected constriction of her throat and forced herself to swallow. She had to be as cool and logical as he was. "I thought when we made love that perhaps I'd broken through, but you have your own agenda and I don't think I like what's written on it."

"Kelly, the store isn't going to come between us."

"I thought when we made love that we were, in effect, discussing love, but it turns out we were discussing business."

"We were making love." He spoke the words softly and with a tenderness that asked for her trust. "Damn it," he said in another moment when she failed to answer him, "we have to talk. What in hell's wrong with you?" She felt his breath hot against her cheek. "You want nothing to change. You don't even want success."

"I don't know what you're talking about. I only know I want to hold on to what I have, the way I have it." She saw the luxury ship gliding through black waters and added without even knowing where the words came from, "Otherwise *he'd* win."

"Otherwise he'd win? Kelly, you're not making sense."

She looked at him, a little confused. What had she said? "Tony, our paths are going to cross and crisscross. Help me. Just help me. We're going to have to pretend last night never happened."

"Not on your life. Not in this world or any other."

Her emotions seemed to be laid out before her, tangled branches caught in a windstorm. She was a little frightened of what was happening between them. Being in love put her at a disadvantage, and she had spent her life making certain she was never at a disadvantage. Yet she knew beyond a doubt that her hunger for him would never be satisfied. She pulled her hand out from under his and opened the door without another word. She stepped out into the corridor and went straight to the elevator. *Otherwise he'd win.* The words haunted her.

CHAPTER ELEVEN

A LIGHT TAP on her office door the following morning signaled Kelly's assistant, Gail Esterbrook, who opened the door without an invitation and stepped in. "Emergency," she said hurriedly. "Can I?"

Kelly automatically checked the time. The store had scarcely opened for business and apparently the first emergency of the day was being dumped in her lap. "What's up?"

"Security thinks we should call the police on this one," Gail said, coming across the office. "A half-dozen leather jackets in the Italy Selects boutique are gone."

"*What?*"

"They're not where they're supposed to be, Kelly. Miriam," she said, referring to the floor manager, "insists she locked them up, as usual, just before she left last night."

Kelly was out of her chair and heading for the third-floor leather boutique when Gail caught up. The exclusive line imported from Italy was expensive even by Lambs' standards. They were displayed in an antique armoire and locked up at night. Each morning, shortly before the opening bell, the armoire was unlocked. The jackets remained on display in the cabinet. Each

was discreetly fitted with a tag that would trigger a
warning light at the front exit if they were stolen.

"Miriam discovered the robbery just before the
opening bell," Gail explained, "when she went to unlock the armoire."

"Was the lock broken?" Kelly started for the stairs
at a near run.

"No, and that's what's so troubling," Gail said.
"The double door was unlocked and she specifically
remembers locking it."

"What does security say?"

"The chief said it has to be an inside job."

"Where is he now?"

"Back in his office, marshaling his forces. He really
wants us to go to the police on this one."

"You told me."

Policy was to handle minor thefts in-store, but this
one looked bad. Kelly's mind went to Charlie, the
night watchman who came on at midnight and stayed
until eight in the morning. She didn't believe a thief
could have moved anything past him.

As to the earlier watchman, also a veteran of long-
standing, stealing garments with him around wouldn't
be easy at all. Also, someone usually worked late—
herself, the members of the display department, her
buyers or office personnel.

"Anyone check the display department?" she
asked. "They're crazy enough to consider using
leather in a summer display. And they're a little casual when it comes to borrowing merchandise."

"I didn't think of it, Kelly, but we grilled Miriam a
dozen different ways. She locked up the jackets and

then put the key in the desk as always. Remember, the desk has a combination lock."

"Which combination the buyer knows, security, Miriam and our Saturday floor manager. And so do I, come to think of it." Kelly headed into the coat department. Miriam was busy with a customer. Summer raincoats formed the major display in the department, but leather was a hot seller year-round; many of Lambs' customers were from the southernmost tip of South America where winter set in about June.

"What's the exact damage?" she asked Gail.

"Six fur-lined leather jackets worth almost twenty-five hundred apiece."

The armoire still held a half-dozen other jackets, but the space struck Kelly as being yawningly empty. Somehow seeing the remaining jackets in the display brought home the size of the theft. "Well, this is one time we can't blame our tragic little kleptomaniacs. I suppose everybody's touched the doors and they won't be able to lift fingerprints."

"You're too right, Kelly."

Kelly sighed and caught the floor manager's eye. Miriam had been with the store for more than a quarter of a century and considered the coat department her private bailiwick. "I'll see you later," she said when Miriam gave her a pained and apologetic smile.

"Let's see the desk," Kelly said, going into the tiny, claustrophobic space reserved for the department buyer. The cubicle was piled with sample fabrics, photographs, sketches and all the other paraphernalia needed to keep a busy department going. She could find no signs that the desk drawer that held the keys had been forced. "Think somebody with sanded fingers had a go at the combination lock?"

"Spend time fiddling with a combination lock in order to obtain a key to undo another lock? That doesn't make sense," Gail remarked. "Why not go right to the source?"

"Why not, indeed? Okay, this is a job for security."

Gail glanced at her watch and said something about a promotional meeting scheduled in a couple of minutes.

"Run ahead," Kelly told her. "I've asked them to push ahead on their Christmas plans. Terro is going to have to approve the budget and I want it nice and clean and well thought out without the possibility of a single glitch." Gregory would have merely waved his hand as though it were a magic wand.

You approve? he'd ask.

I approve.

Then so do I.

But not Terro; she was certain of that. And at the rate things were going it was possible Lambs wouldn't even be in a viable condition to celebrate Christmas.

"I'll tell them not to go off half-cocked," Gail said, rushing off.

Kelly headed for the security department, uncertain whether to inform the police of the theft. The store could absorb the loss, but it would be sending the wrong signal to the thieves. Shoplifting and theft were problems that weren't new to Lambs. Other stores used visible means of discouraging theft—posting guards at every exit, monitoring dressing rooms, mounting reflecting mirrors on ceilings and installing elaborate clothing tags and alarm systems. Lambs, on the other hand, used subtle, old-fashioned forms of security: well-trained guards in street dress and alert sales personnel. The only contemporary addition was merchandise tags that could trigger a flashing light at the store's exit, but were removed at the point of sale. First-time shoplifters who were actually caught in the act were discreetly detained and then released after a warning. Caught a second time, they were prosecuted. Larger thefts were uncommon, and in the time Kelly had been with the store, no thefts of comparable size to this one had been committed by members of her staff.

Kelly caught up with her security chief just as he was leaving his office. "What do you think?" she asked.

"I've just had Charlie on the line. He's offered to come in. Said it was an unusually quiet night."

She asked about the watchman on the earlier shift, and was told the man was out and couldn't be contacted. "What point are you at now?" she asked.

"We've been going over the place with a fine-tooth comb. Want to make certain it wasn't a prank or that they weren't just taken out of the cabinet and moved elsewhere in the store—that sort of thing."

"Do you think the theft has anything to do with the fur coat stolen last week?"

The security chief shook his head. "If you mean was that a trial run, it's possible. We kept that one quiet, although the insurance company is making noises about why we didn't report it. This one we can't sit on if you expect to make an insurance claim. But let me make certain the garments aren't on the premises."

"Let me know before you call them," she said briefly.

"Let's hope we don't have to."

"I hate the thought of it," she said. She shuddered at the idea of the police swarming all over the store, questioning personnel.

Back in her office she picked up a dozen messages. None she saw, leafing quickly through them, were from Tony. Her face flushed at the memory of his touch, at her rash abandon in his arms, at his assumption that she was now on his side and wouldn't be any trouble at all. A day and a night had gone by since she had left him at his hotel, but he had never been far from her thoughts. She knew instinctively that he was waiting for her to break her silence, to come to him. In fact, she had reached for the telephone a dozen times since she'd left him, but each time had drawn back. Now she'd have to call him about the theft. The money involved was substantial and there was no reasonable excuse for holding out on him.

Among her messages Kelly noticed a return call made by Rudy Marchetta. She had called him when she came to work that morning. She dialed Rudy first, if only to steady her nerves for the job ahead of calling Tony. She'd been trying to reach the lawyer with a question that now took on fresh importance.

"How much room for maneuvering do you suppose I have," she asked Rudy at once, "in trying to find a buyer for Lambs?" Now that she'd asked the question, Kelly wondered about its propriety, then decided propriety be damned.

"Kelly, you don't own stock in the company. That's about how much room you have."

"I don't like what might happen to the store," she said. "If, on the other hand, someone were to buy it who happens to understand what it means to the community..."

"Forget it. You might be able to find a buyer that would interest Terro, but the Campbells mean to pull down the building, period."

"Not if I have anything to say about it."

He was silent for a few moments. "There isn't anything you can do. Back away. Ask them to release you from your contract if you're unhappy. Peddle your talent somewhere else."

"Ah, but I'm not unhappy with my contract or my job. That's the point. I wish to stay happy and to keep everybody happy around me."

"Times change. Move with them, Kelly."

"Rudy, do me a favor, even if you think I'm all wrong. See if there's a Good Samaritan interested in keeping a landmark store intact."

"What does Gregory have to say about all this?" he asked.

"Just what you said. Rudy, just check around, please."

He was silent again. She waited patiently. He was a cautious man but fair and they had always had good feelings about each other. "Okay. For you, Kelly."

"Love you." She hung up, knowing that if it were possible, he'd find someone. His loyalty was still to Gregory, but Gregory, as far as she was concerned, wasn't the least bit interested in the fate of Lambs, and anyway, he no longer owned the store.

Her phone rang almost immediately after. "Mr. Campbell here to see you," Gail told her when Kelly picked up the phone. "Are you available?"

"I'm not going anywhere." Kelly put down the receiver, wondering what kind of drumroll her heart was about to play. It didn't take her long to find out. With a light rap of knuckles, the door opened and Tony strode in. She held on to the arms of her chair tightly, merely to prevent herself from running to him.

Then she realized with a queer little pang that something was wrong. But she didn't believe the news of the theft could have caused the closed, hard look he gave her. His mouth was a taut white line, and he glanced quickly around the room like a predator surveying his territory. When he took a seat opposite her, his eyes never left her face.

"Come in," she said, trying to keep her voice light. "Have a seat."

"Kelly, it isn't going to work," he said after a moment.

Her heart did a drumroll, but the sound was deep and funereal. "What isn't going to work?"

"I spent yesterday and this morning trying to keep away from you."

She gave him a puzzled but relieved smile. "I'm sorry. I'm a little confused. Exactly why are you trying so hard to keep away from me?"

"You've got a short memory."

"I'm sorry, Tony. I don't understand."

"Staying away is only the tip of the iceberg. The reasons why you ran away comprise the bulk of the differences between us."

Of course, she had run away from him. It seemed so long ago now, and so inconsequential, running away, when all she remembered was the feel of his arms around her and the love they had made. "You've known that all along," she stated. "You have your set of priorities and I have mine. I don't think continual discussion is going to settle them."

"In other words," he said, getting up and restlessly pacing her office, "you'd be willing to forget something as good as what happened between us the other night for a pack of fool notions. Antiquated, sentimental, totally unprofessional notions at that."

"Do you see what I mean?"

"I thought you were a fighter who'd stick around just for the pleasure of slugging it out."

"Usually I do. Maybe there's too much at stake. I've a lot of power in my left hook, but you're made of concrete."

He laughed, but she sensed no mirth in the sound. "You admit it, then," he said. "It's a lot easier to throw in the towel when you're going to lose no matter how many rounds you get through."

"Persistence and right thinking sometimes pay off, Tony. I never said I intend to throw in the towel."

"What are we talking about?" he asked. "I don't want to lose what we had the other night, not through some notion you have about holding Father Time at bay."

She stared at him, astounded. "Will you listen to yourself?"

"I am. I'm listening to a lot of things—my heart for one."

She felt a long shiver course through her, but his very words called up the truth that needed speaking. She released her hold on the chair, stood up and turned to the window. "What happened between us was a mistake, Tony. An aberration. A foolish moment." Her voice dropped away. She knew her words were scarcely audible.

"That's what you really believe?"

"Yes."

"You little fool." He came up behind her and began to stroke her neck. "Monday morning quarterbacking, is that the expression you Americans use? If only you hadn't pushed me into Mrs. Laurence's pool. If only you hadn't come back for me. If only you hadn't gone to the Carlyle. What is it you want, Kelly? We made love then and we should make love now, this minute, in full view of your neighbors across the way, if need be. And it should end without your running away and, in fact, with a promise to repeat it every day for the rest of our lives."

She felt the heat of his touch, the heat of his words, but didn't turn around. "I'm the president of Lambs. You're the CEO," she said quite simply. "What happened makes me feel . . . damn, I don't know exactly what it makes me feel. Wrong, I guess."

"Wrong? An odd word, coming from someone who seemed to revel in every moment we made love together."

She stared at the clock repair shop across the way. A customer came in. The watchmaker greeted her, waving his hands effusively. Kelly suddenly longed to be there with them, discussing something as mundane as a broken timepiece.

The silence in the office became heavy, almost stifling. Tony didn't move. His hands rested on her shoulders. She closed her eyes and leaned her head back against him. "Don't make things worse than they are," she said at last.

"I'm not going to stop wanting you."

"Please," she said quietly. Then the sudden ring of her phone made her jump.

"Damn it," he said as she turned back to pick up the receiver, "I told your secretary to hold your calls."

"*I* didn't," Kelly said dryly. Her secretary at the other end told Kelly the chief of security was waiting for her. "Send him in," she said, grateful for the interruption.

"I'll see you later," Tony said, heading for the door.

"No, stay. There's something I have to tell you. At least I gather you haven't heard."

"Heard what?" He looked at her sharply, but before she could answer the chief of security came in.

"We searched the place from top to bottom," he said at once. "Even the air ducts. I don't think we have any alternative but to call the police." He cast a quick glance at Tony, nodding to him, as if expecting the head of the company to know what was going on.

"What are you talking about?" Tony asked.

Kelly told him briefly what had happened and then added in a lame manner, "We've been hoping to find them on the premises."

"Whoever stole them planned the job well," the security chief said. "As far as we can tell, they were moved out under the nose of the night watchman."

"Two exits, one closed with a gate, the other guarded twenty-four hours a day," Kelly reminded him.

"And the windows?"

"Barred. Lock untouched," the security chief said.

"The garments were taken from the third-floor coat department," Tony said, striding to the door. "Is that right?"

"From a small boutique of exclusive leather clothing designed for us in Italy," Kelly said.

"Shall I call the police?" the chief of security asked, following them out.

"Hold it until I tell you otherwise," Tony said.

"We don't want to wait too long on this one, Mr. Campbell."

"Because of insurance, for one," Kelly explained.

"Right." Tony took the stairs two at a time, with Kelly racing to keep up with him.

There was only one customer in the department when they arrived. Miriam, the floor manager, came rushing over to them. "Oh, Miss Aldrich," she said, "I feel so sick about it all."

"The garments were taken out of the armoire," Kelly pointed out to Tony. "The door was unlocked."

"Who has access to the keys when you're not around?" Tony brusquely asked Miriam.

She was a tall, slender woman who always wore black, with a necklace of pearls that were clearly very expensive. She gave Kelly a nervous smile. "Who has access to the keys? No one except me and security. And the buyer. And Miss Aldrich."

"You're not here on Saturdays?"

"No, someone else has the job on Saturday."

"Someone who can make a duplicate key," Tony said in an annoyingly persistent manner.

"It isn't Saturday," Kelly pointed out.

Tony ignored her outburst, focusing his attention on the floor manager. "What routine do you generally follow?"

She looked nervously at Kelly, as if for help. "You mean about locking up the armoire?"

"That's what I mean," he said wearily.

"I lock up and return the keys to the desk, which is secured with a combination lock." She kept her eyes on Tony, all the while fingering her pearls. "In the morning I pick up the keys and unlock the armoire. That's when I discovered the jackets were gone." She turned to Kelly almost pleadingly. "I almost had a heart attack."

"I understand," Kelly said in a soothing tone. "Now don't worry. I'm sure you did everything you were supposed to."

"How many more in the department?" Tony asked.

"Besides the buyer?"

"Besides the buyer." His manner scarcely disguised his impatience, which only made the floor manager more nervous.

"In the department altogether?" She looked at Kelly for confirmation.

"We have some part-time help," Kelly explained. "There are half a dozen to cover the entire floor at any one time. This particular area is covered by two saleswomen, plus fitters who come in to alter the jackets and coats, if necessary."

"Any new employees?"

Kelly shook her head. "We hold on to our employees for years, part-timers included. But, yes, of course, there's the occasional turnover."

"We don't allow anyone else near this merchandise because it's so expensive," Miriam said. "You know that, Miss Aldrich, don't you?"

"It's okay, Miriam. No one in the department is to blame."

"You know that for a fact," Tony said, regarding her with a fixed smile.

"Thanks, Miriam. Don't worry about anything," Kelly said, patting the woman on the arm and walking quickly away. When they were on the staircase heading for the sixth floor, Kelly whipped around and said, "I don't want you bullying my employees and making them nervous."

"And you feel a sense of protectiveness toward them that's a lot stronger than your desire to find out who stole nearly ten thousand dollars' worth of merchandise."

"If it's someone in this store," she told him, "we'll find the thief without undermining our loyal employees. I'd stake my reputation on Miriam. And the way you treated her! I guarantee she's in the ladies' room right now, crying."

"I'm touched by your devotion to the people who work here," he said, "but an inside job means someone here can't be trusted. I presume security does a check on everyone who's hired?"

"It's always been our policy. We'd be fools not to do a thorough vetting of people we're about to hire. If you'd like to see the records..."

"That and a whole lot more. Perhaps our entire security system needs an overhaul, like just about everything else around here. For one, your sales staff is too old and entrenched. They treat each other like family, and the trouble with family is you tend to overlook their problems."

"Just a minute," Kelly said, turning on him furiously. "I don't think I like what you just said. We've had a relatively smooth, safe operation with very little theft because we trust our employees and our customers. Now when a minor theft occurs, in you come, blasting at everything in your path. Tony," she added, "take a deep breath and then go away. Let us handle it."

A couple of women came down the steps past them, laughing over something. Kelly flattened herself against the wall to let them pass. Tony waited until they were out of earshot. He stepped up to her, pressing his hands against the wall, effectively caging her in. "You'd like that, wouldn't you, my going away?"

"Yes, as a matter of fact. But if you won't, then just step back and let us get on with our work. Good Lord," she said with a light laugh, hoping to ease the tension, "haven't you anything better to do?"

"Yes. I came in this morning to see you about us. We never finished our conversation, Kelly."

"Odd," she said in a faint voice, "I thought we had." His breath was warm on her face as he leaned close.

"Not finished to my satisfaction. And right now," he added, "I can think of the perfect way to be satisfied."

"Tony," she said, "you're not going to . . . I mean, this is a public stairway."

"No one around right now."

He bent and kissed her softly, as if in tender reminder of what they had shared. Then, in another moment, the kiss deepened.

She pulled away, drawing her hand across her lips. "Are you mad? What if someone sees us?"

"Let them." He kissed her again, pulling her close.

The same strange heat soared through her that she'd never felt with anyone else. She opened her mouth to him, giving in to forces she didn't understand. He let out a satisfied sigh, joining his tongue with hers . . . until she came to her senses.

"God, we're fools," she said breathlessly, pushing him away and rushing up the stairs.

She went past her secretary, who tried to hand her some messages, and slammed her door shut, leaning heavily against it. She was having trouble breathing, and it took several minutes for her to calm down. He had walked into her office and told her it wouldn't work between them and then proceeded to do everything he could to convince her otherwise. On a public stairway with her employees just feet away. She felt the heat stain her cheeks.

"Oh, I could kill him," she said aloud.

"Miss Aldrich?"

She looked over at her sofa and found Isabella there, tucked into the corner. "What . . . what are you doing here?" Isabella worked only three days a week at Lambs, and Kelly was a little surprised to find her at the store on an off day.

Isabella jumped to her feet and straightened her skirt. "Your secretary said I could wait here. I mean, the door was open and everything."

"Yes, yes, of course. What's the problem?"

At that moment her secretary opened the door and looked in. "I hope you don't mind."

"It's all right," Kelly said, glad of the distraction. She took her messages and sifted through them as Isabella came over to the desk.

"Do you think I could get a job here, working full-time?"

"You mean for the summer?"

Isabella nodded enthusiastically. Kelly glanced at her, surprised. She'd taken it for granted that Isabella would work her usual hours over the summer, and that, as usual, she'd give them a hard time by coming in late and complaining over every assignment given her. Perhaps Kelly's trip to Staten island had paid off, after all, in spite of Tony's doomsday scenario. "Well, I'm delighted to see you so enthusiastic," Kelly said, "but I'm not certain they'll have that much work for you in the fitting department."

"I'd like to be a salesgirl," Isabella explained. "I mean, I think it's a lot more fun. And I could see what sells and stuff. You know, what *works*."

"Isabella," Kelly began kindly, "the first roster we fill are salesladies' positions. We tend to take college graduates so that we can move them up the ladder. At any rate, you're not going to move your career along by selling, you know. You want practical dressmaking experience. Just think of all the delicious things that are going to come up in college. You'll be that far ahead of the other kids."

Isabella looked downcast. "I ought to work full-time."

"That's very wonderful of you to want to help out at home," Kelly said. "Tell you what. Let me call Job-Up and see what they have. Perhaps a garment manufacturer. It's a little late, but we can always pull a few strings.''

"But I want to stay here," Isabella said.

Kelly went over to the girl and put an arm around her shoulders. "Well, I'm greatly flattered. We want you here, too. Okay, you're not wishing for the moon. Not even a blue one."

"Huh?"

"Let me talk to personnel," Kelly said. "There's always somebody about to retire or somebody who wants the summer off to go to Europe. Maybe all the positions haven't been filled."

"Great, thanks, Miss Aldrich."

"As long as you're in today, you ought to see if they can use you in the fitting department. An extra day's pay wouldn't hurt."

"Gee, thanks again, Miss Aldrich."

"How's your mom?"

"Okay, I guess."

Kelly walked her to the door. She wished she knew what was really on the girl's mind. She had the oddest feeling that needing the extra money was only a part of her problems. After Isabella left, Kelly checked in with security, found nothing new had developed and cautioned the chief not to call the police until he heard from Tony.

Then she picked up her messages and arranged them in order of importance. She didn't want to think about Tony, nor his kisses, nor the foolishness of how she had let him kiss her and break down all her defenses.

CHAPTER TWELVE

TONY SLAMMED his fist against the office door, totally unconcerned about how the sound might affect those on the other side. His whole world was in danger of standing on edge. He'd been acting like a schoolboy, grabbing Kelly in the stairwell as though she were the prom queen and he a teenager with no control over his libido. She had every reason in the world to turn tail and run. Sebastian, in his darkest moments, hadn't been nearly so lunatic.

He sank into his chair and after a moment or two managed to steady his breath. He wasn't bothered by the small, cramped office Kelly had managed to gouge out for him at the back of the newly expanded dress department. The trappings of success meant little to him. He felt no need to impress anyone else. He liked an office in which the size of his desk or the distance from desk to door purchased what they were supposed to, convenience and ease, and that was all. And if it weren't for Kelly, he wouldn't have bothered entering the Lambs domain, any more than had his brother. Lambs was real estate. Lambs was a product to be bought and sold. He had no interest in the place otherwise.

The store was on the block and the premises, once emptied, would be demolished to make way for Terro

Towers. In fact, he had that morning penciled in a luncheon date with the principals of a large women's clothing retailer. Palace Limited sold medium-priced goods and wanted a flagship store in New York. Since their expansion plans included stepping up several notches in the kinds of clothes they sold, they were looking more than favorably at Lambs.

To Tony the last thing his company needed at that moment was police business and the petty thievery involved in the disappearance of some overpriced leather jackets. He knew the easiest way to handle the incident was to block an investigation even before it began. And the only way to do that was to find the culprit himself, if such a thing was possible.

There would be no stopping Kelly if she made up her mind to pursue the robbery in order to make an insurance claim. She was anxious to prove security wasn't lax and her employees could be trusted. Tony wasn't nearly so charitable. A guard nearing retirement age had the midnight shift. He might suffer from poor vision, poor hearing or be unable to stay awake through the long, quiet night. He'd have to find out how many rounds the man made every night, and how often he left his post.

It was also possible the theft occurred a lot earlier. The culprit might have devised a way to exit the building at a reasonable hour, perhaps counting on high visibility to accomplish the theft right under the noses of the guards. Which meant starting again at square one with the floor manager of the coat department to find out if her memory were all that good.

Five minutes later Miriam was startled to see Tony again, but when he asked her to go over the events of the evening before, step by step, she willingly complied. She had obviously told and retold the story to anyone within earshot and had it down pat. Pat was exactly how he didn't want to hear it. He wanted a few embellishments.

"Is there anyone new in the department?" he asked.

Miriam shook her head. "We're all one big family here."

Family. If he heard the word one more time, he'd begin a lobbying effort to excise it from the dictionary.

"There are a couple of part-timers at the other end," she went on, "but they're long gone by the time I close up."

"And you proceeded as usual," Tony said. "You locked up the cabinet, put the key away and secured the desk drawer. Then you went home, as always."

She watched him through careful eyes, as though hearing for the first time the rigors of her daily routine.

"Well," she admitted, "of course it doesn't happen pell-mell, like that. Sometimes the telephone rings for the buyer, or the buyer stops me for a moment, or well, I change into walking shoes. After a full day on the job." She shrugged, as if in apology for the shape of her feet. "Or I go to the powder room."

"And possibly left the keys out or the door unlocked."

She flushed, uncertain now.

"Meaning someone in the department could have gone into the office and removed the keys while you were in the powder room or changing your shoes."

"Of course not. No one would ever," she said huffily. "These are old and trusted employees. Anyway, they'd all gone home."

"There are five stories to the building," he reminded her gently.

"I'm sorry. There was no one around except for a couple of employees sitting in one of the dressing rooms sewing a garment. They were working overtime on a coat to be photographed today. The hem needed redoing."

Tony asked the next question on a long, drawn-out breath. "Do you have their names?"

Miriam's hand darted to her lips. "Well, you don't think—?"

"I don't think anything. I'd just like the names, please."

HE FOUND ISABELLA at the back of the fitting department, holding a pair of scissors and a tray of notions while the head seamstress fitted a customer for a bright red satin evening gown.

"Can you spare Isabella?" he asked the seamstress.

She recognized him and nodded, smiling around her mouthful of pins.

"Follow me," he said tersely to the teenager.

"Is it all right if I get my bag?" Isabella asked, flushing.

He nodded and stepped out of the room when the customer being fitted glared at him. Five minutes later, still cooling his heels in the designer dress department, Tony knew he'd been had by a very bright, very scared teenager.

He was on his way out through the perfume department on the ground floor when he came face-to-face with Kelly. "See Isabella?" he asked without preliminaries.

"This morning. Why?"

He took her elbow. "Come on, let's go."

"Go where?" She pulled back. "I have a luncheon engagement."

"Get your secretary on the phone. Cancel it and ask her for Isabella's home phone number."

It clearly didn't take Kelly long to figure out what was on his mind. "Wait a minute. You don't suspect her in the theft, do you? Yes," she said, after closely examining his face, "that's just what you think. She's upstairs in the fitting department."

"No." He shook his head. "She's not."

"What did you do? Reduce the possibilities to the lowest common denominator, namely, one of the kids from Job-Up?"

"Kelly, I want to talk to her mother, find out her haunts. I can guarantee she's not on her way home."

Still Kelly held back. "You accused her of stealing, didn't you?"

"I didn't have to accuse her of anything. I told her I wanted to talk to her and she took a powder."

Without a word Kelly marched over to the service desk and picked up the phone. When she came back she'd already talked to Mrs. Sanchez. "Her boyfriend Robbie shares an apartment with a couple of friends in SoHo. She gave me the phone number but has no idea where the apartment is. Security has some contact with the local precinct. Said I should call back in ten or fifteen minutes. What the devil are we doing in the middle of the store, acting like a couple of five-and-dime detectives?''

"Kelly, your favorite Job-Up program is in jeopardy. You know that, don't you?''

She blanched. "You'd better be sure of your facts, Tony. I don't care if you own this store or the whole world. No one person can put the program in jeopardy. It's a fait accompli and it works.''

"Find out what address that telephone number is attached to," he said. "I'm trying to hold on to your program and I want to keep the whole incident out of the press.''

"The press isn't interested in the theft of some leather coats.''

"No. But they are interested in the future of Job-Up.''

"You went specifically after Isabella, didn't you?'' Kelly said contemptuously.

He took her arm and drew her toward the exit. "I don't think you want your customers to see you hot under the collar.''

"You zeroed in on her, Tony.'' She let him push her through the door but stood her ground outside.

"On the contrary, I keep hoping she's innocent.''

"And what led you to your amazing deduction, Mr. Holmes?''

"Persistence, my dear Watson. I kept after Miss Miriam until she remembered she wasn't alone in the coat department when she locked up. Isabella and a Mrs. Langan were there, to be exact, sewing on a garment.''

"Oh, damn, I remember. We were lending it to Town and Country for a shoot today.''

"Apparently Isabella volunteered for the job. I remember listening in on a conversation you had with her once."

"Eavesdropping."

"Listening. She complained about sewing hems, and here she was volunteering to do precisely that. Makes a man stop and think, Kelly. It's all in the amazing gray cells. Come along, I'll tell you everything on the cab ride down to SoHo."

"I'm coming along," she said, just to prove you're barking up the wrong tree. Today Isabella asked if she could work full-time. She needs the money for school."

"Stitching hems?"

"No," she said after a moment. "Not stitching hems."

The kid who answered the door in the SoHo loft a half hour later was overly polite in a faintly swaggering manner. He was big and good-looking and expensively dressed in the current fashion of oversize clothes. His haircut was short and his face smoothly shaved. He claimed not to know anyone named Robbie or Isabella Sanchez. Music blared behind him, but he didn't seem to notice it.

"A pretty girl," Kelly said hopefully, raising her voice to compete with the sound. "Short spiky hair, dark with highlights. Makes all her own clothes."

"You her parents?"

"You know we're not," Tony said. He kept calm when all he wanted to do was blast his way into the place, turn the sound down and kick over the furniture.

The kid clearly understood the menace behind Tony's words, however. "Right," he said after a moment's hesitation. "Now I remember. She doesn't have a father."

Tony already had the notion that he was talking to Robbie. "What's your name?"

"Duane."

"Duane?" Tony exchanged a smile with Kelly. "Funny, I could've sworn it was Robbie."

"It's Duane."

"Duane, want to start it all over again and tell me where Robbie is? Or Isabella?"

Duane shrugged. "She said something about working today."

"And when did she say that?" Kelly asked, frowning. "She couldn't possibly have known. She didn't even know when she came in today—" She stopped, leaving her sentence unfinished.

The boy seemed a little disconcerted, and Tony took the moment to push his way into the loft and look around. A wide, nearly empty space, it held a small open kitchen, a large bed in the center, the blaring stereo and some upended boxes around a kitchen table, which he supposed were used as chairs. He went rapidly over to a metal locker, but when he swung it open, he just discovered some clothes that must have belonged to the owner. As for the leather jackets, if they were in the loft, they'd have to be hidden under the floorboards.

"Hey," Duane said, recovering from his surprise and running over to Tony. "You have no right to come barging in like that. I could call the cops."

"Go ahead," Tony said. He glanced back to Kelly at the door. She shook her head in disgust, as if to tell him he was a bully and undoubtedly breaking the law. He whipped around to the young man, who was watching him with a fixed smile. "Suppose you tell me where you think Isabella might be when she's not at work."

"How do I know where she is? Maybe she's home."

"She's not."

"The park, maybe."

"Which park?" Tony was beginning to lose his patience.

"Washington Square."

"And where does she eat? Where does she go in the evenings? Who are her friends?"

"Hey, come on, man, I've got to get to work. You're holding me up."

"The names first. Then you can go to work."

The kid took a heavy step toward him, but all Tony did was laugh. "Tell you what, Duane. I want those leather jackets back in the store by tomorrow. No, I'll give you a little longer than that. Day after tomorrow."

"Hey, man, I don't know what you're talking about."

Tony took out his pen and notebook. "The names of the joints where Isabella hangs out."

"TONY," Kelly said as soon as they were back outside, "you're looking for a needle in a haystack. Do you know how big this city is? How many people? Isabella will go home eventually and we'll pick her up there."

"No," Tony said. "The trouble is she won't go home, and that's precisely where I want her to be when I get finished with her."

"You really puzzle me," she said. "You go off on a mad toot to find her only to make sure she'll spend the night in her own little bed."

"Maybe," he said tersely, "I'm just trying to save you."

The park at Washington Square was a broad, open space with an arch at one end. On a sunny summery afternoon it was crowded with children, young people, chess players, strolling musicians, giving the casual viewer the impression of watching a carnival under leafy trees.

"Where do we start?" Kelly asked. "She could be ten steps ahead of us and we'd never see her."

"Then we'll split up," Tony said, "and meet back at the arch in fifteen minutes, with or without Isabella."

Tony traversed the park quickly, reminded of London on a warm day when everyone was out visiting Hyde Park. Even as his eyes scanned the present scene for sight of the teenager, he felt a surprising nostalgia for London. He planned on moving his permanent overseas operation to Manhattan. He knew Kelly would figure somewhere in his plans here, but he wanted to take her to London and Cornwall, as well, to introduce her to his past, to the elements that formed him. And to his father who hinted often enough that it was time his younger son settled down.

"Nowhere in sight," Kelly said when they met again. "Are we going back to beat up Duane and get a confession out of him?"

"Check Mrs. Sanchez" was all Tony said. "Make certain Isabella hasn't gone home."

"I hope she has," Kelly said, "and if so, I want you to leave her alone."

"She ran away because she's frightened," Tony told her. "I haven't any doubt she was a party to the theft. How and why are what I want to find out."

"NOT HOME," Kelly said a few minutes later. "And I checked the store. She never returned there, either. Which reminds me, I've a pile of work waiting for me. I trust Isabella to return home tonight. I'm even sure there's a reasonable explanation for her behavior. To begin with, she knows she was in the department where the theft occurred. She just ran scared. And your bullying tactics probably didn't help, either."

"Bullying tactics? I was the picture of calm. Let's go. I'm persistent about finding needles in hay-stacks."

Their needle in the haystack turned up at nine that evening in a noisy disco in Greenwich Village that catered to underage youngsters and served only soft drinks. She sat at a crowded table with a glass of Coke in front of her. Her unhappiness struck Tony at once.

"There's your pet project," he said to Kelly when they first spotted Isabella.

"All right, she's safe. I don't want to hear from you about the way she looks. She's dressing for her peers, not for you." Isabella's lipstick was nearly black against a pale face, and her hair was drawn up into shiny spikes. Her clothes were the ones she'd worn to work—a small black dress, black stockings and a big-shouldered khaki-colored jacket.

"Stay here," Tony ordered. He didn't want Kelly taking the girl's side in a confrontation.

"Just a minute," Kelly began, but he was already striding across the dance floor, pushing his way through the swaying bodies.

He pulled an empty chair from the next table and straddled it in front of Isabella, ignoring the kids she was with. "I don't like people running away from me," he told her.

Isabella stared at him as though at an apparition. Then she said, "My mom send you to find me?"

He held back a laugh. She was just a kid, after all. He took in her companions at a glance. A shy lot, he guessed, pretending insouciance. They sat there, silently watching him, as though he had landed from another planet. The music bleated, and colored lights turned swiftly in ceiling fixtures, striving to give the impression of a certain frenzy, but he was hard put to find it. One thing he knew, these kids were indeed traveling in a separate time zone from his.

"Come on," he said, getting up and holding out a hand for Isabella. "I've got somebody waiting to meet you."

"Honestly, I don't know anything," she said, letting him drag her reluctantly along. He wondered how, as a young man, he'd ever put up with being young himself. It seemed more of a chore than a pleasure.

Kelly put her arms out and gathered Isabella in. "We've had quite a time looking for you. Why did you run away?"

"I didn't," Isabella began.

"Come on, we're taking you home," Tony said, heading for the door.

"Are you going to tell my mother?"

"Not unless we have to." Once outside, deciding they'd better get their talk out of the way first, Tony looked for a quiet place where they could sit down. He found one on the corner, a tiny café dominated by a huge coffee urn on an antique mahogany counter. The place was still open for business and half empty. He ordered espresso for himself and Kelly and hot chocolate for Isabella.

"Before we take you home I want to hear the whole story from you, Isabella, from start to finish." He gestured to a chair near the window. "Sit down."

Her face, even under the heavy layer of makeup, had gone pale, and she sat down on the edge of the chair, hugging her arms tightly.

"You know why we've been looking for you. That's why you ran away in the first place, isn't it?" he asked.

She shrugged, casting a glance at Kelly, as if expecting to find help there.

"Who's Duane?"

"Duane?"

"Lives on Prince Street in a loft. Tall, short-haired, well-dressed, polite."

She gave a sudden, childish giggle, which turned into a sob. "That's Robbie. *Duane.* He's crazy."

Kelly reached over and took her hand. "Isabella, you know as well as we do that there was a theft last night of very expensive leather jackets from the coat department. How come you ran away when all Mr. Campbell wanted to do was ask you if you saw or heard anyone?"

"I . . . I thought Mrs. Langan said something—"

"Mrs. Langan left a half hour before you did," Tony said. "In fact, when I spoke with her, all she expressed was surprise at your zeal."

"Huh?"

"Surely you must have heard or seen something unusual last night," Kelly said with the first signs of impatience she had shown.

"But I didn't, Miss Aldrich, honest."

"Of course you didn't," Tony said soothingly, leaning back in his chair. "After all, you weren't listening for anything except the sounds of the night watchman's footsteps or for Miriam coming back from the powder room."

The girl picked up her shoulder bag, zipped it open and began rummaging through it while Tony talked. At last she fished out a lipstick and a mirror.

The waiter came by with their order. Isabella took a sip from her cup and made a face. "Too hot."

"You know you're in a lot of trouble, don't you, Isabella?" Kelly asked the question gently, touching the girl's arm.

"Yes. I mean, I think so."

"What happened?"

"It's Robbie," she said in a near whisper.

"Duane?" Tony asked, unable to hide the sarcasm in his voice.

"I'm scared of him," Isabella said. The lipstick and mirror lay forgotten on the tabletop.

"What do you mean?" Kelly's voice was breathless, and it occurred to Tony that whatever had gone wrong in Kelly's life, she'd never been deeply afraid of anyone, not even her scold of a father.

He turned to Isabella. "Tell me exactly why you're afraid of Robbie. Tell me exactly what he said."

Isabella began to squirm in her seat. She fingered the mirror, the lipstick, the handle on her cup of hot chocolate and twisted her ankles around the legs of her chair. "Well, you know," she began, averting her eyes, "he has this way of looking at me. I mean, like he had me up against the wall. Like, you know, his eyes would get so dark, and he would say to me, "'You know you're my woman.'" She glanced over at them with unexpectedly shining eyes, as though in a way she was proud of being his woman. "And he says, 'You do what I say, and you don't cause me grief, and everything will be okay. But if you cause me grief, then everything ain't gonna be okay.'" She added after a moment's silence, "'And you better get those jackets, or else.'"

"But why didn't you come to me?" Kelly asked. "We would've helped you."

"Maybe you don't even know what I'm talking about, Miss Aldrich. Maybe you don't know what scared is."

Kelly drew her lips together, clearly taken aback.

Tony felt a tug at his heart. Damn, how had he gotten into this? He'd come on a crusade, ready to take the kid apart, and here he was, wanting to give her fatherly advice, let her know he'd be there for her. He exchanged a quick glance with Kelly, who obviously shared his concern. "Isabella, I want you to remember one thing. Promise me."

Isabella looked at him out of tear-stained eyes. "I promise."

"You're not alone anymore. Do you understand that? You've got me."

She pressed her lips together, then rubbed her hand to her eye, dragging down a large black smudge. Kelly reached into her bag for a tissue and carefully wiped at the smudge. "Want to tell us exactly what happened last night?"

Isabella discovered her lipstick and mirror and began shuffling them around on the table. "Robbie said the store's insured. It doesn't matter if something is, is . . ." She let her voice die away.

"Miriam went to the powder room after locking the leather jackets in the armoire," Tony said for her. "She thinks maybe she neglected to lock the desk drawer. You were conveniently close by, weren't you, hoping for just such a moment?"

Isabella stared at him, her face completely blank.

When she didn't answer, Tony continued. "You went over to the desk, removed the key and unlocked the armoire. Then you put the key back in the drawer. After Miriam left you continued to sew the garment, waiting for activity on the floor to come to a halt. Then you went over to the armoire, opened the doors and took the jackets out. Unless you walked out of the store under the eyes of the early-shift watchman, and if you couldn't remove the seals, you had to have an accomplice. And furthermore, if you hadn't been fortunate enough with the keys, he'd instructed you to break the armoire lock, right?"

She moved the lipstick to the right of the mirror and then back again. "Robbie," she said at last. "I opened the ladies' room window and slipped the jackets through the bars."

Tony leaned back. "Wonderful. Bars on windows that allow dress goods to be squeezed through them."

Kelly loosed a sigh. "Okay, Sherlock, you've made your point."

"Then you went back to the fitting department," he went on, "which works late in the best of times, and handed in the completed hemming job. You walked out of the store with the other seamstresses and went home to Staten Island."

"What are you going to do?" she asked out of tearful eyes. "I really never would have done anything like that if I wasn't scared of him. I thought he would hurt me or something."

"We might settle for the return of the merchandise," he said.

"I can't. Robbie would kill me. Besides, I don't know where the coats are."

Tony suddenly thought he knew where the jackets were. The boxes in the loft used for chairs around the kitchen table. He doubted they were empty.

"Tell you what, Isabella," he went on. "We're going to go back to see Robbie now. We're going to let him know what scared is."

"Tony, that's *enough*," Kelly said. "We're taking you home, Isabella. I'm really greatly disappointed in you. You've put the whole Job-Up program in jeopardy."

"Do I still have a job?"

Kelly and Tony exchanged a glance. Would the girl never learn, he wondered. "Isabella," he said, reaching for her hand and holding it lightly. "You must understand the seriousness of your actions."

She nodded her head enthusiastically. "But I do, honestly. I do."

He released her hand and leaned back. So far he wasn't taking any bets on it. "You're an adult now, Isabella, and you have to take responsibility for what you do every minute of the day. You're going to have to stop and think just how your actions affect other people—your mother, your siblings. And consider your own future. Being scared of Robbie is no excuse. You had people to come to, sympathetic people who would've given you the right advice. You have to learn that you can't steal. You can't bend the law to suit yourself or an oversize bully. Tell me," he said, looking gravely into her eyes, "if Robbie had said, 'I want you to hurt somebody,' would you have?"

An expression of horror spread over her face. She shook her head.

"You know, Isabella, if we wanted to press charges against you, you'd land in jail. A judge wouldn't take, 'I was scared,' as an excuse."

"I know," she said in a faint voice. "I'm sorry. I really am."

"Look, you're a bright, hardworking young woman when you put your mind to it," Kelly said. "What you've got to do is take a minute and pretend you're looking into a crystal ball. Your future is pictured there, but it's the future you're going to draw for yourself. If you hang around with the Robbies of this world, you can guess how you'll end up."

Isabella nodded. "I know."

"Or you can see yourself as a successful woman, taking charge of her life, proud of herself, knowing she's doing a good day's work and really contributing, operating at the top of her abilities.''

"Yeah, I know," Isabella said.

"What do you see in the crystal ball?"

"Being a rich, famous fashion designer?" Isabella responded.

"How about settling for a good designer?"

"Uh-huh."

"Rich and famous can happen, of course," Kelly said, softening her tone, "but it's being good at what you do that counts. Isabella," she added, "I'm going away for a week to England."

Tony started at her remark, but she shook her head briefly, as though to tell him they would talk about it later.

"When I come back, Isabella, I'm going to have a talk with you, and you'll tell me how you want to live your life."

"But do I still have my job?" Isabella asked.

"You have your job," Kelly said with a nod of confirmation from Tony. "And you can come in full-time to help out in the fitting department."

"On probation," Tony said. "One month, with me keeping an eye on you, and I don't want to hear one tiny whine out of you, Isabella. I don't care what assignments they give you. Oh, and incidentally, I expect you to show up on the button. And," he added, "do something about that hair."

Isabella sent him a little look that held something of defiance in it, but nodded when she saw he wasn't about to put up with her nonsense. She drew her hands through her spiky hair, but it refused to press down.

She'd be difficult, he thought, but perhaps she had to be to survive.

"Okay," Kelly said, "let's take you back home."

"All the way to Staten Island?"

"All the way to Staten Island."

Tony fished in his pocket for some change. He kept his smile to himself. He could think of worse ways to end the evening than be with Kelly on a ferry ride across the bay. And then there was the matter of her going away for a week. Perhaps he might be able to move more swiftly on certain of his projects without her around, but at the moment the idea didn't appeal to him.

CHAPTER THIRTEEN

RUDY MARCHETTA CALLED Kelly three days after her foray with Tony into Manhattan's Greenwich Village. The intervening time had been a relatively calm one for Kelly, although every so often a memory would slip in and a shadowy vision, half hidden in darkness, would make her feel the warmth of an embrace, the touch of lips against hers, the promise of something precious.

Tony had started on his chase after Isabella, as though she were the crumbling lodestone of Lambs. Lax security, indifferent personnel, criminals underfoot: his script cast Kelly as a poor chief executive, the store itself a burden that was best sold off to the highest bidder. He may not have changed his perception of Lambs, but now he and Kelly were held together by the most tenuous of knots, a rebellious teenager whose future was important to both of them.

Although she had been warned by Sebastian Campbell that the store might be sold, Rudy's call nevertheless came as a shock.

"No need putting out feelers any longer, Kelly. Palace Limited is looking with increasing interest at your operation."

"Palace! Are you sure?" She fell weakly back in her chair.

"You asked me to do a little fishing. I did. It's all on the quiet, so you haven't heard it from me."

"Palace. That's the last company I'd have gone to," she said. It was a well-known fact that Palace wanted to establish a base in New York. A large, successful medium-price clothing chain operating out of California, its style was simple, unprepossessing, without daring. Linking the two names together might help Palace; it could ultimately destroy Lambs.

"Don't look at the downside," Rudy told her cheerfully. "Mary had a lot of little Lambs, and maybe that's what the country needs, too. Incidentally, if it's any consolation, I've heard the company is a fine one to work for. They do well by their executives."

"Thanks, Rudy, but it's no consolation."

She had scarcely hung up when Gail asked to see her. Her assistant bounced into the office, wearing a wide smile. Kelly, who was about to blurt out the business about Palace, held her tongue. Gail was a jewel and would survive any change of ownership. In fact, she'd undoubtedly do well in a large corporation where intelligence, enthusiasm and creative flair were usually in short supply.

"Today a big carton arrived in shipping," she told Kelly, her eyes twinkling. She had been informed of Isabella's foray into larceny and agreed being caught, put on probation and forced to change her hairstyle were adequate punishment for a first offense. "No return address. Destination, third-floor coat department. Contents?" She paused and Kelly waited, knowing perfectly well what the contents were. "Guess," Gail said.

"Blue suede shoes?" So Tony had been successful in convincing Robbie to return the jackets. She didn't even try to imagine his methods.

"Every last jacket that was stolen."

"Fantastic."

"In perfect condition."

"I'm really pleased," Kelly said. "I suppose we can write finis to the whole episode." Just another problem, she thought, solved by the Masked Rider and his faithful sidekick, Kelly Aldrich.

"Of course, there's the problem of beefed-up security," Gail said. Immediately after the episode, Terro had ordered a study of the best methods for securing the store. "There are already grumblings by the staff about the way they're being treated when they check out at night."

"The times they are a-changing," Kelly said.

"I hate being a suspect when about the worst thing I've ever done is chew the end of a company pen," Gail said on her way out. Then, winking, she said, "I'm a positive treasure, aren't I?"

"You are," Kelly said.

Gail was about to say something else but seemed to understand that Kelly wasn't in a happy mood. Gail let herself out, closing the door softly behind her, and once she was gone, Kelly wanted to call her back. It was as though Rudy's call had signaled the end of everything—including her certainty. Was she really trying to hold on to a dinosaur just because her ego told her the world needed dinosaurs?

Kelly stood up and stretched. She needed an aspirin. She needed a drink. She needed a new life. She thought, with a little ache, that she needed Tony and that perhaps the only way she could have him was to throw in the towel. At what point she had deluded herself into believing that everything was wonderful, that her father was right, that success was *success*? For the past decade she'd been living in a tinsel land with fake clouds and an endlessly sunny sky. Well, the yellow brick road had certainly come to an end, and what she'd found wasn't Oz; it was Takeover City. And the architect of her future was the most unlikely man in the world for her to fall for.

She had slipped on her mother's pearls that day and now touched them tentatively. They felt good, warm and familiar. She cherished her mother's memory and missed her. Sometimes, in the dark of night, when all her mistakes seemed illuminated on the wall, her mother's comforting presence would make itself felt, as now, when the word *success* seemed the most unappealing and unpoetic in the world.

She felt suddenly stifled in her office and thought with increasing interest of her impending visit to Great Britain. She had—ages before, it seemed—penciled in the vacation. She remembered clearly discussing the trip with Gail during the charity fashion show at the Metropolitan Museum of Art. Those were the days of her near-innocence when exhaustion and the need for vacations were the result of hard work and not emotional turmoil.

She'd almost forgotten her plans when her secretary had asked about booking the flight and hotel room.

Now it was an inevitable week away, and she was looking forward to it. She needed space and time to think. If reordering her priorities was required, it would have to take place far away from the world she had built and burrowed in twenty-four hours a day. She reached for her calendar: schedules could be changed, appointments put forward.

She went outside to her secretary's desk, meaning to discuss booking a seat on the Concorde in the next day or two.

"Hello, Kelly, I was just asking for you."

She was surprised to find Diane Bourne standing there, carrying an armful of packages bearing the Lambs logo.

"Diane!" She greeted the woman with genuine enthusiasm, glad of the diversion.

"Did I come at the wrong time?"

"The right time," Kelly said, and meant it. "Come on in." She spoke a few words to her secretary, asking for a schedule and immediate available space on the Concorde. Then, asking that her calls be held, she brought her visitor into her office.

Diane dropped her packages onto the sofa and then sat down at Kelly's invitation. She wore a green linen suit and print blouse that suited her flamboyant red hair, and Kelly was struck with her poise and sophistication. Yet despite her smile and nonchalant air, Kelly recognized tired circles under her eyes.

"You've certainly shopped the store," Kelly said of the Lambs packages strewn about. "I wish I'd known you were here. I'd have arranged for a store discount. After all, you're an employee of Terro."

"Never thought of it," Diane said. "Typical of my wild, extravagant ways. I've never saved a cent, haven't the faintest idea how to curtail my spending, and ought to be in the market for a husband with a very large fortune. You wouldn't have a spot of something for me to drink, would you?" She gave an unexpectedly hearty laugh. "Do you have one of those hidden bars that are part and parcel of the successful executive's office?"

"Yes, as a matter of fact I do," Kelly said, going over to an antique cabinet and pulling the doors open. Something was up, she decided, and also decided the drink wouldn't be Diane's first of the day. Nevertheless, Kelly joined her in a Scotch and soda, swallowing the sharp mixture with distaste, but hoping the liquor would dull the edge of her own anxiety.

"Speaking of men with large fortunes," Diane began, "have you heard from Gregory?"

Kelly shook her head. "We used to talk every day, but of course there's no reason to now. I do miss him," she added. "How I miss him!"

"Well, I suppose things are different with Tony. He's not exactly a man with a sympathetic ear for the way women deck themselves up. Then, of course, he knows nothing about the retail business, although at least he has the goodness to admit it."

"Yes, he does that." Diane's real relationship with Tony had never been quite settled in Kelly's mind, and although she knew it was over, the thought of something having once been between them still poked at her occasionally. "Diane," she said, without giving herself a chance to think about the consequences of her next remark, "I thought you and Tony were—"

"Not a chance," Diane broke in, giving her a sharp, canny glance, which brought a spot of color to Kelly's cheeks. She wondered whether Tony had been talking about her. "Oh, we've had some good times together," Diane continued, warming to the subject. "Tony's nothing if not a gentleman, but he was never serious about me. Never serious about anyone, for that matter. He's a Campbell, and they don't do too well by their women."

"I'm sorry. I don't understand," Kelly said, aware of a certain shakiness in her voice.

"Campbell, Sr., had two wives, and look what happened to them," Diane said with the certain air that Kelly knew all about the family. "The Campbell boys were brought up to collect and discard women like trophies. There's really only one kind of woman for them, the kind picked by their father."

"Was Sebastian's wife handpicked?"

Diane gave a smug smile. "Certainly. Why in the world would he have married Patricia otherwise?"

"Tony doesn't strike me as someone who'd allow that sort of thing," Kelly said.

Diane's laugh was brittle. "Tony's managed to escape so far, but believe me, for four hundred years his class has only married among themselves. He's a product of that history and isn't about to break with it. Anyway, the truth is, both Tony and his father are exactly alike."

"Four hundred years," Kelly echoed, thinking with a heavy tug at her heart that being involved with Tony Campbell was a lot more complicated than she was prepared for. A girl from a mill town wasn't material for the Campbells of Cornwall, apparently.

"Nothing comes before Terro, not even women," Diane added.

"As someone who has the same relationship with a store, I can understand that," Kelly mused, adding to herself that if Tony's marriage was to Terro, then it followed she was merely a temporary convenience.

"You two should make beautiful music together under those circumstances," Diane said in a flippant manner. She downed her drink quickly, as though to steady her nerves. "The truth is, I came to talk about Gregory."

"Oh? What about Gregory?"

Kelly didn't want to hear about Gregory Solow. The truth was, she wanted Diane to leave so that she could think about Tony and what had gone on between them and how her future stacked up. As for Gregory, she was still angry at him for his lack of interest in her problems, for leaving her swinging in Terro's breeze.

Diane got up and went over to the bar, where she poured herself another drink. "I've been married three times," she said, turning and looking at Kelly as though daring her to be shocked. "Each marriage was worse than the previous one. A lout, a drunkard and a womanizer—in that order. I've no sense, obviously, when it comes to picking out a mate. And I've had my share of lovers outside the bonds of matrimony. I don't know why I'm telling you all this," she went on, wandering over to the window and staring down at the traffic below. "Yes, I do. I want to talk about Gregory Solow. I've got no women friends, you know." She came back, sat down on the sofa and gave another of her brittle little laughs. "I've always had my share of confidants, but men, of course. Lovers or friends who'd lend an ear and tell me I was perfect just the way I was, to change nothing. Gregory asked me to marry him." The last was said quickly, as though to catch Kelly off guard.

Kelly, leaning against her desk, arms folded, gave a start, then colored lightly when she found Diane looking curiously at her.

"Are you worried about him?" Diane asked. "I mean, in relation to me. You knew his wife, I suppose."

"Yes," Kelly said. "He was very devoted." She didn't even try to answer Diane's question, and for a long while the room remained silent but for the sound of traffic below.

"I imagine she was very beautiful," Diane said at last.

"Yes."

"But now he's fallen in love with me." She cast Kelly a defiant glance. "He's older than I am and rather settled in his ways. I don't know whether I love him or not. For once in my life perhaps I'm afraid to. I told him about me, about everything."

"Of all the things Gregory might be," Kelly remarked, "stiff-necked isn't one of them."

"I think he's sorry as hell that he asked me to marry him," Diane said.

"And you want me to find out just what he thinks?" Kelly asked.

Diane nodded.

"And you'll bow out gracefully if you find he's sorry?"

"Yes, I think I would."

Kelly turned and picked up her phone. She dialed Gregory's number, found him in and was in turn invited for cocktails at his apartment, followed by a concert at Carnegie Hall. Gregory was a member of the board and held a box on the first Thursday of every month.

They'd have dinner at intermission, he promised her, and Kelly remembered that these dinners with Gregory often lasted the length of the second portion of the program. When she turned to Diane, she found her gathering her packages together. "I won't put in a good word for you," Kelly told her.

"But not a bad one, I hope."

Kelly laughed. "I just meant that I don't want to interfere. You said you're uncertain about whether you love him or not. Maybe he's no longer the Gregory Solow I remember. Perhaps I'll never forgive him for selling the place, but I want him to have all the happiness he can. He deserves it."

"Yes, he does. I don't want to be the source of unhappiness for him. He's a wonderful man."

"But you don't love him."

"I don't think I know what the word means."

Perhaps I don't know, either, Kelly thought. *I've certainly worn blinders with Tony.*

Diane came over to her and spontaneously kissed her cheek. "I had a presentiment that you were the one person I could talk to about Gregory. I'm sorry he sold Lambs also, even though it resulted in our meeting. The Campbell boys are hard-nosed and all business. At least you know to expect the worst from them. Well, I wish you luck."

Seeing her out, Kelly thought that she and Diane were more alike than not. They were both wary of falling in love, or having fallen in love, were afraid of the very word. In her case it didn't matter. The Campbells of Cornwall were clearly a breed apart.

There was no room for Kelly in either Tony's future or his heart.

AT SIX KELLY was in the Solow apartment, surprised to find she wasn't the only visitor but that at least a dozen people were in the elegant antique-filled drawing room.

"You're looking very lovely tonight," Gregory said.

"Thank you." She pretended a curtsy. Under a sheer silk jacket she wore a slim print dress with spaghetti shoulder straps. The night was warm, and she knew that concert houses, in spite of air-conditioning, tended to heat up in direct ratio to the size of the audience.

"I think you know everyone," Gregory said to her.

"Yes, I do," she whispered, "but I thought I made it clear on the phone that I wanted to talk to you."

"Not about business, angel. I've lost interest," he said.

"You're a beast, but you're going to talk to me, anyway, even if I have to hog-tie you and sit on your chest. And you'll be happy to know it isn't about business." She tucked her arm through his and drew him through the open doors onto the terrace. "I saw Diane Bourne today. Is that enough of a conversation starter?"

The black look he gave her set Kelly back for a moment, but then he went over to the terrace doors and closed them firmly. He came back and took her arm. "You always were a bit of a busybody," he told her. An iron bench stood against the brick wall, and it was there that he led her. "As I recall, you're always interfering in your employees' lives,'' he said, sitting down next to her.

"Still am," she said. "And proud of it. Interfering may be the most interesting thing I do."

"Except Diane isn't your employee. She's Terro's."

"But she saw the Mother Hen in me, Gregory."

"No," he said, shaking his head slowly. "I think she's a little more calculating than that. She figures you're a direct conduit to me. How much did she pay you to extol her virtues and tell me she's the most beautiful and exciting thing in the world?"

"Oh, scads."

"You don't have to, anyway," he commented. "I admit I find her exciting and beautiful, but then so are tigers. She's been married three times. Did she tell you that?"

"Yes, quite openly."

"She's extravagant and would like nothing better than to marry a man with money. Did she tell you that?"

"Yes."

"Perhaps she's more calculating than even I imagined. She's had far too many lovers. She's a woman men fall in love with and live to regret."

"Have you talked to many men who've regretted it?"

Gregory looked at Kelly with a degree of surprise and then burst into a hearty laugh. "Maybe I should find one. I confess I'm a little out of practice in discussing those things with anyone—anyone at all."

"So you've fallen in love, but being sensible old Gregory, you've politely written her off."

"And Diane wants to know whether she still has a chance with old money boots," Gregory said. His voice held a tinge of regret mixed with sarcasm. "Three husbands, a shady past and a yen for all the good things in life. I wouldn't be the last man to fall for a woman like that, except for one thing—I know when to run and how fast."

"I think she's afraid to fall in love with you."

He gave a low grunt. "I wonder whether she'd feel the same way if I didn't have a cent."

"You wouldn't have met, so it's a moot point. Gregory," she said, taking up his hand, "don't throw away something that might be good for you. After all, Diane's been honest with you. She needn't have been, you know. She could have rushed you through a wedding if money were the only thing on her mind. Isn't that something in her favor? Write a prenuptial agreement—that sort of thing," she added brightly.

Gregory tilted her head and kissed her on the nose. "Mother Hen, mind your own business. I was married to one woman for thirty-five years. I'd be a fool to take on someone almost young enough to be my daughter, someone with a . . . a history like hers. I wasn't looking to fall in love with her," he added, as though an explanation were necessary to himself. "I fell in love with the surface, the glamour, the need to be entertained and to believe the world's a good place with happy endings. There are no happy endings, pet. Have you learned that by now?"

"Happy endings, happy beginnings," Kelly intoned. "I seem to remember a poem my mother wrote about that."

He kissed the tip of her nose once more and said with the air of a man who had heard one too many of Mrs. Aldrich's poems, "She was a genuine philosopher, your mother. Did she ever tell you, in rhyme, to mind your own business?"

"The only thing I was ever told to mind was my nose to the grindstone. And that was by my father."

He glanced at his watch. "Satisfied with the outcome of our little conversation?" he asked.

She stood up. "I know, your guests are wondering where you are. Are you going to stuff them all into your box at Carnegie Hall?"

"Only the musical among them," he said. "You haven't answered my question."

"Whether I'm satisfied or not means nothing, Gregory. That's between you and Diane. And incidentally," she said, reaching out and pretending to straighten his tie. "I've heard that Lambs is up for sale and that Palace Limited wants to buy it."

Before he could say anything, she headed inside, losing herself in the crowd.

SHE WAS GLAD of the concert, glad to be sitting in Gregory's box in the beautiful white-and-gold hall, but every now and then her mind was distracted and she stared straight ahead, unmindful of the music. Before leaving the store she had successfully booked a seat on the Concorde for the following day. She'd be in London for a couple of days without appointments or her retinue of buyers who usually accompanied her on such trips. She'd be able to wander the streets alone, to see her life from a fresh perspective. Gregory, upon learning her plans, had offered her the use of his house on Belgravia Square. She'd accepted quickly, knowing the place well from the times she had visited with both Gregory and Suzanne.

Shortly before the intermission there was a slight rustle at the back of the box. She turned to find Tony enter with a slight, apologetic smile, his eyes lighting up when he saw her. She turned around, feeling the music well up around her, wanting desperately to lose herself in it. Gregory, reaching out, touched her hand as if to tell her he was glad she had come along. She returned his smile, all the while aware of Tony sitting behind her.

She glanced out over the audience below in their bright red plush seats, sitting attentively as the music drew to a crescendo. She had dreamed as a teenager of sitting in one of the world's great concert houses, dressed as she was now in a glamorous gown and in the company of elegant men and women. She thought of the measure of success she had attained, and the price she was paying for it.

Her work consumed her life twenty-four hours a day, seven days a week. It was a life filled with business engagements and the social engagements that grew out of them, a life of relationships that were superficial: the peck on the cheek, gossipy lunches, concerts she scarcely heard because her mind tingled with the day's events.

She'd thought she was filling her life with important work, but now wondered whether her work was a subterfuge, an excuse for not living like other people, for not allowing things to reach her on a personal level. The truth was that while running herself ragged she didn't have the time to make personal decisions, even a decision about whether to take a lover or whether a relationship with a man could be serious for a while, even if the future didn't look promising.

Perhaps her first feelings of dissatisfaction had begun in a subtle way when she took on Job-Up. She found unexpected joy in working with kids and seeing them blossom. There was excitement at Lambs, but she never received the visceral charge over her customers she had had from saving the futures of talented kids.

She was beginning to believe heading an elite store for the very rich wasn't all it was cracked up to be. The job was keeping her from smelling the roses.

She felt a light touch on her bare shoulder and then his breath against her cheek. "Shall we get out of here?" She felt warmth suffuse her body but turned to Tony and solemnly shook her head. Maybe she'd purposely picked a man like Tony to fall in love with, a man who wasn't serious about her. She closed her eyes as the music ended and the applause exploded. Tony lifted his hands to clap. She joined the applause, opening her eyes, watching the conductor exit the stage, then come back in as the applause continued.

Perhaps she was fooling herself about Tony. Perhaps she was in deeper than she thought. She suspected that what she felt for him didn't even have a name. She knew he'd discovered from Gregory that she would be there that night and somehow she knew she had to escape him.

Kelly wasn't one to give in to impulse, but all she could do was lean over to Gregory and kiss him lightly on the cheek. "I'm leaving now. Thanks for the loan of the apartment. I do like Diane, you know."

As she hurried out of the box and away from Tony, who was talking politely with his neighbor and couldn't get away, she thought of Diane's words and knew she had to prepare herself. No matter how far up in the world she traveled, she was still a girl from a mill town and Tony was still the son of an English viscount. The only similarity between them was that Tony would do what his father expected, just as she'd always done what her father had programmed her to do.

CHAPTER FOURTEEN

THE HOUSE IN BELGRAVIA SQUARE, in one of the most prestigious sections of London, was a four-story white stone structure wedged into a row of look-alike buildings. Gregory had warned Kelly she'd have the place to herself; his servants had been given time off when he returned to the States and weren't expected back for a couple of weeks.

"Suits me fine," she'd told him "I'm hankering for complete privacy."

The interior was impressive, a compendium of burnished antiques, curtains of silk brocade held with passementerie, and a collection of English eighteenth-century artworks. She wandered the rooms, recalling better days when the Solows were a couple and life seemed simpler. She chose a simply furnished rather feminine bedroom on the second floor, the one she had occupied previously. She unpacked, then without even taking a cup of tea, lay down and fell into a deep sleep.

The next morning, Saturday, Kelly awoke to a fog that seemed to hold a gray, damp, mournful threat, but she was up early and out with a set purpose in mind. She needed to leave London for a while, to let a country breeze ruffle her hair, to smell country air and rest her eyes on the English landscape. She longed for a sense of renewal, a perception that she had some control over her life.

Her rented Rover proved to be smooth and powerful, although driving on the left side of the road took some getting used to. As to the gearshift, her left hand seemed to have developed a mind of its own, and a forgetful one at that.

She followed the map to Oxford, arriving a little before noon. She had lunch at a small, crowded pub that served a favorite of hers, steak and kidney pie. She ordered a half and half, then played darts with several young men who flirted with her and offered to show her the ancient town.

She refused their offers with a twinkling smile, flattered and no longer feeling quite the antique she had upon disembarking at Heathrow the day before.

The fog hadn't lifted and kept the air wet as she made her way along worn cobblestones in the courtyard of Balliol College. Kelly knew why she had settled on Oxford for her day's outing. Tony had attended Balliol, and it seemed imperative that she see the place, to trace some moments of his life. Now that she was getting closer to losing him, she wanted, no *needed* a memory upon which to anchor her heavy heart.

Kelly had never believed in love at first sight. Yet she could no longer remember the moment when she didn't love him. Nor had she believed one could love only once, nor that there was only one road in life. Yet she knew now that she'd never meet another man like Tony. She was mourning a loss that hadn't quite happened but was as surely in her path as the steepled building ahead.

That was when she turned her back on the town, knowing she shouldn't have come, that she was peeking into a past to which she had no right.

On the leisurely ride back to London Kelly made a valiant try at fighting her depression. As the city drew nearer, she began to succeed somewhat. She knew and loved London and had spent many happy hours there. Along the way, she picked up some fish and chips, and when she returned to the house in Belgravia Square, she showered, then slipped into a warm jogging suit and sat cross-legged in front of the television, eating her dinner. Thoughts of New York, of Lambs, even of Isabella's problems, were neatly stored away under a file marked Hold in Abeyance. She was alone, and hardly anyone even knew she was in London. Such luxury had to be sinful.

Deep into a rerun of an American program she had never seen back home, Kelly jumped when the doorbell rang—three short blasts that were angry, insistent, even bossy, a sound that raised the hairs along her arms. She sat very still, her eyes closed against the flickering images on the screen, trying to calm her heavily beating heart.

The three short rings were repeated, and as she got slowly to her feet, Kelly knew only one person in the world would tap out such a message.

The front door was locked, chained, bolted, secure for the ages. She carefully undid each one and pulled the door open without even checking through the peephole.

Tony stood there, hair mussed, drops of moisture clinging to his raincoat from the damp night air. He looked tired and, more surprising, confused. In another moment Kelly felt a surge of joy so intense that it seemed her heart would expand and burst in her chest. She didn't care why he was there, just that he was, although payment would undoubtedly come due for her momentary happiness.

"Going to ask me in, or do we waltz out here?" he asked.

"Oh, my manners, forgive me." She gave a light laugh to cover her emotion. "Come in, Tony. It's just seeing you—"

"Left you speechless. I know." He went past her, tearing off his raincoat. "Can you make a strong cup of British tea?" He headed straight for the kitchen without asking where it was.

"How'd you know where to find me?" She followed him helplessly, not even questioning why he seemed to know the house.

"I spied your itinerary on Gail's desk. Did I tell you I passed upside down reading in my last year at university?"

She thought of her trip to Oxford and how she had come away filled with images but empty of memories. "On the honors list, as I remember. Tony, why are you here?"

He glanced around the kitchen, avoiding her eyes. He spotted the kettle, filled it with water and, only when it was sitting on a flame, did he answer her. "I came because suddenly New York seemed empty and deserted."

They stood several feet apart, Tony at the stove, Kelly holding on to the table for support. She needed every bit of help she could get to resist him. They were caught at both ends of a seesaw: if one dropped off, the other fell to the ground. The trouble was she could no longer trust any move he made. "Maybe the city *was* empty," she said at last. "It's summer, you know. For every tourist, ten citizens leave. It's the law."

"Is it the law that you can run out on me whenever the mood hits you?"

"You knew I was coming here."

"Why did you run out of Carnegie Hall the other night?"

"I was tired," she said. She faltered and couldn't answer his question directly.

"Go on."

"The kettle," she said. "It's boiling." She hurried for the teapot, put in tea and brought the pot over to him.

"Damn the tea," he said roughly, taking the pot and putting it down with a little crash. "Damn everything except you and me." He took her in his arms, and with his lips hard on hers, held her in a vise that grew tighter and tighter. She tried to tell him no, it couldn't be, that he was the most wonderful man she'd ever known but that they had no future together. Diane Bourne had said so, and Kelly had seen she was right. For him, women were conveniences until that day he'd marry one who was suitable—one picked and approved by his father.

Tony felt her resistance and let her go suddenly, his eyes flashing anger. "All right, out with it."

"You shouldn't have come here. Perhaps you ought to leave." She was fighting for breath as she turned and left the room. She was halfway to the front door when Tony came up behind her and swung her around, gripping her arms.

"Kelly." His voice softened. "What's wrong?" Then, after examining her for a long moment, he stepped back, as though satisfied that he had found the answer. "All right, I understand. It's about Palace, about the building, about your bloody job. You've been trying all along to mix up our personal lives with business and apparently can't separate them, don't want to separate them."

"Are you trying to tell me Terro doesn't mean everything to you?"

"That's a stupid question."

"And that's no answer."

"I'm not leaving, Kelly, any more than you want me to." He went into the library where she found him poking calmly into the bag of half-eaten fish and chips. The television set was still on, the sound turned low. "Like lonely evenings at home with television and a bag of fish and chips?"

"I like escaping from the pressures of my daily life, sure."

He took out a chip and stuck it in his mouth. "Too much vinegar."

Yes, she thought, too much vinegar, and he wasn't referring to the chip. She stared at the flickering pictures on the television screen, a blond family smiling around a kitchen table. Middle-class happiness with cheap, throwaway problems.

The trouble was that she had always reached for the stars. She'd been programmed that way, reached for them and won them, but now she wanted a star that was beyond her reach.

"Tony," she began just as he pronounced her name. With another step forward he had pulled her into his arms.

"I came halfway across the world to hold you in my arms," he said. "Don't spoil it." He covered her lips with his, and after that it didn't matter what Diane had said or even what the future held. Perhaps Kelly needn't even succeed in holding his love. The moment alone mattered. She couldn't let it go. She took his hand in hers and led him up the mahogany stairway to her room.

She had no idea how their clothes came off, only that they were naked, entwined under the sheets, crushing each other with kisses.

There was no time for languid, leisurely lovemaking; need was in every breath, every sigh and touch. She was ready for him, aching, pulsing, craving, scarcely aware of her nails digging into his flesh.

They caressed each other feverishly, kissing wildly. She barely heard his whispered words, only his hot breath on her mouth, her throat, her breasts, that made her blood rage like a fire in an autumn woods. She hurried him, wanting him in her, wanting him to take possession and never let go. She, for whom control was so necessary, was now burning out of control.

She angled herself under him, opening as the fire consumed them both and exploded in a burst of frenzied passion.

Then, just a little later, before he fell into a deep sleep, Tony murmured, "You're coming with me to Cornwall tomorrow."

She shook her head, but he didn't see the gesture.

THE NEXT DAY, Sunday, saw the lifting of the fog and
a warm sun that drew a long, bright wash over the
world. The Jaguar Tony drove took to the British
country roads like the sleek animal it was named after.

"Just the countryside, Tony," Kelly had cautioned
him over breakfast that morning. "I don't want to see
the old family home or meet your father or anyone
else."

His eyes had flickered visibly, but when he'd spo-
ken the tone was light. "I don't even want to share you
with the birds."

Once on the road, they didn't speak much, as
though silence would fill the gaps better than words.
Or perhaps because neither knew the right words to
say. They were treading on dangerous ground, tiptoe-
ing around problems that wouldn't go away despite the
love they had made. Occasionally, however, he would
take his hand from the wheel and touch her, as if the
contact were absolutely necessary. She slept part of the
way, reflecting that her sleep the night before had been
broken by demons telling her she was walking open-
eyed into disaster.

They stopped a hundred miles into the journey near
Salisbury for a picnic lunch, buying food at a local
market. They camped in a field bordered by a small
forest that appeared to delineate the line between two
farms. The weather was serene, without a cloud on the
horizon. From somewhere behind a hillock they heard
the soft mooing of a cow and the deep jangle of bells.

Kelly went to the top of the hillock where a ridge of
wild roses were still in bloom. Below, a herd of soft-
eyed black-and-white cows moved in the grass. Here-

fords? she wondered. And for a long moment she stared at them with fascination, as though she had never seen a cow before. Perhaps they weren't Herefords. Her ignorance of the country and things that belonged to the country was abysmal. She bent over the pink blossoms and took in the sweet, powdery aroma.

When she came back down, she found that he'd spread out the contents of their picnic basket: wine, cheese, bread and pastries. "Imagine! I've taken out time to smell the roses."

He filled a glass with wine. "Shall we toast a minor miracle?"

"If you'll call it a major miracle, sure."

"Here's to smelling the roses," he said, clinking his glass with hers.

They sipped their wine in silence. Then Tony's manner suddenly turned serious. "Mind telling me what put a bee in your bonnet about not wanting to meet my father?"

For a moment her heart sank. He'd asked the one question she dreaded hearing. She sat for a long while without answering. "I didn't come to England to be seduced by the land," she said at last, "nor the atmosphere, the people or personal relationships. The truth is, I came away from what was beginning to be too stifling an atmosphere. I need time to take stock and think, that's all. I don't want any new impressions that are going to interrupt my pattern of thought. I just want to establish contact with myself and my priorities. Does that make sense?" she added lamely.

"I had no idea you needed a reordering of your priorities."

"Just what do you think you've done to me on a personal and professional level?"

"And that's why you ran away? To escape my clutches?"

She turned and tentatively touched his hand. "Oh, Tony, let's not think for today. I hadn't counted on seeing you, being with you, and here you are. Let's just picnic and look at the sea and—"

"Make love."

"And not visit your old homestead or your father, and we'll worry later about how the day will end."

"I don't think I'm worried about that," he told her. After a moment's silence, he said, "I think you'd find my father rather an interesting character."

"I'm not looking for him," she said quietly.

He ignored her remark. "He's quite impressive. Even when I was very small, the possibility that I might displease him sent me into a state."

"I'm afraid you've just described my father to a T."

"Sebastian and I have different mothers, you know."

She took a sip of tea and heard the soft mooing sound again and the tinkle of a cowbell, as though they were musical accompaniments to her thoughts. "He isn't very much like you, is he?"

"Lord, I hope not," he said with a laugh. "Sebastian's mother came from a neighboring estate, an only child and heiress to a large fortune. She married my father when she was quite young. One day, when Sebastian was scarcely more than a baby, she left him behind and ran off with her lover, who happened to be the manager of the estate."

"And your mother?"

"Ay, there's the rub, Kelly. My father has a fatal fascination for women who are bound to treat him roughly."

She thought once again of Diane's words, of how both father and son were married to Terro.

"She stepped into the picture just long enough to produce me. Poor Sebastian. He thought he'd at last found a proper mother, and then she left for Australia. My father brought us up and had the good sense not to marry again."

"What's she like, your mother?"

"Nice. I didn't meet her until I was twenty-one and made my first trip Down Under. She's fun-loving, irreverent, and totally self-absorbed. She must have amused my father at first. I suppose his bearing, his manner, his credentials impressed her. All the signs were right for a good marriage except the most important one—a deep, abiding love."

Kelly gazed up at the sky. High above, beyond a wheeling hawk, was an airplane heading west, a shining, silent winged creature.

"She runs a guest house in Sydney," Tony went on. "A rather posh place. And she's still a beautiful woman with an eye for men. I believe she set herself up in business because she knew my father would disapprove."

"Does he disapprove of women in business?"

"Running a boarding house? Almost as bad as running a bawdy house in his books." Tony smiled. "Let's go," he said, reaching out and pulling her up. "I want you to see the land where I grew up."

"TONY, YOU'RE NOT—"

"I'm afraid I am."

"But you promised . . ."

"I promised no such thing."

Kelly stared in dismay at the pale yellow stone manor house that stood high above the deep gray sea. Gazing out to the moors that cut a path to the water, Kelly thought she could hear the echoes of centuries of ships caught in a sudden gale or on the jutting rocks. Though a warm sun burned down, she thought the place seemed to exude a chill of its own, particularly because half the building was charred and in near ruin.

"Burnt in the seventeenth century," he said, noting her curiosity. "I used to play among the ruins when I was a child, letting my imagination run wild."

"Sort of reminds me of a certain slag heap outside the town where I grew up. We used to go there to play. The town fathers talked of turning the place into a park, but it never happened, at least not while I lived there."

"I wish you'd stop throwing your privileged childhood up to me, Kelly. I refuse to be impressed." He pulled the car up at the front entrance. "Welcome to Campbell Hall."

Welcome, indeed. As Tony held the door for her, Kelly hesitated a moment before stepping out. He couldn't be playing a game to amuse himself. Diane was wrong about Tony. He was warm and dear and was inviting her home to meet his father.

The door opened to the manor house and a gray-haired man rushed to greet them. "Sir, welcome home."

"Radley, this is Miss Aldrich. She'll be staying with us for a couple of days. Is my father here?"

"He went out about an hour ago but said he'd be back about now." The butler then turned to Kelly and gave her a welcoming smile of unexpected sweetness.

It was clear Tony's father expected them. For the first time that day she felt truly relaxed.

"Oh, and, Radley, we'll have tea in the garden room," Tony said. He reached for Kelly's hand. "Come along. There are no monsters around. I promise you."

They entered a huge central hall constructed of stone with an immense fireplace at one end. "That fireplace is as big as my first apartment," Kelly said.

"The house was built four hundred years ago when they hadn't quite perfected central heating."

"There wasn't perfect central heating in my first apartment, either." In spite of the warm weather the house exuded a decided chill. Kelly rubbed her arms. "Nothing wrong with the air-conditioning."

"Just the shades of a couple of dozen family ghosts at their annual gathering. Don't let them bother you. Let's see if we can't find a little warmth in the garden room. If not, I have a foolproof way of heating you up."

"No, I'm fine," she said hastily. "It was just that swarm of ectoplasm we swam through back there."

The garden room was long and narrow. Through its floor-to-ceiling mullioned windows was a view of a sloping lawn and the sea beyond.

The room was filled with plants and worn, flowered chintz sofas and chairs. It had a pleasantly seedy country air to it and seemed precisely right for an elderly English bachelor who needed one comfortable room in his house. Fireplaces at either end were cold, but the room wasn't cold and was lit by the deepening sun's rays.

"We'll warm the cockles of your heart with a nice spot of tea," Tony said, leading her over to a couch and sitting down beside her. "Sorry you came?"

"Ask me again after we meet your father."

"Kelly, you and he are going to get along splendidly. Trust me."

"Anthony." The voice from behind was forbidding, deep and resolute.

Tony got quickly to feet. "Ah, Father." His first uninhibited and excited smile changed at once to something more reserved. Kelly turned and found coming toward her a tall, exceedingly handsome man, an older, more severe image of his younger son. Without even realizing it, she sprang to her feet, as though upon command.

"Father, this is Kelly Aldrich," Tony said, keeping his expression distant. She noted the way they shook hands before Tony made his introduction; they might have been casual acquaintances, meeting on a street somewhere. Then she found herself staring into deep blue eyes that held not a drop of warmth nor tenderness, certainly none of his son's humor. She put her hand out and he grasped it.

"How do you do, Miss Aldrich." A small curve to his lip indicated an attempt at smiling. "It's a pleasure to meet you."

His touch was cold, his handshake without friendly pressure. Kelly had the distinct impression that he had just lied to her.

CHAPTER FIFTEEN

"TONY, where are we heading?"

"They know the way."

The dappled mare Kelly rode, was gentle and sure-footed. Tony's roan stallion, ordinarily frisky, kept protectively close, nuzzling the mare, pushing and directing it. The sun in a bright, clear late-afternoon sky highlighted each crag along the moors that edged the sea, each stone and boulder, each blade of grass and wheeling bird. The weather was warm, almost tropical, interrupted in bursts by gusts of chill wind that fanned around them as though hurrying them along.

"Happy?" Tony asked.

"Very, though the truth is I'm not certain what I expected," she said.

"What did you think you'd find? A fine mist over the moors and dark, brooding horsemen ready to sweep up unsuspecting women and drag them back to their castles?"

"I was thinking about your father, Tony." She realized she had touched a nerve when she saw him stiffen.

"Does my father make you nervous?" he asked.

"He is rather formidable."

"Don't let his manner put you off, Kelly. Mark it down to traditional British reserve with strangers. He'll warm up."

I doubt that, Kelly thought. It would take a heat unknown on earth to warm that man up. He certainly wasn't about to thaw out over the American his son had brought home.

"You'll see," Tony remarked, as though he understood what she was thinking.

"I'm sure," she said without conviction. "Just nerves on my part, nothing more. And that unexpected wind. It's chilly and not nearly playful enough."

"Come on." Tony prodded his horse. "I'm going to show you a bit of the historical Cornwall. We take our myths seriously here. Sites associated with King Arthur are pointed out with a great deal of reverence, much as you do in the States with sites associated with George Washington—places where he once slept and so forth."

"But King Arthur was a myth," Kelly said. "George Washington was real. After all, our history as a nation is a short one and extensively surveyed by eyewitnesses."

"And here, in Cornwall, the line between myth and history is fudged. The myths contain a lot of history, and the history a lot of myth. There was a warrior, possibly a Cornish chief, who fought the Saxon kings at the end of the fifth century. Out of his exploits the myth of King Arthur was developed and embellished through the centuries, For instance, the story of Tristan and Isolde. It dates from about the twelfth century, and somewhere along the line was incorporated into the Arthurian legends.''

"Oh, I remember that one well enough," Kelly said. "Tristan was bringing Isolde back to Cornwall as a bride for King Mark, only someone slipped them both a love potion, and those two kids weren't ever the same."

Tony gave her a wry, fond grin. "Anybody slipped you a love potion lately?"

Felt like it last night at the house in Belgravia, she thought, but the clarity of a sunny day told her to keep all her senses intact. She would need every last one of them.

They rode along silently for a while, Tony's horse leading. The land split into a gorge. They took the zigzag path down, crossed a stream, swollen from recent rains, and slowly mounted the other side. In a while they spotted an ancient fortress high on the moors overlooking the sea. The late-afternoon sky turned a pale blue almost bordering on white. As they came closer, Kelly discovered the building was in ruins. It looked like a surrealist sculpture, with towers and windows opening upon the vast and solitary landscape.

Tony drew his horse up and Liz came alongside him. She had watched him from a distance, seeing him enter a world that was alien to her. He leaned over the saddle and kissed her, as if he wanted her to share that world.

"Shall we explore on foot?" he asked.

"Love to."

They dismounted and tethered their horses. "This way," Tony said, taking her into the courtyard of the ruin, which was filled with rubble and dust.

"Do you know where you're going?" she asked, scampering after him over the fallen stones.

"Like the back of your hand."

"King Arthur country?" she asked.

"If you look close, you'll see a sign that says King Arthur slept here."

She was seeing a boyish side that he'd kept hidden in New York. Even his speech had taken on a slower cadence. "You love these old places, don't you?" she asked.

"Yes, of course. They're part of my soul."

"Part of your soul?"

"You know, one of those things most of us come equipped with."

Do we come equipped with souls? she wondered. Looking up, she saw that clouds had suddenly appeared in the east, rolling swiftly toward the setting sun. She thought that moment was the most bittersweet of her life. She traced the feeling back to the instant she'd looked into the elder Campbell's eyes and seen the set of his mouth. She'd once thought she was in control of her fate but had learned better. Perhaps Sir Sebastian controlled his own fate. Clearly he determined the destiny of all those around him. Maybe she'd try to snatch Tony away from him under his nose. But the odds were decidedly against her.

"When we were small we spent a lot of time searching for Excalibur," Tony was saying. "Everywhere, every nook and cranny, every cave. Even now

I dream of discovering it, a gleaming blade in a rock, waiting for me to pull it free and conquer the enemy."

"Do you always search for something you have no hope of finding?"

"It's amazing what you find when you don't give up hope," he said softly. Then with a grin he added, "Just think of me as a knight in shining armor. Have you ever been made love to among the spirits of ancient kings and lost legends?"

She shook her head, fighting the warning that slithered down her spine. She looked over to the horses and found them contentedly feeding. The sun hovered above the water, as if reluctant to take the final dip toward night. The magic of the scene was working its spell, and when she turned back to Tony, she found him watching her, his gaze smoky.

He reached out and took her hand, then drew her up. He grabbed the saddlebag, removed a blanket and led her through the remains of an old wall that was overgrown with vines. He brought her along a path and under a weathered terrace, then across a small stream. They came upon an archway half open to the sky where stone steps led to a tiny square of soft, thick grass. A gnarled and ancient tree stretched powerful leafy limbs toward them. Tony set the blanket down and silently took her into his arms. They both sank to the ground.

"What if someone comes?" she managed as his lips closed over hers.

"I'm the only one who knows this place, Kelly."

"What if—" He closed her mouth with his lips. With quick, deft touches he had their clothes off, then wrapped the blanket around them. "Cold? I have every intention of keeping you warm, you know."

She reached up and pushed his hair from his eyes. "I don't remember complaining." She held him, listening at first to his labored breathing, feeling the pounding of his heart as it kept time with hers. She gathered him close, clinging with a fastness that astounded her. She lost all sense of time and place. The clouds traveled rapidly across the sky; the sun still held suspended above the water. The sensation of being one with the elements, earth, water and sky, sent their lovemaking soaring.

Their mouths held fast as his body moved over her, laying claim, possessing, demanding, as though expressing the need to connect at all points. Warm flesh pressed against warm flesh.

Neither moved when it was over, aware that a moment both strange and wonderful held them. With light, heated whispers Tony enclosed her in his arms and buried his face in her hair.

"Think the sun will ever set?" she asked sleepily.

"We have extraordinary twilights."

"Still, it's a long way back to your castle." She sat up and reached for her clothes.

He drew his finger down the length of her back. "You're beautiful. Do you know that?" His voice was hushed.

She bent to kiss him. "We still have a long way to go."

He laughed and made a playful grab for her. "So we do, but not in the way you meant." His lips found hers. Then, before their lovemaking grew serious again, he stopped, looked at his watch and let out an expletive.

"Well, thanks a lot," Kelly said. She reached once again for her clothes.

"Sebastian and Patricia are on their way down from London. They'll be arriving for dinner."

"Oh, Tony." She felt her heart sink. *Patricia*. She knew nothing about the woman but Diane's few words. Patricia, who had been selected for Sebastian by his father.

"I'm sorry I forgot to tell you," he said. "They like to take stock of the place every so often, counting the silver, et cetera. Patricia is redecorating, incidentally, turning the clock back, so to speak."

"Turning the clock back? Whatever for?"

"She has a passion for restoration, and my father has given her a blank check to bring back the past, polish the crest, so to speak, turn on the Campbell history spigot."

"You go for that kind of thing," Kelly said. "It matters, doesn't it?"

"If you've got it," he said, giving her a sideways glance, "why not flaunt it?"

"Yes, of course, why not?" She looked at him, suddenly feeling as if she had been led into a trap, warned too late to escape.

"MADAM?" A servant materialized at her side, holding a silver platter containing partridge and browned potatoes, with delicately prepared, thin string beans forming a frame around them. Kelly helped herself to a spare serving, reflecting that the scene in the small, paneled dining room was enough to curb her appetite. They sat around an oval table with the head of the family at one end and Patricia at the other. Kelly sat next to the elder Campbell, with Tony on her right side and Sebastian opposite. The atmosphere, in fact, seemed to hold the same chill as the old house.

"Lambs. Where did the name Lambs come from?" Patricia Campbell fixed Kelly with an interested eye. She was a tall, thin woman, with a long, narrow nose and dark hair pulled severely back and tied with a black ribbon. She wore the habitual bewildered expression of a person who'd been awarded a prize only to have it yanked away. "Has it been in your family long? The store, I mean, not the name," she added with a self-deprecating laugh.

"If so, I'm afraid my family wasn't apprised of the matter," Kelly said. Marriage to Sebastian had done nothing for Patricia's self-image, Kelly supposed.

"Of course," Patricia said, "you were the woman who single-handedly turned Lambs around. Sebastian's told me all about you."

"She exaggerates, as usual, don't you, my dear?" Sebastian said. "Not about your success with Lambs," he added hastily to Kelly. "I explained you run a tight ship and have everyone's respect."

"Of course, dear, that's what I meant," Patricia said with an apologetic little laugh somewhat like a cough.

Kelly watched the interplay between husband and wife and marveled at the elder Campbell's awful silence. She was being made painfully aware of how the scions of the establishment conducted themselves away from the rarified climate of Terro.

Plates of condiments occupied the center of the table between heavily ornate silver candelabra. The design on the bases of the candelabra were becoming familiar to her now. It was the same design she'd seen on Sebastian's tie in New York, the same design ensconced on the various fireplaces and furnishings around the manor house: with one foot on a snake, another upon a boar, a dragon reared its head in victory.

She took a sip of the excellent wine, hoping it would relax her, make her less nervous of Sir Sebastian Campbell, whose silent presence dominated the table. He had a talent for rendering one impotent, she decided, a lethal power that kept everyone avoiding his glance.

"Does the crest have any special meaning?" she asked Tony.

"Carpe diem," Sebastian said a little impatiently. "Don't you see the banner above the dragon's head?"

"Seize the day," Tony said. "The motto by which Terro lives."

"And the name Terro?" Kelly asked.

"Terro, like *terra*," Sebastian said. "Earth, real estate. Quite simple, really."

"No, I believe Terro was named after grandfather's mistress," Tony said. "There was such a trade with Italy once upon a time, and enough wrecks of Italian ships to these shores to change the faces of the land forever. And the names, too. Our late grandfather was the last in the line of fun-loving Campbells."

"Tony, the story's apocryphal, and I wish you'd stop telling it," his father said.

"Mea culpa," Tony said to Kelly. "You'll find that on the crest, too."

There was a little clatter of noise as Sir Sebastian put his knife on his plate. Tony had apparently gone too far. Kelly hastened to fill in the uncomfortable silence that followed.

"Are you familiar with New York?" she asked Patricia.

"I go there once in a very great while," Patricia said, casting a glance at her husband. "Sebastian prefers to travel alone on business trips," she added with an awkward laugh. "He says I distract him."

"New York is the most distracting place in the world," Kelly said, trying to save the other woman embarrassment. "It's all one can do to concentrate on the matter at hand." She was talking irrelevancies.

"And so Mr. Solow plucked you out of graduate school," Sir Sebastian said suddenly, as though their conversation had gone on a long time. "He says you fulfilled his every expectation." His comment had a nuance, an underlying suggestiveness that set her on edge.

"I'm glad he feels that way. He taught me the business and then handed me the reins when he thought I was ready."

"And you have negative feelings about Terro's plans."

Kelly glanced at Tony, hoping for a clue about how to respond, but he was watching his father. She wasn't certain whether or not the man was baiting her, trying to provoke an argument, but she wasn't about to be drawn in. A small cough caught her attention. Two servants stood at attention near the door, their chins raised toward the ceiling, their eyes fixed glazedly at some distant point. She imagined they had been witness to some major squabbles in the room.

"Father, let's save this kind of talk for some other time," Tony said. "I didn't invite Kelly here to discuss Lambs or Terro."

"You realize she's going to be an obstacle," Sebastian said, as though Kelly weren't at the table, "if she persists in that business with the Preservation Society."

Tony's voice held the same coldness as his father's. "I run the international operation, Sebastian. Totally."

Including me, Kelly thought, including me. She wondered what kind of fool she was to have opened the door to him in London, to have come with him to Cornwall and to have let him make love to her.

"Perhaps Sebastian is better able to acquaint her with the benefits of cooperating with us," the elder Campbell began. Obviously he'd brought up his sons to compete, not only with the rest of the world, but with each other.

"Come on, Kelly," Patricia said with a nervous laugh. "Let me show you the rest of the house, and leave the men to their squabbles and cognac."

Kelly got to her feet quickly. "Yes, yes, of course, thank you."

Patricia took Kelly's arm in a loose fashion, talking quickly and with enthusiasm, although Kelly heard her words as though from a long way off.

"This is the smaller dining room. The Shelby Room is used for banquets and balls. I'm in the process of redecorating now."

"Patricia has taken courses in restoration, haven't you, my dear?" Campbell's voice revealed a softer tone as he gave his daughter-in-law a cold smile. "Do show Miss Aldrich our world."

Kelly, without a backward glance, followed Patricia from the room. Damn the man, she thought. Every word he spoke was calculated to let her know she wasn't one of them. She had met mildly insensitive characters who'd stomp all over people, smiling benignly, unaware of the debris in their wakes. But Sir Sebastian Campbell was of a far different cut. His method was deliberate, calculated to make her run with her tail between her legs.

"Of course I'm dying to live here full-time," Patricia was saying. "Sebastian doesn't mind the commute, but I detest it. I'm a country girl at heart. I could do wonders with the place if I had the time."

"Why don't you move, then?"

"Good heavens, Sebastian won't allow it. He prefers London, even though Campbell Hall will be his eventually."

"But I suppose your father-in-law must be lonely," she ventured. "All those years rearing his sons alone."

"Good Lord, he's seldom alone here. And he interferes in our lives entirely too much as it is," Patricia said in a slow voice. She stopped in the hall and picked up a silver urn. "I think I'll have to get after the servants," she said. "I can't abide tarnished silver."

AT MIDNIGHT, far in the distance, chimes sounded the hour. Black mist rolled over the land like galloping ghosts. Sitting at her window, Kelly listened to the creaks and moans of the house as it sank deeper into the night. The curtain moved in the breeze. She thought of how she would like to escape the night, to flee back to London and the safety of the house in Belgravia Square. She wasn't able to fathom Tony's motives for bringing her to Cornwall. He'd made love to her as though she mattered, but afterward had set her loose among the cannibals. Perhaps he was testing her mettle, seeing how she'd survive his loathsome family. Suddenly she longed for her own, dear, warm brothers. She lived far apart from them through circumstances, not desire, through pursuit of their respective dreams, American style, as decreed by their father. But no competition had ever developed between them, only abiding love.

She had excused herself after coffee, claiming that she was tired. Once in her room, however, Kelly had found she couldn't sleep, couldn't even shut her eyes, and instead found herself replaying the dinner scene over and over, concluding that even Tony was outdistanced by his father.

She thought perhaps he might come to her, but one by one she heard good-nights outside her door, heard footsteps going down the corridor and doors slamming until at last she was certain the house had simply closed in upon itself. And Kelly was glad Tony hadn't come, even though the night stretched ahead and sleep eluded her.

After a while she reached for her robe and the flashlight that sat on the guest table. She made her way through the darkened house to the library with the intention of finding a book to read. She needed to soothe the edges that the senior Campbell had frayed.

She entered the book-lined room and turned on a desk lamp with a green glass shade. The library was cold, although embers still glowed in the fireplace, so she held her hands over them, hoping to capture some heat.

Lithographs and tinted prints in antique burled elm frames were hung along the window wall. Floor-to-ceiling shelves held hundreds of leather-bound books. She ran her finger along the spines, checking titles, occasionally pulling a book out and glancing through its pages, at last settling for a thick volume entitled *British Poets of the Nineteenth Century*.

An ancient afghan had been thrown over the sofa, and when Kelly sat down, she reached for it, discovering too late that a file was half hidden in the folds. The file slithered off the sofa onto the floor, spilling its contents. Kelly scrambled to the floor and began gathering the scattered papers, pushing them back into the folder. She stopped only once to gaze at a familiar logo on buff-colored stationery. Solow Enterprises. Gregory's familiar, flamboyant signature was at the base of the letter.

Intrigued, her eye slipped over the contents of the letter. "I have no quarrel with the two percent of Terro that I now own," she read, "but I'm a little discouraged over the clause in the contract that prohibits me from disclosing my association with Terro." She closed the folder and was just about to put it down when she heard a sound at the door.

"Find anything of interest, Miss Aldrich?"

She looked back to find Sir Sebastian standing there, still dressed in his formal dinner clothes. She hastily put the folder back on the couch. "I tipped the

whole business over when I reached for the afghan,"
she explained, stuttering her apology and knowing he
didn't believe her. "I'm afraid I couldn't sleep."
Whirling in her head was the news she had just learned
about Gregory, news that explained his lack of interest in what happened to Lambs. He was, after all, part
and parcel of Terro, with a sizable interest in the corporation.

"And in a room lined with the classics you found
some dull business correspondence more to your lik-
ing."

"I'm sorry," she said quietly. "I really did knock
the folder over. The truth is, I read part of a letter
from Gregory Solow, and frankly it answered a question for me."

"I see." He came into the room and picked up the
folder, then advanced with it to his desk where he
placed it in a drawer. "And what question was that?"

"Why he was so uninterested in the fate of Lambs."

"And now you know."

"Yes. He was bought for two percent of Terro. I
feel a bit betrayed."

Campbell sat down behind his desk. His face was
molded into strong planes by the shaded light, outlin-
ing the strength and purpose that was such a natural
part of him. She just wished he were on her side.

"I'm afraid Gregory Solow had his reasons for not
wanting you to know he was part of the corporation," he told her. "But we aren't hiding anything.
Gregory Solow was given an opportunity to make a
very great profit and still have a minority say in the
company that bought out his interests. A case of hav-

ing his cake and eating it, too." He studied her for a long time.

"I never really thought he liked cake that much," Kelly said wistfully.

"You're a very bright and witty young woman," he said. "I wonder if you can't be tempted in some way to step away from Lambs."

"I'm sorry," she said. She was about to leave when she thought, no, she wouldn't be harassed, especially not by her reluctant host. "You don't like me, do you?" she asked as matter-of-factly as she could.

He gave a dry laugh and ran his hand along his chin. His eyes darkened. She felt his gaze almost reach under her robe to touch her flesh. "On the contrary I like you immensely, but not as a wife for my son. It's nothing personal, I assure you," he said. "If I thought you were just another woman in my son's life, I wouldn't react to you at all."

She closed her eyes for a second and let the joy wash over her. Tony loved her. The notion gave her added strength. Yet she knew that the battle with his father was far from over, and if Tony truly wanted her, it was a fight he'd have to wage all by himself. She wished fervently that he would, but understood the power of his adversary.

"Sebastian thought his brother was a little too taken with you," Campbell went on. "You've never made any bones about who you are and where you come from."

"Does Sebastian spy on his brother all the time?"

"In my business people report things of interest to me. My oldest son, others. There was that incident of a pool in someone's apartment on Central Park South.

I believe you stayed the night with Tony at the Carlyle.''

"Was it Diane?" she asked quietly.

"Diane Bourne can be managed," he said. "My concern is that you can't. My sons will inherit Terro, and frankly I want nothing to go wrong. Terro is my life and my sons are my life."

"And I come from the wrong side of the tracks and haven't got personal wealth," she said.

He didn't answer her, merely offering her a cold smile of acknowledgment.

"I'm afraid one's antecedents aren't of much interest to most Americans," she said, the heat rising to her face. She felt no need to defend her family, rather a latent dose of pride about them suffused her bones. "As a matter of fact," she added, "we admire individual accomplishment above everything."

"Oh, we appreciate individual accomplishment," he said. "Which is why we hope you'll stay on with us. It may take time, but perhaps you'll learn to understand the abyss that stands between you and my son."

"There is no abyss," she said, "except in your imagination. I'm really very sorry," she added, but let her voice drop away. No, she was sorry about nothing. When she next spoke, she had to strive to keep her voice from cracking. "Then I'll wish you good night." They were the hardest words she had ever had to say, because she was not only taking leave of his father, she was also saying goodbye to Tony. At the door, however, she turned back. "I'm not, you know. Wrong for your son."

But she saw from the smile on his face that he understood his power. And she well understood the potency of a father's ambition for his children. Tony was under his father's influence, whether he'd admit it or not. Of one thing she was certain, she had stepped into mined territory and didn't want to walk gingerly around the little explosions that would keep occurring. In the world where the Campbells held sway, love obviously held very little value.

When she reached her room, Kelly began to pack, holding back the tears, feeling an emotion so naked that it didn't bear examining.

It was clear to her that Sebastian Campbell, Senior, was the real power behind Terro, and she suspected she'd lost her job as well as Tony. One thing Kelly had learned early on was the impersonality of life in the stratosphere. Her contract with Solow Enterprises hadn't guaranteed her future into infinity. It only gave her a little bargaining power for a little while.

Gregory had sold Solow. She was part of the merchandise, and if Terro wanted to dispose of old goods, they would. She'd come away solvent—there would be other jobs—and the only spot damaged would be her heart. A little repair work, the application of some glue and paint, and it would work as good as new.

She'd order a car in the early-morning hours to take her to the airport, away from the lord of the manor and the power he held over the man she loved.

CHAPTER SIXTEEN

"VICTOR ALDRICH."

"Hi, big brother."

"Hey, Kelly!" Where are you calling from? L.A. airport, I hope."

"Nope, New York. How are you doing, Vic?"

"I'm fine. It's wonderful to hear from you, Kel. About time you called, too."

"You now, you could call once in a while," Kelly said. She pretended annoyance, but the supreme happiness she felt upon hearing her brother's warm, loving voice took the edge off the depression she had felt ever since leaving Cornwall. The call was one she needed to make, although she knew she couldn't discuss Tony with him, not from that distance, not just out of the blue. Vic's usual advice was that she was too good for whoever had momentarily broken her heart.

"I know, I know," Vic was saying, "the phone works two ways, but there's always that three hours' difference between California and New York. By the time I decide to call you, I figure you're in bed asleep."

"Funny, it's six in the evening," she said, keeping her tone light. "I've just come in from Britain and here I am, calling you first thing. Ah, me, you're the same old Vic. No wonder you're such a successful lawyer."

"Kelly," he said after a brief silence, "I'm not sure I like the way you sound. I think the description is *faintly lugubrious*. You were never very good at hiding your emotions. Something wrong?"

"No, not really," she answered with a sigh. "As I said, I just arrived on these shores and I've had a sudden, incredible urge to talk to you and somehow make contact with my past."

"I think they call what's happening plain, old-fashioned jet lag."

"Not this time. I took the Concorde."

"Hey, I'm impressed with my baby sister. The Concorde stands for success with a capital *S*."

"I suppose it does, although I sprang for the tab myself."

"More power to you."

The tab for the flight had been large, but Kelly had picked it up without a second thought. She had become used to traveling first class, to being first class, to saluting her own success. Only she had been shot down on a remote corner of the English coastline. "I've been thinking a lot about Mom, too," she told her brother, "particularly her poems."

"Ah, yes, our poetic mother, the wraith who presided over breakfast every morning, not quite knowing how she'd burnt the toast."

"You're a brat, Vic Aldrich. She was a poet—unlike the rest of us who'd pursue the dollar to the ends of the earth."

"Hey, as far as I'm concerned, I've reached a pretty good end right here in California. Why don't you come out? There's a box of her stuff in the attic. We'll haul it down and have a poetry reading. Wine and cheese served to all comers."

"Vic, I know I really need to touch some bases, but what I'd like right now is for you to send the box to me by express. Frankly, I just want to sit in a quiet little corner and read her poetry all alone. I promise to get the whole works back to you."

"No problem," her brother said good-naturedly. "You can keep the stuff. Her poetry always meant more to you than to Jim and me. I'd rather touch base in person."

"So would I, big brother, and I promise we'll see each other soon. Now let's get on to the good stuff, like how's everything? Have you talked to Jim recently?"

When she hung up ten minutes later, Kelly felt a little more relaxed. She hadn't told Vic about any of her problems. He'd have been upset enough for the two of them, she supposed, and couldn't have helped, anyway. What she wanted now was a shower and an early night. She turned the sound low on her telephone and clicked in the answering device so that she could have it both ways. She hoped Tony would call, but didn't want to speak to him.

KELLY STOPPED at the door to Gail's tiny office and peered in. "Hi, how are you holding up?"

"Oh, jeez, Kelly, we've been worried. You take off with barely a word about your itinerary. You okay?"

She gave her assistant a smile. "Right as rain. Fill me in on everything I've missed. Oh, and here's a little present from the wars." She pulled a package from the Harrods shopping bag she carried.

"Oh, you wicked woman," Gail said upon discovering the rich confections the store was famous for.

"Well, that's something Harrods has that we don't. Come on, we've got work to do."

Kelly picked up her mail from her secretary, stopping long enough to present her with a gift from the same store. "Oh, and hold my calls," she said. "I don't care how important. I've got a backlog and a lot of catching up to do." Tony might call, from Cornwall, from London, perhaps even in-flight if he was coming back to the States. She still didn't want to speak to him about anything.

"Even Mr. Campbell, for instance?" her secretary asked. She clearly stood in awe of the CEO of Terro.

"Everyone."

When Gail came into her office with a scheduling book and two cups of coffee, Kelly was already at her desk, sifting through her mail. "I cancelled my appointments for today before I left," Kelly said without looking up. "Let's see if we can't activate a few of them for later this week. I'll want a staff meeting at noon, which we could pencil in for an hour. It'll kill everybody's luncheon plans, but that can't be helped. Better lay on coffee and pastry."

Gail nodded. "All your messages are in your incoming box in ascending order of importance. I handled the ones I could and explained to the others that you weren't due back until the end of the week. Something told me you weren't going to be ready to jump back into the rat race at once."

"Does it show on my face?" Kelly asked.

"No, just in the slump of your shoulders. Want to borrow mine to cry on?"

Kelly shook her head. "Keeping busy is the best revenge."

"Incidentally, there's this luncheon meeting with the board of Job-Up tomorrow noon. I said you couldn't make it."

"Call them and tell them to expect me. Isabella being a good girl?"

Gail's face exploded in a broad smile. "Teacher's pet. If she turns any more obliging, I'd say she had a lobotomy."

"Is that good?"

"I don't know. If she's scared, that's good. If she's decided not to fight the system, that's bad. We don't want to destroy the best part of her talent."

"I'll go down and see her later. While we're on the subject, fill me in on security. I feel as if I've been gone a year. Everything working?"

"On hold. We thought Mr. Campbell would be around, à la Gregory Solow, and he took off instead, leaving the store under the care of the merchandise manager, who wasn't about to tackle security."

"Okay, don't blame him a bit. If Mr. Campbell wants to turn us into a maximum-security prison, that's his business. Let's get to work." Work was best. Work kept you busy and your heart on hold.

They spent the morning clearing up her desk, skirting those issues that were potentially worrisome. She checked with her secretary for incoming calls three times. Several were important. None were from Tony. After her noon staff meeting, she had lunch alone in her office, handling what telephone messages she could. The day was speeding by, just the way she liked it to when she needed to keep from thinking. At four in the afternoon she took her usual tour of each department, starting on the top floor, chatting with office personnel, and as she made her way down, customers and salespeople.

When she reached the fitting room, she was surprised at the feeling of anticipation that bubbled through her. Off in the corner before a tripod mirror she found a familiar figure bent in front of a dress form fitted with a bright red gown with a flame hem.

"Isabella?"

The girl looked up and got quickly to her feet. "Oh, Miss Aldrich, hi." She flushed, backing up against the form.

"But, Isabella, you look so beautiful." She had cut and reshaped her hair so that it fell around her face like a cap. The colored spikes had been washed out and her natural color restored. She wore soft shades of lipstick and mascara. Her young, fresh complexion needed no other makeup. Tucked into a denim skirt that was cleverly worked with delicate silk flowers across the hem was a white silk shirtwaist blouse.

"I didn't know you were back," Isabella said shyly. "I was waiting for you."

This splendid young creature was more Tony's creation than hers. Longing to thank him, Kelly wished he were there. But all she could do was ask an empty question. "Is everything working out all right?"

"I think so."

"Well," Kelly said, stepping back and admiring her anew, "I'm really impressed. What's the problem with the dress?" She pointed at the gown the girl had been working on.

"Oh, the hem," Isabella said. "They call it a flame hem because it's like a flame, only the stitches are coming apart. You have to hand sew them. Miss Aldrich," she went on, "could you call my mother maybe sometime? She wants to thank you. I mean, about my hair and all. She doesn't know about the other stuff. I mean, Robbie got good and scared when Mr. Campbell made him give the jackets back.'' She put her hand to her mouth to hide her giggle. ''He doesn't want to see me anymore. He says I'm trouble.''

''Of course I'll call your mother.'' Kelly spontaneously hugged the girl. ''And maybe we can do something about those hems. You come and see me tomorrow and we'll see if we can't have you promoted to sleeves or something.''

Isabella giggled again. ''Sleeves. Oh, Miss Aldrich.''

Oh, Miss Aldrich, she thought as she left the fitting room. Miss Aldrich always had time for a funny word. Miss Aldrich was Miss Fix-it. Something was repaired that had been broken, something even more vulnerable than a heart. Isabella's grateful smile sent a thrill of accomplishment racing through her, a new feeling, one that kept her grinning as she headed through the dress department for the stairs.

Something odd was happening to her, and only when she reached the first floor did she understand. Nothing had changed. Lambs was still intact. Gremlins hadn't arrived in the middle of the night and turned the place into a giant discount supermarket. The atmosphere was as colorful and charming as ever, and as busy. The scent of perfume flowered the air with a lovely rose topnote. But something had changed nevertheless.

She went behind the counter displaying a new jewelry collection—Designs by Geri. ''How are they doing?'' she asked the salesgirl.

"Runaway bestsellers. People like them big and chunky, and these are so light on the ear."

The earrings were large and clever, each pair hand-made and witty. She picked up a pair and slipped it on in front of an oval mirror.

"Lovely," said the salesgirl admiringly.

Kelly thought the earrings transformed her, or was it her imagination? She looked like a young girl, not the president of a store who had forgotten how to live. She removed the earrings. "I'll take these. Put them on my charge, will you?" The thought struck her that she was getting ready to say goodbye, and the idea wasn't sending cold shivers down her back. In fact, what she felt was a quirky, perverse anticipation, as if she were about to make a leap into the unknown.

When she returned to her office, she went swiftly through her telephone messages. Tony hadn't called, although Mrs. Laurence had several times. It wasn't like the woman to check on a scheduled meeting, and Kelly had already confirmed she'd be there. She fidgeted over returning the call; the incident with Isabella had been played close to the vest, but she couldn't count out the possibility of a leak somewhere. If a scandal were imminent, Mrs. Laurence might quit the program, and everyone involved with hiring Job-Up kids would question its efficacy. She drew her arm across her brow. What in the world was she thinking, making lakes where there were only puddles?

"I'm so glad you're back," Mrs. Laurence said at once when she heard Kelly's voice. "You'll be happy to know we're rid of the pool."

Was that the reason for the phone call? She smiled. That evening with Tony seemed long ago and far away. "What about the goldfish?"

"The aquarium was happy to have them."

And a sizable donation, Kelly had no doubt. "What have you put in its place?"

"A marvelous miniature Japanese landscape. Lots of sand and rocks. *Wonderful* for contemplation."

"Safer, anyway," Kelly said. The longer they talked about pools, the farther away from Job-Up they'd be.

"Well, that's neither here nor there. You know, of course, that Tony called me and told me about Isabella Sanchez and the leather coats. These teenager girls nowadays," Mrs. Laurence went on before Kelly could put her thoughts into order, "they think they're in love and behave like perfect little idiots. But never mind her at the moment. I think we've been wrong about how we're handling the program, doing it piecemeal, I mean. We'll work this all out tomorrow, but I want you on my side, Kelly."

Kelly let out the breath she had been holding. "Go on."

"We have to approach these children in a *holistic* manner, so to speak—their schoolwork, their talent, the jobs they need, their home life, the works. You do agree?"

"Absolutely."

"We need a professional staff and a full-time administrator, and we'll leave fund-raising to our ladies who lunch. They're charming, they're enthusiastic, but a little inattentive to important details such as the psyche of the youngsters enrolled in the program. Now, my dear, what do you think of that?"

"If I had ten votes on the board, I'd give them all to you."

"One will be sufficient. I'm willing to sweeten the fund-raising drive with a sizable donation. I want you to think of where and how we'll go after professional staff and a first-class administrator. Promise me that."

"I'll promise you more than that. I promise personally to find you the best administrator in the world. See you tomorrow, Mrs. Laurence."

"And for heaven's sake, call me Edna. We've known each other long enough."

Hanging up, Kelly swiveled her chair around and let out a Texas yell that brought her secretary to the door. "Anything wrong?"

"Imagine having a real staff and working with the kids from the ground up, making them fully rounded human beings."

"I thought you had a real staff," her secretary said, nonplussed.

"Oh, it's wonderful!"

"Right." Her secretary raised her eyebrows, shrugged and disappeared quickly.

Imagine going to schools, Kelly thought, interviewing talented youngsters, seeing them through the system, working out their problems, watching them graduate and enter the work force as fully committed human beings.

Of course, with an administrator and full-time staff she realized her own role in the program would be somewhat diminished. She'd be relegated to fund-raising. Damn, why had she agreed so readily?

Her baby was growing up and leaving home and the thought was unexpectedly depressing. *Damn.*

She'd still organize all those fund-raisers at the Temple of Dendur, all those fashion shows, all those tables decorated by Manhattan Florists, then hand over the takings to some social worker. Her future was written out for her whether she worked for Lambs or

Palace or some other house. She'd help collect the money and turn over the best part of the program to some stranger.

"Hey, Pop, you were wrong," she said out loud. "You don't measure success by how much money you make, or where you last had dinner. Or those box seats at Carnegie. You measure it by accomplishment, by connecting with others and helping them grow. I might have loved being a social worker. Long live Lambs, but I'm beginning to believe it isn't for me, not anymore."

"Talking to yourself?" Gregory had opened her door without knocking and stood on its threshold. "Your secretary was away from her desk. You don't mind, do you, my barging in?"

"Not one bit," she said dreamily. "It's amazing how we're all expected to fulfill other people's dreams."

"You fulfilled mine."

"I was talking about my father. My mother paid a price for her dream. She might have been a successful poet if my father hadn't nipped her efforts in the bud."

"Don't try to rewrite history, Kelly." He sat down on the sofa, patting the cushion next to him as an invitation to join him.

Kelly came around from behind her desk, but instead of sitting next to him, pulled up a chair. "And if my father were here right now, I'd tell him he was a Little Caesar and I'd have no more of his lectures about making it in the real world."

"Kelly, can you come down off your soapbox? I'd like to talk to you about something."

"I know about it," she said in a crisp manner, coming back to earth, "the two percent reason why I received no cooperation from you on the matter of the building."

He ran his hand nervously along his beard, shifting in his seat like a little boy caught stealing apples from the supermarket. "How did you find out?"

"It doesn't matter. I just wish I'd known about your contract with Terro. I'd have been less hard on you."

"Kelly, I wish you had, too. I should've told you, anyway, and now I've come up with even more bad news. About the Preservation Committee. I had a talk with Francine Marshall. I'm afraid the wheels are going to grind too slowly to save the building. Kelly, even if my hands weren't tied, I couldn't have made the difference."

"We could always strap ourselves to the building when they come to tear it down," she said. "Make enough noise to embarrass Terro into the next century. But let's not talk about that. Tell me about you and Diane. Anything settled?"

Gregory didn't smile at the bluntness of her question. He didn't even appear to be uncomfortable with the subject, surprising her when he said, "I think we're going to take a trip together. See if we're really compatible."

"Smart idea."

"She's not at all like Suzanne," he said quietly.

"But she shouldn't be."

"I'm almost ashamed, but damn it, I'm willing to take a chance on being happy."

"Then do it, with no regrets."

He got up and came over to her, picking up her hand and kissing it. "Nonjudgmental Kelly. I appreciate that more than I can express. I miss you, miss this place.''

She smiled, scarcely able to keep back her tears. ''I miss you, Gregory. Nothing's the same, is it? I feel as if I'm teetering on the edge of wanting to stay and wanting to go, of caring about what happens under Terro and not caring. Do I make sense?''

''I think we call it the turning-thirty crisis. What about you and Tony Campbell? He dashed out after you when you left the concert the other night and came back looking a little dejected. After that soaking in Mrs. Laurence's pool and the way you dragged him off, I had the impression you two were—''

''We aren't.''

''No?'' He looked at her shrewdly.

''Gregory, when you sold your business was it because you wanted to take time out to smell the roses?''

''Smell the roses? Yes,'' he said, as if the idea were new to him. ''I suppose you could say that.''

''That time when you didn't show up at the Temple of Dendur? I mean, when we had the charity event for Job-Up? There was something so extraordinary in the air that night. Everything seemed a little haywire, dreamy, *different*. Tony blamed it on the blue moon. I ran away with him to Central Park and this incredible concert. And fireworks. And I thought about how I'd had no time to be young and crazy, and that I was missing everything, and that I didn't *have it all*, the way I thought I did. I've never even seen the Temple of Dendur without table settings in it for three hundred.''

''Quite nice,'' he told her. ''You must see it, then. I find it very mysterious and mind-clearing. If you concentrate, you can be transported back in time.''

"I could use a little time travel," she mused.

"The museum is open late tonight," he said. "Dr. Solow's cure for you is a visit, pronto. Would you like me to come with you and point out the sights?"

"Tonight. Yes," she said spontaneously. "I think I'd like that."

"At eight, then? That will give us about forty-five minutes to commune with the spirits before the museum closes."

"Fine. I think I'm going to take the museum in bits and pieces, not all at once. Eight it is, at the Temple."

"PACKAGE FOR YOU, Miss Aldrich," the doorman said when she came in a little after six that evening. "Came by express. It's a little heavy. Want me to bring it up?"

She saw her brother's familiar handwriting on the label. She hadn't expected the carton of her mother's poetry quite that quickly, but evidently Vic had caught the anxiety in her voice.

"No, I'll manage, thanks," she said, reaching for the carton as though it were something precious.

Once in her apartment with the door closed firmly behind her, she allowed the tears to form in her eyes. She ripped open the wrapping and came upon the tongue-in-groove wooden box Vic had made in grammar school.

She kicked off her shoes and carried the box into the living room, tucking herself into a corner of the sofa. She opened the box slowly, finding the cache of school notebooks in which her mother had written her poems. She reached for the top notebook and began searching it at once for her favorites.

"'An Hour in the Woods,'" she read out loud. "Oh, I remember this one." She turned around, fiddled with the sofa pillow so that it fitted more comfortably into the small of her back, and settled down to reading.

After an hour had passed, she stopped reading. The notebooks lay scattered around her on the couch. Kelly placed them back in the box and closed it securely.

Dear Mom, she thought. An hour in the woods, a walk on the beach, a sunset over the hill, the design in a fall leaf. Christmas arriving once a year. All the time Kelly had believed her mother to be a poet on the order of Emily Dickinson. As a little kid, being read a poem at bedtime was all the beauty she'd needed. She saw now that her mother's lovely, slanted script revealed nothing more than rather simple, innocuous poetry without originality or artistic flair. Just sweet little poems to entertain one's daughter before bedtime.

How sad, she thought. What a sad discovery to find her mother wasn't special, merely a dreamy creature who had chosen not to face reality and always burnt the toast.

Burnt toast and poetry at bedtime.

Kelly got up and made herself some tea and toast, unburned, but then Kelly was a model of efficiency. She was her father's daughter, after all.

She went back into the living room and watched the evening news without quite hearing it. Her mind was on her father and how she had possibly misunderstood his motives. She thought now that he'd been protecting her mother from ever finding out that she never *could* be published, letting her blame him for his callousness. He had sacrificed honesty so that she could have her dream.

It was a theory, of course, one she'd have to discuss with her brothers. Right now her father's actions seemed plausible. But then again, maybe her mother *was* something special. Kelly was judging by the word *success* again. Success was a lot of things, none of which had to do with the ordinary reading of the word.

Her mind reeled with how she'd have to reorder her thinking. Only right now she had a date with Gregory. She rushed to get ready, wondering if she'd tell him about her discovery.

One should always have a dream, not a father's dream, but one's own. And what was hers? Her mind slipped to Isabella and Isabella's talent. She thought of Lambs and the charming building the store inhabited—a building that was about to come crashing down. She thought of Designs by Geri and all the kids she'd helped along with their careers. She thought of that unknown social worker who would become administrator of Job-Up. And of how everything was coming to an end for her.

AN EXHIBITION of French Impressionists on the second floor drew most of the visitors to the museum at that time of night. The walk through the Egyptian exhibit to the Temple of Dendur in the outer reaches found only a sprinkling of people gazing intently into glass cases. Her heels clicked eerily on the stone floor as she made her way, the quiet echo the only sounds in the vast, high-ceilinged rooms. Once she passed into the sacred precincts, the atmosphere changed. The ancient edifice, seen in the reflecting pool, was lit by lights carefully angled to reveal its shadowy majesty. And just rising in a pale early-evening sky was the moon, which had gone through all its phases since she had last been there and was now once again white and swollen—the second full moon of the month.

Gregory hadn't arrived. She stood alone, deep in contemplation, transported back to a time when life was defined in simpler terms. When she heard footsteps approach, she started, almost sorry she had agreed to meet Gregory there.

She spun around and found Tony coming toward her, carrying a bouquet of wild roses and a bottle of Dom Perignon. The rhythm of her heart took several leaps before settling down. She had believed he was gone from her life forever. "How did you—?"

"Gregory sends his apologies. He called me. Said you needed to smell the roses."

She took the roses and buried her nose in the blossoms and inhaled the powdery fragrance. "No thorns."

"Had them surgically removed. You know, don't you, that I can solve all your problems?" He bent over and placed his lips against her cheek in a brief kiss.

"You're not my problem, Tony. You never were. Not you, not Terro, not that old temple of a building standing on Fifty-seventh Street."

"You should never have left Cornwall," he said. "You're going to have to learn to trust me."

"Did your father tell you he found me riffling through his papers? It wasn't true, except that I had a glimpse of Gregory's note."

"He told me. He also told me you're a bundle of dynamite, the kind the Campbell clan should stay away from. Both of his wives packed your kind of dynamite, he told me, and he's still reeling from the experiences. I think he wants to save me from you before the going gets rough. I told the old reprobate to mind his own business."

"I thought you were a good and obedient son."

"I am. Once upon a time I would have even let him choose my wife because, back then, I didn't think it was such a big choice. Now I know better. And it's love that chooses us, not the other way around."

"I thought you followed your father's ideas the same as I've followed my father's program. No questions. You just follow orders. I wonder," Kelly said after a moment, "what you would've thought of my father. He was the rough-and-tumble sort and ambitious for us. He didn't want me to turn into a clone of my mother, but now I realize why. He didn't want us to go chasing after dreams that had no hope of coming true. He believed in the concrete, a future you could all but feel, touch and smell. He wanted us to excel, because he was afraid for us."

"And you accomplished what he thought was important," Tony said.

"Yes, but now I'm going to do what I think is important."

He put a hand to her lips. "Kelly, know what the champagne is for?"

"Terro sold another building or bought another building or tore another building down."

"We're going to keep the building intact and build up and around it. Palace has bought Lambs and will use the space as its flagship store. You're going to be able to name your price with them."

"That's wonderful about not taking the building down and keeping the integrity of the store, but I'm changing the rules midstream,'' she said. ''The price is breaking my contract. I've just taken an administrative post with Job-Up. Of course, Mrs. Laurence doesn't know it yet. No one does. I hardly know it myself. Oh, Tony,'' she said, reaching up and drawing her arms around his neck, ''I want to take kids who start life with no hope and help them with their dreams no matter what their dreams are. I want to see their faces when things work out right for them.''

''Is that all you want?'' he asked gently.

''I'm afraid to ask for more.''

''I'm afraid you won't.''

''I want you,'' she said.

He took her in his arms. ''Amazing how wishes can be fulfilled near this displaced old temple. Must be something in the shifting sands of time.'' He held her tight, tilting her chin and kissing her.

The moon dipped behind a cloud, and when it re-emerged, it shone bright and clear on the small jewel of a building and the two people caught in an embrace that would last through many a blue moon.

**From America's favorite author
coming in September**

JANET DAILEY

For Bitter Or Worse
Out of print since 1979!

Reaching Cord seemed impossible. Bitter, still confined to a wheel-chair a year after the crash, he lashed out at everyone. Especially his wife.

"It would have been better if I hadn't been pulled from the plane wreck," he told her, and nothing Stacey did seemed to help.

Then Paula Hanson, a confident physiotherapist, arrived. She taunted Cord into helping himself, restoring his interest in living. Could she also make him and Stacey rediscover their early love?

Don't miss this collector's edition—last in a special three-book collection from Janet Dailey.

If you missed *No Quarter Asked* (April) or *Fiesta San Antonio* (July) and want to order either of them, send your name, address and zip or postal code along with a check or money order for $3.25 per book plus 75¢ postage, payable to Harlequin Reader Service, to:

In the U.S.:	In Canada:
901 Fuhrmannn Blvd.	P.O. Box 609
Box 135	Fort Erie, Ontario
Buffalo, NY 14269	L2A 5X3

Please specify book title with your order

JDS-1

HARLEQUIN
American Romance®

THE LOVES OF A CENTURY

Join American Romance in a nostalgic look back at the twentieth century—at the lives and loves of American men and women from the turn-of-the-century to the dawn of the year 2000.

Journey through the decades from the dance halls of the 1900's to the discos of the seventies . . . from Glenn Miller to the Beatles . . . from Valentino to Newman . . . from corset to miniskirt . . . from beau to significant other.

Relive the moments . . . recapture the memories.

Watch for all the CENTURY OF AMERICAN ROMANCE titles in Harlequin American Romance. In one of the four American Romance books appearing each month, for the next nine months, we'll take you back to a decade of the twentieth century, where you'll relive the years and rekindle the romance of days gone by.

Don't miss a day of A CENTURY OF AMERICAN ROMANCE.

A CENTURY OF
AMERICAN ROMANCE
1920s

The women . . . the men . . . the passions . . . the memories . . .

If you missed #345 AMERICAN PIE or #349 SATURDAY'S CHILD and would like to order them, send your name, address and zip or postal code, along with a check or money order for $2.95 plus 75¢ postage and handling ($1.00 in Canada) *for each book ordered*, payable to Harlequin Reader Service to:

In the U.S.
3010 Walden Ave.,
P.O. Box 1325
Buffalo, NY 14269-1325

In Canada
P.O. Box 609
Fort Erie, Ontario
L2A 5X3

CAR-1RR

You'll flip . . . your pages won't!
Read paperbacks *hands-free* with

Book Mate · I

The perfect "mate" for all your romance paperbacks

**Traveling • Vacationing • At Work • In Bed • Studying
• Cooking • Eating**

Perfect size for all standard paperbacks, this wonderful invention makes reading a pure pleasure! Ingenious design holds paperback books OPEN and FLAT so even wind can't ruffle pages — leaves your hands free to do other things. Reinforced, wipe-clean vinyl-covered holder flexes to let you turn pages without undoing the strap . . . supports paperbacks so well, they have the strength of hardcovers!

Pages turn WITHOUT opening the strap.

SEE-THROUGH STRAP

Reinforced back stays flat.

Built in bookmark

BOOK MARK

BACK COVER HOLDING STRIP

10" x 7¼", opened.
Snaps closed for easy carrying, too.

Available now. Send your name, address, and zip code, along with a check or money order for just $5.95 + .75¢ for postage & handling (for a total of $6.70) payable to Reader Service to:

Reader Service
Bookmate Offer
901 Fuhrmann Blvd.
P.O. Box 1396
Buffalo, N.Y. 14269-1396

Offer not available in Canada
*New York and Iowa residents add appropriate sales tax.

BM-G